The Encyclopedia of Business Letters, Fax Memos, and E-Mail

By
Robert W. Bly

CAREER PRESS
Franklin Lakes, NJ

ENCYCLOPEDIA OF BUSINESS LETTERS, FAX MEMOS, AND E-MAIL
Cover design by Barry Littmann
Printed in the U.S.A. by Book-mart Press

To order this title, please call toll-free 1-800-CAREER-1 (NJ and Canada: 201-848-0310) to order using VISA or MasterCard, or for further information on books from Career Press.

The Career Press, Inc., 3 Tice Road, PO Box 687, Franklin Lakes, NJ 07417

Library of Congress Cataloging-in-Publication Data

Bly, Robert W.
    The encyclopedia of business letters, fax memos, and e-mail / by
Robert W. Bly.
        p.   cm.
    Includes index.
    ISBN 1-56414-375-9 (pbk.)
    1. Business letters.   2. Memorandums.   3. Facsimile transmission.
I. Title.
HF5721.B59   1998
651.7'5--dc21   98-45170

Dedication

To the memory of Burton Pincus, one of the greatest letter-writers of all times, and to Bob Jurick, who has mailed more letters than anyone I know.

Acknowledgments

Thanks to the many organizations and individuals who allowed me to reprint their letters in this book.

Thanks also to my editors at Career Press, Betsy Sheldon, John J. O'Sullivan, and Stacey A. Farkas, for making this book much better than it was when it first crossed their desks.

INTRODUCTION

The era of long, leisurely letters is gone.

The chatty correspondence of yesteryear has been replaced by concise letters, crisp memos, fast faxes, and instant e-mail.

Your reader doesn't have time to waste. And neither do you. That's where *The Encyclopedia of Business Letters, Fax Memos, and E-Mail* can help.

Here you'll find the most complete and up-to-date collection of model business correspondence for every conceivable occasion—sample letters, faxes, memos, and e-mail you can use as is or adapt for your own purposes. The result: You eliminate hours of wasted time and effort composing correspondence; we've already done the work for you. You can get your message across clearly, easily, and *quickly*...so you can cut down on writing time and focus on more important tasks.

How the encyclopedia works

This encyclopedia contains hundreds of model letters with instructions for adapting each to your particular situation. Letters are organized into chapters by category—sales letters, credit and collection letters, customer service letters, cover letters, among others. The detailed table of contents and index are both designed to quickly guide you to the letter that best meets your needs.

When you turn to the model letters, you'll find a variety of pointers and guides to help you adapt them to your own needs, including:

- **Descriptive heading.** A clear heading identifies the type of letter and lets you rapidly assess whether a particular model letter fits a specific situation.
- **Introductory comments.** In a few quick sentences, you gain a working knowledge of the category of correspondence, including background on why people send such letters and the results they typically achieve.

- **Model letter.** In simple and straightforward categories, a single sample letter is presented. In other cases, several variations in tone and style are offered so you can pick the one that suits your situation best.
- **Customization tips.** Some of the letters are written to a specific formula for that type of correspondence. I'll show you the formula and how the model letter follows it. This lets you understand the model letter better and also enables you to write your own letters following the formula, if you wish.

In this way, you not only benefit from having a time-saving collection of pre-written letters, but you also find what you need in minimum time. You'll be able to quickly and easily adapt it for immediate use.

You may be a creative person and an original thinker. But when it comes to routine correspondence, why reinvent the wheel? *The Encyclopedia of Business Letters, Fax Memos, and E-Mail* puts graceful, concise, persuasive correspondence at your fingertips. Hundreds of businesspeople and writers spent countless hours sweating out and refining these gems so you don't have to. Just pick them up, apply polish if you like, and send them on their way. As a busy manager or entrepreneur, you'll treasure *The Encyclopedia* for a lifetime. Here's to quick—and painless—writing!

P.S. I do have a favor to ask. If you've written or received a letter you think is especially effective, why not pass it on to me so I can share it with readers of the next edition? You will receive full credit, of course. Contact:

Bob Bly
Center for Technical Communication
22. E. Quackenbush Avenue
Dumont, NJ 07628
phone: 201-385-1220
fax: 201-385-1138
e-mail: rwbly@bly.com
Web site: www.bly.com

1

Quick Tips for Better Business Writing

Several years ago, I interviewed Burt Manning to gather information for a book I was writing on careers in business. In the course of our conversation, Mr. Manning, who is vice chairman of the J. Walter Thompson Company, complained about the lack of basic writing skills in the young people who seek employment with his agency.

"We get people who have college degrees," said Manning, "and they can't write a sentence in English."

Functional illiteracy is nothing new, but among advertising people whose business is words? I was skeptical until I turned on the television that evening and heard a commercial describing a new television series as "the most unique show of the season." This seems a strange claim to make, since *unique* means, "one of a kind" and it is therefore impossible for anything to be the most unique. Or *very* unique, or *quite* unique, or *somewhat* unique, or even, as one advertising executive used the phrase modestly, a *little* unique.

But the television network is not the only corporation guilty of turning business communications into what E.B. White calls "the language of mutilation." A Detroit automobile manufacturer based a recent series of print ads around the theme "new innovations." This may lead one to believe that there can be such a thing as an *old* innovation.

One of my clients, normally an articulate and intelligent marketer, changed some ad copy I had written for one of his products, a wire splint that helps keep loose teeth in place. The advertiser decided that what the product *really* did was "to stabilize mobile dentition." Dentition is what you brush with Crest. If someone should punch you in the dentition, my client believes that the dentition may become mobile, but certainly not loose. (If they fall out, the dentition fairy may deposit some monetary compensation under your pillow.)

Increasingly, the skills of clear communication are waning. "I'm chagrined at the decline in the writing skills of college graduates," says Hugh Farrell, president of Hammond Farrell, Inc., a New York business-to-business advertising agency. "Roughly half of the cover letters accompanying resumes that cross my desk contain errors, and I don't think that was true 15 years ago. And good writing is important, even with account people. If a person can't write a lucid, clear, correct report, he or she shouldn't be in this business."

Jargon, double-talk, and weak, watered-down prose proliferate in business writing. A brochure for a storage silo informs us that material is "gravimetrically conveyed"—not dumped. Sony's advertisement for cassette recorders explains that my tape recorder captured Burt Manning's voice so perfectly because "a counter-inertial flywheel keeps the tape speed constant." True perhaps, but did I really need to know this? And, of course, every system, product, and service now sold to businesses is said to be "cost-effective." How refreshing it would be to read of a product that was inexpensive, low in price, or just plain cheap.

Certainly, such obfuscation has not always been embraced by English-speaking people. Approximately 70 percent of the words in Lincoln's Gettysburg Address contain less than six letters. Winston Churchill, faced with Hitler's armed forces, said to Americans, "Give us the tools and we will do the job." He did *not* say: "Aid our organization in the procurement of the necessary equipments and we will in turn implement the program to accomplish its planned objectives." (Today's MBA would be likely to call Churchill's troops the "key target market segment" for defense manufacturers.)

Happily, academia has now recognized the problem and is working toward a solution. *Forbes* reports that undergraduate engineering students at MIT will be required to take a course in English composition. And *The New York Times* notes that the number of writing courses at colleges throughout the nation is now on the rise.

As a result of improved education, today's students should be able to write letters and reports that other people can understand (at least we hope so). Those of us who may never see the inside of a classroom again would do well to heed this bit of advice from the essayist and co-author of the writer's resource book *The Elements of Style*, E.B. White: "When you have said something, make sure you have said it. The chances of your having said it are only fair."

12 secrets of clear writing

The average manager in industry cannot write clear, lucid prose. He or she may know the basics: sentence structure, grammar, punctuation, exposition. But most businesspeople have a few poor stylistic habits that mar their writing, making it dull and difficult to read.

Why do so many professionals write so poorly? Many feel that writing is time consuming, unimportant, and unpleasant. Others lack confidence in their ability to communicate, or simply don't know how to get started. A third group has the desire to write well, but lacks the proper training.

In seminars given at New York University, American Chemical Society, the U.S. Army, American Institute of Chemical Engineers, and numerous corporations, I have surveyed hundreds of professionals to discover which problems occur most frequently in their writing. Below are solutions to the most common problems in business writing, along with tips on how to recognize and solve them.

1. Get organized. According to the survey, poor organization is the number one problem in business writing. As writer Jerry Bacchetti points out, "If the reader believes the content has some importance to him, he can plow through a report even if it is dull or has lengthy sentences and big words. But if it's poorly organized—forget it. There's no way to make sense of what is written."

Poor organization stems from poor planning. While a computer programmer might never think of writing a complex program without first drawing a flow chart, he'd probably knock out a draft of a user's manual without making notes or an outline. In the same way, a builder who requires detailed blueprints before he lays the first brick will write a letter without really considering his message, audience, or purpose.

Before you write, plan. Create a rough outline that spells out the contents and organization of your document. The outline need not be formal. A simple list, doodles, or rough notes will do; use whatever form suits you.

By the time you finish writing, some things in the final draft might be different from the outline. That's okay. The outline is a tool to aid in organization, not a commandment cast in stone. If you want to change it as you go along—fine.

The outline helps you divide the writing project into many smaller, easy-to-handle pieces and parts. The organization of these parts depends on the type of document you're writing.

In general, it's best to stick with standard formats. These formats allow for an easier time writing, as well as understanding. A speech begins with an introduction, presents three to four key points in the body, then closes with a summary of the main points made in the body. An operating manual includes a summary; an introduction; a description of the equipment; instructions for routine operation, troubleshooting, maintenance, and emergency operation; and an appendix containing a parts list, spare-parts list, drawings, figures, and manufacturer's literature.

If the format isn't strictly defined by the type of document you are writing, select the organizational scheme that best fits the material. Some common formats include:

- **Order of location.** An article on the planets of the solar system might begin with Mercury (the planet nearest the sun) and end with Pluto (the planet farthest out).
- **Order of increasing difficulty.** Computer manuals often start with the easiest material and, as the user masters basic principles, move on to more complex operations.
- **Alphabetical order.** This is a logical way to arrange a booklet on vitamins (A, B-3, B-12, C, D, E, and so on) or a directory of company employees.

- **Chronological order.** Here you present the facts in the order in which they happened. History books are written this way. So are many case histories, feature stories, corporate biographies, and trip reports.

- **Problem/solution.** Another format appropriate to case histories and many types of reports, the problem/solution organizational scheme begins with "Here's what the problem was" and ends with "Here's how we solved it."

- **Inverted pyramid.** This is the newspaper style of news reporting where the lead paragraph summarizes the story and the following paragraphs present the facts in order of decreasing importance. You can use this format in journal articles, letters, memos, and reports.

- **Deductive order.** You can start with a generalization, then support it with particulars. Scientists use this format in research papers that begin with the findings and then state the supporting evidence.

- **Inductive order.** Another approach is to begin with specific instances, and then lead the reader to the idea or general principles the instances suggest. This is an excellent way to approach trade journal feature stories.

- **List.** Articles, memos, instructions, procedures, and reports can be organized in list form. A list procedure might be titled "Six Tips for Designing Wet Scrubbers" or "Seven Ways to Reduce Your Plant's Electric Bill."

2. Know the reader. When I admit to doing some direct-mail copywriting as part of my consulting work, people turn up their noses. "I always throw that junk in the garbage," they say. "Who would ever buy something from a letter addressed to 'Dear Occupant'?"

They're right, of course. Written communication is most effective when it is *targeted* and *personal.* Your writing should be built around the needs, interests, and desires of the reader. Know your reader, especially his or her job title, education, industry, and level of interest in your message:

- **Job title.** Techies are interested in your compressor's reliability and performance, while the purchasing agent is more concerned with cost. A person's job influences his or her perspective of your product, service, or idea. Are you writing for plant engineers? Office managers? CEOs? machinists? Make the tone and content of your writing compatible with the professional interests of your readers.

- **Education.** Is your reader a Ph.D. or a high-school drop-out? Is your reader a Web designer? Does he or she understand computer programming, thermodynamics, physical chemistry, statistics, and the calculus of variations? Write simple enough so that even the least technical of your readers can understand what you are saying.

- **Industry.** When plant managers buy a reverse-osmosis water purification system for the town water supply, they want to know every technical detail down to the last pipe, pump, fan, and filter. Fishermen buying portable units for fishing boats, on the other hand, have only two basic questions: "What does it cost?" and "How reliable is it?" Especially in promotional writing, know what features of your product appeal to various markets.

- **Level of interest.** A prospect who has responded to your sales letter is more likely to be receptive to a salesperson's call than someone who the salesperson calls on "cold turkey." Is your reader interested or disinterested? Friendly or hostile? Receptive or resistant? Understanding state of mind helps you tailor your message to meet the reader's needs.

If you don't know enough about your reader, there are ways of finding out. If you are writing a letter to potential customers, for example, visit their Web site to get background on the company and study it before you write. If you are presenting a paper at a conference, look at the conference brochure to get a feel for the audience who will be attending your session. If you are contributing text to product descriptions, ask the marketing or publications department the format in which the material will be published, how it will be distributed, and who will be reading it.

3. Avoid "corporatese." Anyone who reads business documents knows the danger of "corporatese." Corporatese, by my definition the pompous, over blown style that leaves your writing sounding as if it were written by a computer or a corporation instead of a human being, is language more complex than the concepts it serves to communicate. By loading up their writings with jargon, clichés, antiquated phrases, passive sentences, and an excess of adjectives, technicians and bureaucrats hide behind a jumble of incomprehensible memos and reports.

To help you recognize corporatese, I've assembled a few samples from diverse sources. Note how the authors seem to be writing to impress rather than to express. All of these excerpts are real:

> *"Will you please advise me at your earliest convenience of the correct status of this product?"*
>
> –memo from an advertising manager

> *"All of the bonds in the above described account having been heretofore disposed of, we are this day terminating same. We accordingly enclose herein check in the amount of $30,050 same being your share realized therein, as per statement attached."*
>
> –letter from a stockbroker

> *"This procedure enables users to document data fields described in master files that were parsed and analyzed by the program dictionary."*
>
> –software user's manual

This same verbal gobbledygook in the business world that tries to pass for English has turned the word "fired" into any of the following pieces of gibberish:

- ▤ Downsizing.

- ▤ Eliminating redundancies in the human resources area.

- ▤ Indefinite idling.

- ▤ Involuntary separation.

- ▤ Managing our human resources down.

- ▤ Restructuring.

- ▤ Realignment.

- ▤ Reductions in overhead, process improvements, facility rationalization, and purchasing and logistics savings.

- ▤ Reengineering.

- ▤ Right-sizing.

- ▤ Volume-related production schedule adjustment.

How do you eliminate corporatese from your writing? Start by avoiding jargon. Don't use a technical term unless it communicates your meaning precisely. Never write "mobile dentition" when "loose teeth" will do just as well. Legal scholar Tamar Frankel notes that when you avoid jargon, your writing can be easily read by novices and experienced professionals alike.

Avoid clichés and antiquated phrases. Write simply. Some executives prefer to use big, important-sounding words instead of short, simple words. This is a mistake; fancy language just frustrates the reader. Write in plain, ordinary English and your readers will love you for it.

Here a few big words that occur frequently in business and technical literature; the column on the right presents a shorter and preferable substitution:

Big word	Substitution
terminate	end
utilize	use
incombustible	fireproof
substantiate	prove
eliminate	get rid off

Many industries have their own special languages. Industry terms are a helpful shorthand when you're communicating within the profession, but they may confuse readers who do not have your special background. Take the word "yield" for example. To a chemical manufacturer, yield is a measure of how much product a reaction produces. But, to car drivers, yield means slowing down (and stopping, if necessary) at an intersection. That's where knowing your reader comes in as explained above.

4. Prefer the active voice. In the active voice, action is expressed directly: "John performed the experiment." In the passive voice, the action is indirect: "The experiment was performed by John."

When you use the active voice, your writing will be more direct and vigorous; your sentences, more concise. As you can see in the samples below; the passive voice seems puny and stiff by comparison:

Passive voice	Active voice
Control of the bearing-oil supply is provided by the shutoff valves.	Shutoff valves control the bearing-oil supply.
Leaking of the seals is prevented by the use of O-rings.	O-rings keep the seals from leaking.
Fuel-cost savings were realized through the installation of thermal insulation	The installation of thermal insulation cut fuel costs.

5. Avoid lengthy sentences. Lengthy sentences tire the reader and make your writing hard to read. A survey by Harvard professor D.H. Menzel indicates that in technical papers, the sentences become difficult to understand when they exceed 34 words in length.

One measure of writing complexity, the Fog Index, takes into account sentence length *and* word length. Here's how it works:

First, determine the average sentence length in a short (100 to 200 words) writing sample. To do this, divide the number of words in the sample by the number of sentences. If parts of a sentence are separated by a semicolon (;), count each part as a separate sentence.

Next, calculate the number of big words (words with three or more syllables) per 100 words of sample. Do not include capitalized words, combinations of short words (everywhere, moreover) or verbs made three syllables by adding *ed* or *es* (accepted, responses).

Finally, add the average sentence length to the number of big words per hundred words, then multiply it by 0.4. This gives you the Fog Index for the sample.

The Fog Index corresponds to the years of schooling you need to read and understand the sample. A score of eight or nine indicates high school level; 13, a college freshman; 17, a college graduate.

Popular magazines have Fog Indexes ranging from eight to 13. Technical journals should rate no higher than 17.

Obviously, the higher the Fog Index, the more difficult the writing is to read. In his book *Gene Control in the Living Cell* (Basic Books), J.A.V. Butler leads off with a single 79-word sentence.

"In this book I have attempted an accurate but at the same time readable account of recent work on the subject of how gene controls operate, a large subject which is rapidly acquiring a central position in the biology of today and which will inevitably become even more prominent in the future, in the efforts of scientists of numerous different specialists to explain how a single organism can contain cells of many different kinds developed from a common origin."

With 17 big words, this sample has a Fog Index of 40, which is equivalent to a reading level of 28 years of college education! Obviously, this sentence is way too long. Here's a rewrite I came up with:

"This book is about how gene controls operate—a subject of growing importance in modern biology."

This gets the message across with a Fog Index of only 14.

Give your writing the Fog Index test. If you score in the upper teens or higher, it's time to trim sentence length. Go over your text, and break long sentences into two or more separate sentences. To further reduce average sentence length and add variety to your writing, you can occasionally use an extremely short sentence or sentence fragments of only three to four words or so. Like this one.

Short sentences are easier to grasp than long ones. A good guide for keeping sentence length under control is to write sentences that can be spoken aloud without losing your breath (do *not* take a deep breath before doing this test).

6. Be specific. Businesspeople are interested in specifics—facts, figures, conclusions, and recommendations. Do not be content to say something is good, bad, fast, or slow when you can say *how* good, *how* bad, *how* fast, or *how* slow. Be specific whenever possible.

General	Specific
a tall spray dryer	a 40-foot-tall spray dryer
plant	oil refinery
unit	evaporator
unfavorable weather conditions	rain
structural degradation	a leaky roof
high performance	95 percent efficiency

7. Be simple. The key to success in business writing is to *keep it simple*. Write to express—not to impress. A relaxed, conversational style can add vigor and clarity to your work.

Formal style	Informal conversational style
The data provided by direct examination of samples under the lens of the microscope are insufficient for the purpose of making a proper identification of the components of the substance.	We can't tell what it is made of by looking at it under the microscope.
Formal Style	**Informal Conversational Style**
We have found during conversations with customers that even the most experienced of extruder specialists have a tendency to avoid the extrusion of silicone profiles or hoses.	Our customers tell us that experienced extruder specialists avoid extruding silicone profiles or hoses.
The corporation terminated the employment of Mr. Joseph Smith.	Joe was fired.

8. Define your topic. Effective writing relies on a clear definition of the specific topic you want to write about. A big mistake that many of us make is to tackle a topic that's too broad. For example, the title "Project Management" is too all-encompassing for a business paper. You could write a whole book on the subject. But by narrowing the scope, say, with the title "Managing Chemical Plant Construction Projects With Budgets Under $500,000," you get a clearer definition and a more manageable topic.

It's also important to know the purpose of the document. You may say, "That's easy; the purpose is to give business information." But think again. Do you want the reader to buy a product? Change methods of working? Look for the hidden agenda beyond the mere transmission of facts.

9. Create adequate content. After you've defined your topic, audience, and purpose, the next step is to do some homework and gather information on the topic at hand. Even though you're an expert, your knowledge may be limited, your viewpoint lopsided. Gathering information from other sources helps round out your knowledge or, at the very least, verify your own thinking. There is another benefit— backing up your claims with facts is a real credibility builder.

10. Be consistent in usage. Inconsistencies in business writing will confuse your readers and convince them that your work and reasoning are as sloppy and unorganized as your prose.

Good business writers strive for consistency in the use of numbers, hyphens, units of measure, punctuation, equations, grammar, symbols, capitalization, business terms, and abbreviations.

For example, many writers are inconsistent in the use of hyphens. The rule is: two words that form an adjective are hyphenated. Thus, write: first-order reaction, fluidized-bed combustion, high-sulfur coal, space-time continuum, and so forth.

The U.S. Government Printing Office Style Manual, Strunk and White's *The Elements of Style,* and your organization's writing manual can guide you in the basics of grammar, punctuation, abbreviation, and capitalization.

11. Shun dull, wordy prose. Business professionals, especially those in industry, are busy people. Make your writing less time-consuming for them to read by telling the whole story in the fewest possible words.

How can you make your writing more concise? One way is to avoid redundancies—a needless form of wordiness in which a modifier repeats an idea already contained within the word being modified.

Some redundancies that have come up in business literature are listed below, along with the correct way to rewrite them:

Redundancy	Rewrite as
advance plan	plan
actual experience	experience
two cubic feet in volume	two cubic feet
cylindrical in shape	cylindrical
uniformly homogeneous	homogeneous

Many business writers are fond of overblown expressions such as "the fact that," "it is well known that," and "it is the purpose of this writer to show that." These take up space but add little to meaning or clarity.

The following list includes some of the wordy phrases that appear frequently in business literature. The column on the right offers suggested substitute words:

Wordy phrase	Suggested substitute
during the course of	during
in the form of	as
in many cases	often
in the event of	if
exhibits the ability to	can

12. Consider the page layout. To enhance readability, break your writing up into short sections. Long, unbroken blocks of text are stumbling blocks that intimidate and bore readers. Breaking your writing up into short sections and short paragraphs makes it easier to read.

These tips should help eliminate some of the fear and anxiety you may have about writing, as well as make the whole task easier and more productive. Keep in mind that success in writing or any form of communication, is largely a matter of attitude. If you don't think writing is important enough to take the time to do it right, and you don't really care about improving, you probably won't. But if you believe that writing is important, and you want to improve, you will.

2

RULES FOR BUSINESS LETTERS, FAXES, MEMOS, AND E-MAIL

The way a letter, fax, memo, or e-mail *looks* immediately tells the reader how seriously they should take the contents. You can throw a few words on a piece of paper and look like an amateur to your readers, or you can learn the rules for writing business correspondence and look like you know what you're doing. It's all in perception. Knowing when and how to use each of these formats is the sign of a true professional. You don't send a fax or memo to congratulate someone on his or her retirement, and you don't send a formal letter to tell employees that there is a new snack machine in the lobby! The following rules and tips will set your stylistic eye straight.

The business letter

The business letter is used to communicate formal matters in business, jurisprudence, or otherwise. You will use this form of correspondence when you want to write a cover letter to accompany your resume, write a letter announcing business news to colleagues outside your company, or notify vendors of a change in your ordering procedures. You can file an official complaint or compliment with such a letter, or any number of other business occasions. You will want to use the formal format to emphasize the importance of the contents to your reader.

The rules are simple, however make sure not to break them. Business letters should be written in the following manner:

- Print your letter on high-quality white or light-colored paper with black ink.
- Set your margins to 1 to 1 1/2 inches all around.
- Use a colon after the salutation.
- Leave four spaces between the complimentary close and your name.
- Place your signature in-between the complimentary close and your name.

Sample business letter on letterhead paper

There are many formats you can use, but to keep things simple I recommend the full-blocked style in which everything is placed flush with the left margin. (This includes the dateline, inside address, salutation, paragraph openings, complimentary close, and writer's name.) See the sample below:

Fictional Firm Letterhead
0000 Make-Believe Street
Noplace Real, NJ 10000

Dateline: [put the date here]

Inside Address   [This is the company or person you are writing
Street Name   your letter to.]
Town, State zip

Salutation: [This is your "hello" greeting. If you do not know the
                             person's name, use: *Dear Sir or Madam:* and when you
                             are writing to an organization rather than an individ-
                             ual, you can write: *Dear Ladies and Gentlemen:*]

Body: [The body, as its name suggests, is the primary part of
                             the letter. It follows the salutation. Most often business
                             letters are single spaced, unless they are very short
                             and double spacing will better fill up the page.]

When you start a new paragraph, drop down two spaces and begin. In this full-blocked style you do *not* indent the first line.

Closing: [This is where you say, *Sincerely yours,* or *Best wishes,*
                             or *Very truly yours.* Note the first word of the compli-
                             mentary close is capitalized; the second word is not.]

[Your signature goes here.]
Type your name below it

Sample business letter on plain paper without letterhead

If you are writing a business letter on paper without letterhead, put your company's name and address directly above the dateline and then proceed with the same format as above:

Fictional Firm
0000 Make Believe Street
Noplace Real, NJ 10000

Dateline

Dear Salutation:

The fax

The facsimile machine has dramatically changed the pace of business communication in the past ten years. No longer patient enough to wait for overnight express mail, much business correspondence is passed over the telephone lines for instant communication. As with most new pieces of office equipment it can be both a blessing and a curse. Knowing how to correctly and appropriately use this form of quick correspondence will help you boost your business image.

Fax transmission cover form

Not every businessperson has his or her own personal fax machine. Often fax transmissions arrive in a common area and then are forwarded to the proper recipient. The facsimile transmission cover form has been developed to route your communication to the correct person and to provide details you'd find on a business letter, such as the sender's name, address, and date. It also includes subject matter, as well as the number of pages being transmitted. It's smart to keep your fax cover sheet as brief as possible. The fax machine will read all print on the sheet including borders, margins, and lines. Something as simple as a heavy border around the cover sheet can double your fax transmission time.

Be sure your fax communications are preceded by this type of cover form. Here's a simple format you can use or adapt any way you like.

3

COVER LETTERS, RESUMES, AND OTHER HIRING LETTERS

The correspondence you'll find in this chapter will help you get the job that will put you in a position to write lots of business letters. These employment letters include letters to land a job, letters to reject a job, and sample resumes. You will also find the letters you need if you're the one doing the hiring and firing. These letters are models you can adapt to your personal needs whether you are entry level, middle management, or experienced executive. Keep in mind that all business letters in this chapter should be written on letterhead or with proper business formatting and headings (as described in Chapter 1). All the letters below begin with the salutation.

Letters to gain employment

The following letters will help bring your job-search process from application through interview to acceptance.

Recent college grad cover letter (traditional)

Recent college graduates are often (but not always) light on experience. You have a degree like most other candidates, extracurricular activities like most other candidates, and summer job experience that doesn't relate to the position you're seeking. Therefore, your letter should be short and sweet; don't try to cover up your beginner status in the work world with hype.

On the other hand, if you have some experience that differentiates you from the crowd, say you started a successful business or climbed Mt. Everest, the cover letter is the best place to stress it.

Customize your own letter as a recent college grad:

This simple and short letter doesn't waste the recipient's time. It gets right to the point with three main details:

1. Enclosed resume and spotlight on important experience.

2. Request for a job interview.

3. Promise of a follow-up call.

Dear Ms. Rushiski:

As my enclosed resume shows, I am a recent graduate of HigherEd University with a major in English. My experience includes an internship with a large publishing company and word processing a novel for a best-selling author. I would like to meet with you to discuss the possibility of gaining an entry-level editorial position with your company. I will call on Tuesday, October 2 to discuss the possibility of an interview.

My resume is enclosed. Thanks for your time and consideration.

Sincerely,

Recent college grad cover letter (nontraditional)

This letter is a little different, a bit bolder than the conventional cover letter above. The writer of this letter got the interview.

This kind of letter is risky—it may turn some people off, but if it works, it can make you stand out clearly from the crowd. (The person who wrote this letter got the interview).

The only problem with working at the cutting edge of communications is staying ahead of the blade.

To stay ahead, you need aggressive people willing to take chances.

People who are confident, flexible, dedicated.

People who want to learn—who are not afraid to ask questions.

I am one of those people—one of the people you should have on your staff.

Let me prove it. Start by reading my resume. It shows I can take on any challenge and succeed. I want to succeed for you.

But if you're looking for someone comfortable with covering the same old ground, count me out.

If you want to work at the cutting edge, call me. I won't get cut.

Sincerely,

---

your correspondence be sure to use the name in the salutation of your letter. If the ad supplies only the person's title, use that, as in "Dear Creative Director." If you are not given any information about the person the letter is directed to you can either call and ask for a name (if a phone number is give) or you can resort to using "To whom it may concern."

Be careful about responding to blind ads (ads that do not give a company name). Once I responded to a blind ad from an ad agency looking for a copywriter. At the time, I was an advertising manager for an engineering firm. The agency running the ad turned out to be *my* agency! "When we got your letter, we didn't know whether to tell your boss," the account executive confided in me years later. "It's a good thing you didn't," I replied. "I might have fired you on the spot."

Customize your own letter in response to a classified ad:

When you respond to a classified ad be sure to directly state three things:

1. Where you read about the job opening.
2. Your special qualifications that match the needs mentioned in the ad.
3. Your availability for an interview.

RE: Your ad for "copywriter wanted" in *Adweek* magazine

Dear Personnel Director:

Your help-wanted ad caught my attention. You're looking for a copywriter with heavy software background—and that's my specialty.

As my enclosed resume indicates, I've worked on a number of computer-related accountings, including Dell and IBM. An ad campaign I wrote for Parsons software was their most profitable ever.

I can send a portfolio or visit your offices for an interview—whichever you prefer. Please let me know what you want to happen next.

Sincerely,

Cold-call letter requesting an interview

Many firms have occasional or even frequent job openings that they do not advertise. Therefore there is often less competition for these positions.

To be considered, write a letter requesting an interview. The key to this unsolicited request is to establish that you know the company and have a strong interest in working with them based on who they are and what they do.

Since the introduction of Internet accesses for the masses, gaining inside corporate knowledge has become much easier. For example, in the 1970s, when I looked for my first job, the only way to gain knowledge of a company was library research or to get them to send you an annual report, if they had one. Nowadays, crucial information is all but a click away.

Before writing a letter requesting an interview, you should log onto the company's Web site and browse it carefully. The home page should give you a good overview of what the company does. Check the most recent press releases for news items you can work into your letter. The recipient will be impressed that you know what's going on with the company.

Customize your own letter for a cold-call interview:

Make sure your cold-call letter clearly states four things:

1. A piece of company information that shows you are familiar with their operations.
2. A highlight of your business experience.
3. Your interest in an interview.
4. How your skills will benefit their company.

Dear Ms. Parks:

Congratulations on Acme's recent acquisition of Ace Company. This will certainly strengthen Acme's product offerings for digital prepress. That's the reason I'm writing you.

As an area sales rep for Grayco, I have been the number one producer for my company for the past three years. This year, I exceeded last year's prepress equipment revenues by over 65 percent. Now I am looking for my next challenge.

I'd love to interview for any area or regional sales rep positions you have open now or might in the near future. As my resume indicates, I have broad experience in sales of many different products to the printing and photographic markets.

With your newly acquired line of Ace systems, Acme will clearly provide the single-source solution prepress operations are demanding. I think my solution-selling experience is a good fit for your current direction, and would welcome the chance to discuss how I can help increase Acme's market share. Just let me know when and where!

Sincerely,

Requesting an informational interview

Informational interviews, which are interviews with potential employers or sources of referral who have no immediate opportunity to give you directly, serve two purposes: They give you an inside view of an industry and its hot career opportunities. And, they allow you to present yourself to people who would not otherwise see you for a "job interview" because no immediate job position exists that they know of. Do the informational interview well, and you may suddenly find yourself called in or recommended by that person for a "real" interview for the next position that opens up—often quicker than you'd think.

Customize your own letter requesting an informational interview:

In a letter that requests an informational interview, be sure to note:

1. How you know about this person.
2. Who you are.
3. Why you would like to talk.
4. A promise to call to set up the interview.
5. A subtle piece of flattery.

Dear Ms. Tonnely:

Elizabeth Abrams suggested that I write to you. Would you consider meeting with me to discuss instructional design and your experiences in the profession?

Liz suggested you might have some helpful advice for me. I am a computer programmer who became interest in computer-based training six months ago after taking several courses offered through my company.

I have always loved learning, and am now thinking of making a career move to instructional design, emphasizing computer-based courseware in technical skills. I am also currently taking a night course at Generic University.

I'd greatly appreciate it if you could call me. My work number is 123-456-7890. If I don't hear from you in the next week or so, I'll call to see if you have time to meet at your convenience.

Your experiences in training and development would be invaluable to me. Thank you for your time and consideration.

Sincerely,

Accepting an interview offer

If you are offered an interview, confirm it in writing. Also, telephone the day before to ensure that the meeting is still on. You wouldn't want to travel across town to an interview and take a day off from work if the personnel director is out sick with the flu!

Customize your own acceptance letter:

After you confirm your interview, you should send one or two more communications to the interviewer, such as a testimonial letter from a satisfied customer or a clip of an article about the interviewer's industry. This keeps your name in mind and shows that you're thinking of them.

Dear Ms. Parks:

Thanks for your prompt response to my letter. As we had previously discussed, I will meet you in your offices on Thursday, March 22, at 2 p.m. If you have to change the appointment, you can phone me on my private line at 123-456-7890 or send an e-mail to my personal account. The address is: sullivan45@internetprovider.com.

I look forward to meeting you and continuing our discussion in person!

Sincerely,

A thank you note for an interview

Sending thank you notes has become a lost art, yet in today's busy world, people appreciate then more than ever. These factors work to your advantage: Since most people don't send thank you notes any more, yours will stand out and make a lasting impression.

Customize your own thank you note:

Thank you notes are short and sweet. Remind the recipient of when you met and what position you interviewed for. Add an interesting note about something you talked about at the interview and you're done.

Dear Ms. Parks:

Thanks for taking the time to meet with me last Thursday to discuss sales opportunities with Acme Co. I'm excited about the possibility of your creating a new position for an additional rep in the northeast. And I look forward to being considered for the assignment.

Enclosed is the information on the sales training program we discussed. Grayco's training department sends most of the sales force through this program. I found the techniques well worth learning. Overall, we saw a lift in our closing rates.

Sincerely,

Requesting a letter of recommendation

When you want a former employer, supervisor, colleague, customer, vendor, or professor to write you a letter of recommendation for employment, make your request in writing. Be realistic as to whom you send such a letter. Someone who thought highly of you is more likely to comply with your request than a boss you disliked or a professor who flunked you.

You will get the letter you want if you supply the writer with information that does not merely repeat what is on your application. Explain that this company is looking for information about attributes like an employee's ability to work on a team, to meet deadlines, to work hard, and to meet goals. Factors such as perseverance, loyalty, and job commitment might also be included.

Customize your own letter requesting a letter of recommendation:

Letters asking for a recommendation should include:

1. A request for a favor, not a demand. Too many people make the mistake of thinking this request can't be refused and they pose their request as an order ("I need a letter of recommendation. Send it to the address below.")
2. Statement of the skills and attributes you'd like mentioned in the letter. This isn't being pompous; it's being helpful. This makes it much easier for the recipient to dash off a good letter.
3. The complete name and address you would like the letter of recommendation written to.
4. An envelope stamped and addressed to the person to receive the recommendation.

Dear Norman:

Would you do me a favor? I need a letter of recommendation from you to aid in my current job search. Could you write and send such a brief note?

The company I am applying to is looking for someone who is able to work on tight deadlines and stay organized. The employee must have superior communication skills and the ability to work on team projects. Could you please mention in your letter how these attributes were evident in my work with you.

Please send your letter to:

Ms. Jane Smith
XYZ Company
54 Broad Street
New York, NY 10012

I appreciate the opportunities I had while working for you, and I thank you for considering me for this additional favor.

Sincerely,

P.S. An addressed and stamped envelope is enclosed for your convenience.

Negotiating a job offer

When I graduated with a B.S. in engineering in 1979, two firms offered me jobs. I wanted to work for Westinghouse, but the other offer was considerably higher, and I knew Westinghouse could not match it. However, rather than try to puzzle this out, I simply replied straightforwardly to Westinghouse with the facts. This resulted in $2,500 increase in salary over the original Westinghouse offer, and I took the job.

Customize your own letter negotiating a job offer:

If you want to negotiate your terms of employment consider the following and use what's appropriate in your letter:

1. Your performance. Have you done something to warrant better terms?
2. The going-rate in the marketplace. Check the employment classified and talk with colleagues in other firms to find the salary

range for someone with your education and background experience.

3. Other benefits you might consider, such as a company car, in the place of increased salary.

Dear Mr. Smith:

Thanks for your letter and the job offer. I enjoyed our time together and know that I would like to work for you.

However, Koch Engineering in New York City has offered me $23,000 a year. Given that my fellow chemical engineering classmates average $20,000 a year, I just can't accept your offer of $16,000.

If it's possible to increase your offer or add additional benefits, let me know. I'd be interested in pursuing the position with you. If not, I still learned a lot from the time we spent together.

Sincerely,

Accepting a job offer

Years ago, employment contracts were common. Today, they are becoming much less so. Therefore the confirmation letter you send accepting a job offer is a good place to spell out the basic terms and conditions of employment. This gives everyone a clear sense of what has been agreed upon and also documents the offer in writing.

This is an important letter that can save you many headaches down the line. It often happens that when you arrive, no one quite remembers offering you your own office or promising a two-week vacation. Protect yourself with a letter of confirmation that asks for a signature. It shows you're an astute businessperson who leaves nothing to chance.

Customize your own letter accepting a job offer:

Letters accepting a job offer must include:

1. All terms of employment: include starting date, salary, benefits, hours, perks, and so forth.
2. A request for a signature of agreement and an enclosed self-addressed stamped envelope.
3. A positive note of enthusiasm about the new job.

Dear Mr. Mutsakis:

Thanks for your call today.

I accept your offer of a position as advertising manager at a salary of $47,000 a year. Based on our phone conversation, I understand that in addition to Oak Engineering's standard benefits plan, I will receive two weeks of vacation the first year. As discussed, I will also be given a private office (not a cubicle) with a PC, fax, and printer. I will share an administrative assistant with Joe Bulges, your trade show manager. My starting date will be Monday, June 12. Oak will reimburse me for mover's fees for relocating from Baltimore to Secaucus.

If I have understood the terms of my employment correctly, please sign in the space provided below and return to me in the enclosed self-addressed stamped envelope.

I'm thrilled about starting with Oak and look forward to a long and productive relationship. On a personal note, I'm also delighted that you're going to be my boss!

Sincerely,

Agreed: _____   Date: _____

Rejecting a job offer

On a lucky day, you might be able to reject a job offer. This rejection letter should be very professional with no personal information added. For example, if you have a superior offer that you've already accepted, don't boast about it. You might meet that person again some day. I turned down a job offer once and ended up accepting it a year later. If I burned my bridges being snide or boastful that wouldn't have been possible.

Customize your own letter rejecting a job offer:

Note that rejecting a job offer requires some sensitive communication skills:

1. State immediately that you cannot take the offer position.
2. Explain why the company you choose was a better match for your needs. (Or you can skip this part completely if you'd rather not compare companies or explain your reasons.) End the letter on a positive note that leaves the door open for the future.

Dear Terry:

Thanks for your call. However, after much thought, I have decided to take a position with General Motors in Flint, and must turn down your generous offer.

I'm sure I would have enjoyed working with you and the Process Design Group. But the opportunity with General Motors was as a management position, which you know I had aspirations to. This position is more in line with my career objectives than the staff position you had available.

I'm sure we will meet again, perhaps at the upcoming Process Design Society Conference. Perhaps we can meet at your booth for a cup of coffee—on me, of course.

Sincerely,

Resigning on good terms

Company loyalty isn't as crucial as it once was. Employees routinely hop from job to job looking to advance in position and salary. When you find it necessary to move on, don't delay in notifying your employer in writing (and keep a copy for yourself).

Customize your own letter to resign on good terms:

To resign from a company on good terms with, it's best to include:

1. Notification of resignation.
2. Exact date of your leave.
3. An offer to stick around for a specific period while the company looks for a replacement. Never make this offer open-ended by saying something like, "I'll stay until you find a replacement." Give an exact period of time.
4. Indicate that you're willing to be on-call for awhile after your leave.
5. A positive statement about your experience with the company.
6. A reason for leaving, if you choose to. Most bosses understand when you explain that you received an offer you simply couldn't refuse.

Dear Mr. Jones:

This letter is to notify you that I'm resigning from my position at Global Affiliates to take a new position at Associated Systems.

My last day will be October 11. By giving you six weeks notice I'm hoping to provide you with some extra time to find a replacement. After October 11, I'll still be available if you need help locating resources or getting answers to any questions the new employee may have about procedures or records. You will be able to reach me at my new number, 123-456-7890.

For the record, I enjoyed my job and our association here at Global. But the position at Associated has significantly higher compensation, and in our annual reviews, you indicated the salary for someone in my classification could not come near this level. So the decision is mainly a financial one. However, I'll miss you and the whole group in our department.

Sincerely,

Resigning on bad terms

Make this letter simple and straightforward. No embellishments, no explanation. The boss already knows why you are resigning. It's a sore spot, so why bring it out into the open? No one benefits, and it just makes one or both of you look bad.

This is as simple as business letters get. State your resignation and the date you are leaving.

Dear Mr. Smith:

This letter is to notify you that I'm resigning from my position at Global Affiliates to take a new position at Associated Systems.

My last day will be October 11. By giving you six weeks notice I'm hoping to provide you with some extra time to find a replacement.

Sincerely,

Experienced professional resume

John Doe
100 Summertown Drive
Anyplace, NJ
Phone 123-456-7890

Technical Writer
Industrial Copywriter
Training Specialist

TECHNICAL WRITING EXPERIENCE

6/95-present ACE CHEMICAL COMPANY, Boonton, New Jersey
Polymer mixing manual—Produced installation, operation, and maintenance manual for a polymer mixing system used in injection molding operations. I had complete responsibility for the organization, data gathering, and writing of this manual, and I developed illustrations to explain theory of operation, wiring, and parts location. Customers found the manual to be interesting, accurate, and easy to follow.

Other technical literature—Although I am responsible for writing technical manuals from scratch, I also prepare technical papers, press releases, and product literature. For example, I edited and supervised the production and printing of a technical paper on the performance of motionless mixers.

6/92-6/95 LIGHTNING ELECTRONICS INC., Paterson, New Jersey
Shipboard radar manual—Wrote a theory of operation manual on the W-120 shipboard fire control radar system. My responsibilities included setting up a schedule for typing and illustrations through the repro stage.

X-100 radar brochure—Wrote and produced a glossy, four-color, 12-page sales brochure on the X-100 air traffic control radar system. Brochure describes capabilities, performance data, and operation of this airport surveillance radar.

Product information sheets—Wrote product information sheets on the WX-200 modular shipboard fire control system, TCCS air traffic control system, X-100-AR air route surveillance radar, and other systems.

ENGINEERING EDUCATION

9/88-5/92 B.S., Chemical Engineering, University of Rochester, Rochester, NY

RELATED ACTIVITIES

7/92-present Member, American Institute of Chemical Engineers

3/95-present Freelance writer—have published articles in *Science Books and Films*, Baltimore *City Paper*, and *The Rochester Patriot*

REFERENCES AND PORTFOLIO
Will be pleased to submit upon request.

Other sample resumes

Jennifer Smith
1243 Downtown Drive
Gaithersburg, Maryland
Home: (123) 456-7890
Office: (123) 456-7899

OBJECTIVE: Hospital Health Care Director

KEY QUALIFICATIONS:

- More than 10 years experience as a healthcare director for both large and mid-sized hospitals.
- Awarded "Best Supervisor of the Month" for six consecutive months.
- Expertise in promoting open communication with staff members.
- Spanish: Speaking, reading, and writing competence.

EXPERIENCE:

1994–present Assistant Hospital Health Care Director, Sloan-Kettering Hospital
- Developed a total quality management system that cut the time to set up a patient's room by 50 percent.
- Introduced a new computer system that impacted 15 hospital departments.
- Promoted conflict resolution by setting up a weekly forum for more than 200 staff members and an 18-hour emergency training program.

EDUCATION:

M.S. 1994: Nursing, with a special focus on Administration
Thesis: Taking the Pain Out of Logistics Planning
University of Maryland

B.S. 1992: Nursing
Towson State University
Maryland

REFERENCES

Available upon request

3. A request for information that zeros in on specific work skills and characteristics you are most interested in knowing about.
4. A deadline for reply.
5. An offer of confidentiality that will make the recipient more comfortable about telling the truth.
6. A thank you.

Dear Mr. Carlson:

We recently received an application from George Olmstede for the position of master electrician with our firm. We understand he was previously employed by you.

We would appreciate any information you could give us concerning Mr. Olmstead's work habits, expertise as a master electrician, and attitude. We would also appreciate your sharing with us the reason he no longer works for your firm.

We look forward to hearing from you. If you could reply by early March, it would be very helpful. Please advise us if the information you provide is confidential. Thank you for your time in considering this request.

Sincerely,

Rejecting an employee applying for an open in-house position

Inside people don't always have the inside track on new positions, especially if these opportunities are in areas outside of their core skill set. Because the applicant is also an employee, your letter must motivate and encourage even as it rejects.

Customize your own letter to reject a current employee applying to an open in-house position:

A letter rejecting a current employee applying to an open in-house position needs to be carefully crafted. It should include:

1. An opening that acknowledges the employee's application and presents a form of active listening that shows you've read his or her application letter carefully—you understand why the employee is applying for the open position.
2. A clear statement of the skills or training required for this job that the employee does not possess.
3. An acknowledgment that you have a number of qualified applicants and will choose from that pool.

4. A paragraph that praises the work of this employee and opens the door to future advancement in a more appropriate direction.

Dear Dan:

Thanks for your interest in becoming part of SunStar's marketing communications department as a communications coordinator. Yes, I agree that as a sales rep, you know what motivates customers to buy our products. I also appreciate your desire to reduce your travel and make the change from personal selling to mass communications.

Unfortunately, your field sales background has not given you many of the skills this position requires, including copywriting, editing, desktop publishing, database marketing, and mailing list selection and analysis. You also don't have the Internet experience needed; knowledge of Java, Front Page, or HTML is required.

We've received applications from several candidates who, in addition to having these requisite skills, have a background in lines of equipment and markets similar to ours. We will probably fill the current opening from these applicants.

Although you are not being selected for this position, I am aware that you wish to change your department and upgrade your level within the company. I encourage you to do this. Your sales record is good and your appraisal reports are positive. I am sure that we can find a position that best matches your experiences, background, and career goals.

Again, I appreciate your interest and hard work at SunStar, and good luck in all your future promotions.

Sincerely,

Invitation to a job interview

If you are in human resources or a hiring manager, you will need to communicate with candidates for positions open at your firm. Here is a letter you can use to invite an applicant in for a job interview.

Customize your own invitation to a job interview:

A letter that offers an invitation to a job interview should include:

1. A cordial "thank you" for the interest shown in working for your company.
2. An invitation to an interview. You can either state a time or ask the applicant to call your office and set up an appointment at a mutually convenient time.

Dear Ms. Myers:

With great pleasure, I am able to offer you a position at Artech Semiconductor as a quality engineer.

The position pays $38,000 annually, in equal increments, every other Friday. Additionally, you will receive two weeks paid vacation every 12 months, a bonus equaling two weeks' salary the payday before Christmas, health benefits, and $25,000 in life insurance. The position is a one-year agreement, after which it may be renegotiated. Either party can terminate with a two-week notice.

We are very pleased to offer you this position. Your starting date will be April 3rd at 9 a.m. You will report to Ms. Johnson, the senior supervisor. Please signify your acceptance of this offer by calling my office before Friday the 15th.

On a personal note, I think you'll enjoy working at Artech and will fit in well with our department. If you have any questions, please call me anytime.

Sincerely,

New employee introduction

This is an easy note to write. An easy way to get this letter written is to ask the new hire to draft it. Then you simply edit and distribute. If you want a more in-depth profile of the new hire, perhaps the editor of your employee newsletter can work one into a forthcoming issue. Or perhaps the public relations department can prepare a release for industry trade publications.

Customize your own letter to introduce a new employee:

This kind of internal office communication to introduce a new employee may be communicated in letter, memo, or e-mail format. It should include:

1. The new employee's name and position.
2. The new employee's responsibilities and working relationship with other employees.
3. The new employee's background.
4. A request for company employees to make the new person feel at home.

TO: New York office staff
FROM: Fred Guterola
RE: New employee

Starting next Monday, Raymond Starks will be joining our New York office as advertising manager.

Randy will be responsible for all marketing communications activities, except for trade shows (these will still be managed by Ben Buffett). He is the person to see when you need a new ad or brochure, and he will report directly to me. Please go through Randy for any advertising or collateral needs.

Randy comes to the New York area from our Wichita, Kansas, location, where he held the position of technical writer for five years. Since he's used to the wide open plains of Kansas, anything we can do to make him feel more at home here in the Big Apple will be appreciated (I suggest a Friday night trip to the Village for Frank's Pizza!).

Other employment letters

There are a few other instances when you may need to write letters regarding employment. These include writing a letter to ask someone to be your mentor, to refuse a request for a letter of recommendation, and to recommend a job applicant.

Asking someone to be a mentor

Here is a letter I sent decades ago to a direct marketing writer, asking him to be my mentor. Although he refused my offer of apprenticeship in his practice, we met for lunch in New York City's Plaza Hotel and have been fast friends ever since.

Customize your own letter asking someone to be a mentor:

When you write a letter asking someone to be your mentor, be sure to include:

1. An introductory piece of information that shows the person you've been following his or her work and career with admiration.
2. An offer to do something useful for the person in exchange for the opportunity to be nearby in a mentor relationship.
3. A request for a response.

December 2, 1981

RE: Your recent article in *Direct Marketing* magazine

Dear Mr. _____:

I enjoyed your recent article in *Direct Marketing* on "How to Write Copy That Sells." I'm an advertising manager for an engineering firm but a complete novice in direct mail. Frankly, I find your niche of letter writing fascinating, which is why I am writing this letter.

Perhaps from time to time when you take on clients selling technology and business products you find that doing the research to write these letters is time consuming. This is where I can help. Consider allowing me to explain the technology in lay language to these customers, so you can spend less time translating and more time writing your usual sizzling sales letter. I would do this free-of-charge hoping, in turn, to learn direct mail copywriting from a master (I am thinking about becoming a freelancer specializing in direct marketing of high-tech and industrial products).

How does this sound to you?

Sincerely,

Bob Bly

Refusing to write a letter of recommendation

When someone asks *you* for a letter of recommendation, are you obliged to write it, even if you had problems with the person in the past? This is a hard personal decision you have to make, but it would be dishonest to make a positive recommendation if it may hurt a potential employer. This course is better than agreeing to write the letter and then saying negative things.

Tell the person who requested the recommendation why you can't oblige without name-calling or baiting. State the facts as you see them in a gentle but firm tone. Doing so, you have fulfilled your obligation to the request in an honorable fashion.

Customize your own refusal to write a letter of recommendation:

When you write a letter to refuse a request for a letter of recommendation, you should include:

1. A cordial greeting.
2. Your refusal to write the recommendation.

3. A reason for your refusal. This can be a detailed account (while remaining professional and factual), or it can be a simple statement that says you do not share the same business philosophies.
4. A suggestion for finding a positive recommendation.

Dear Will:

Thanks for your letter. It was good to hear from you again. I wish I could be of some help, but unfortunately, after giving it careful consideration, I feel I can't in good conscience write the letter of recommendation that you requested.

You are competent on the technical side of the business. But you and I had (and have) a completely different perspective of being part of a work group. I appreciate your desire to have time for creative thought and contemplation. However, on a project team, my feeling is you can't do so at the expense of meeting deadlines. Other team members can't proceed to meet their milestones if you haven't met yours.

While you were at this company, you worked for a number of other people with whom you may have had a better relationship. I'm sure that one of them would be glad to write you a positive letter of recommendation.

Sincerely,

Recommending a job applicant

The key to this letter is unabashed enthusiasm. The reader knows you're a fan of the applicant, you wouldn't be writing it if you weren't. Don't pretend neutrality and then gush praise. Instead gush praise and admit you're an unabashed promoter of the applicant. Let your enthusiasm shine through.

Customize your own letter of recommendation:

To write a convincing letter of recommendation include:

1. A statement of whole-hearted recommendation.
2. Exemplary adjectives.
3. Detailed examples of positive work habits.
4. A wish to retain the person in your own employ.

Dear Mr. Keyes:

Since you're considering hiring Bonnie Denny as a customer service representative, let me do something I rarely do, and recommend this former employee wholeheartedly.

I have seen customer service reps come and go and their quality varies. But Bonnie is the cream of the crop. Her skills are superb. In addition to being friendly, helpful, and articulate, she knew both our products and our buyers inside and out. By being an advocate for the customer, she is a champion of the firm, and firmly cements the company's relationship with the buyer.

After Bonnie moved east with her husband, who was relocated, a number of customers called me directly and complained that she was no longer available to talk to. If I had an office in your area, I would do anything I could to retain her as an employee and hire her away from you. But I don't, so she's yours to hire.

Sincerely,

4

CORRESPONDING WITH COLLEAGUES

From fellow members of trade associations, to other businesspeople who work out at the same health club we do, we have many colleagues. Our relationship with them may be professional, personal, or both. But unlike co-workers, they don't work for the same company we do. Therefore, our communication with them must not assume knowledge of our product, service, or organization. Unless we've crossed the line from colleague to best friend, these correspondences should always remain professional.

Business greetings

Corresponding with professional colleagues is a terrific way to network. Don't miss out on this opportunity when you have the chance. This section will help you write letters to introduce yourself to a colleague, letters you should write after you have met someone you'd like to keep in touch with, and letters asking for a meeting or get-together.

Introducing yourself to a colleague

In today's teamwork-oriented, outsourced business world, you will frequently be working with, for, or supervising people you don't even know. A simple letter of introduction is a good way to gain cooperation and start the relationship off on the right foot.

Customize your own letter of introduction to a colleague:

Saying hello is easy. Just follow these four steps:

1. Introduce yourself and mention something positive about your relationship with this colleague.

Dear Robin:

I will be in Houston on June 22nd giving a customer service seminar at the Hilton. If you're available, can we have breakfast that morning?

We talked about getting together if I was ever in town so I can get a better feel for what Knight Co. is doing, and so you can get a better feel for whether there's a good fit between us.

This seminar is an ideal time because I will be in your neighborhood with a little extra time on my hands (and the seminar company is paying for travel costs, although I'll spring for the coffee and waffles).

Please let me know whether this sounds good to you so I can arrange my travel schedule accordingly.

Sincerely,

Letters of request

There are many occasions in the business world when you'll need to ask for something. You might need to ask for a favor, or for information, or for the opportunity to speak at an upcoming event. You might need to write for permission to reproduce materials in a project, or ask to serve on a committee. Sometimes you'll need to write a letter to refuse the request of someone else. These are only a few of the instances in which you'll need to ask for something, but the following letters will give you a good idea how to make any request.

Requesting a favor

People are often willing to grant favors—sometimes generous ones—to friends, colleagues, and sometimes even total strangers. But don't assume they will. Ask. In your request letter, be cordial, direct, and clear about what you want. If there is a reward or benefit to the reader for complying with your request, state it if you feel he or she needs extra convincing.

Customize your own letter requesting a favor:

A letter requesting a favor should say so right up front. There's no point trying mask the fact. Make sure your letter includes:

1. A request for a favor.

2. Details about the project you're working on or the circumstances of your situation.

3. An explanation why the recipient of the letter is the best person to grant this favor.

4. The exact specifications of the request (don't assume the recipient knows what you need).

5. An offer of something in return.

Dear Charles:

I have a favor to ask.

We are currently compiling a corporate history. It will be titled *Balson Nuclear: Half a Century of Radiant Progress* and will be privately published as a limited edition hardcover book by the corporation early next year. The main use is as a premium and promotion.

You are a respected professor in nuclear engineering and it was in your senior class that I learned much of what I needed to know to get hired by Balson.

Would you be willing to contribute a brief (200 to 300 word) preface about the importance of nuclear energy as a current and future energy source?

The company can pay you an honorarium of $500. In addition, your preface will be bylined so you can add the book to your list of publications. You will also get five free copies of the book.

Any interest? Please let me know. We would need the preface by June 20.

Sincerely,

Requesting information

When you are requesting important information, it's best to do it in writing rather than over the phone. The written request helps the reader understand exactly what you need, and it gives him or her a checklist to work with. This kind of written correspondence is more likely to get you what you need, when you need it.

Customize your own letter requesting information:

When you need accurate information, be specific so the reader knows exactly what you need:

1. Use numbers to list each piece of information you need.
2. Be very specific by asking questions that require detailed answers.
3. If you ask a question that requires a "yes" or "no" answer, back that up with an "If so, why (or what)?"

Dear Pam:

The questions I have for you are as follows:

1. What is different about this coming crash than previous market crashes? How will it differ (severity, speed, duration, and so forth)? Why? We want to show that this crash is unlike any the reader has experienced.

2. The notion that the stock market will crash is not contrarian, of course. Is there anything about your predictions for the markets that is contrarian? If so, what?

3. How do we explain the recent volatility in the market? Specifically, if a person gets our mailing and sees that the Dow Jones Average went up 78 points that day, what can we say to convince them that it will still go down over the long-run, and soon?

That's it. Please get back to me with some answers as soon as possible.

Requesting a speaking engagement

Are you good at what you do? If so, you can earn some extra money and market your services or product at the same time by giving speeches at seminars, workshops, conferences, and so forth. The first step is to get a go-ahead to be a guest speaker. The following letter will show you how to market yourself to build a schedule of speaking engagements.

Customize your own letter to request a speaking engagement:

When you write a letter that you hope will convince someone that you have something valuable to say, be sure to include:

1. A hook opening that grabs the reader's attention and makes him or her want to know more. This can be an interesting piece of research, a little-known fact, some information that is of immediate benefit to the reader.
2. Your request, directly stating your topic.
3. Your credentials that make you an expert on this topic.

4. A question asking if the reader is interested.

5. A request for a response.

Dear Ms. Smiley:

Did you know that, according to a recent survey in *Engineering Today,* the ability to write clearly and concisely can mean $100,000 extra in earnings over the lifetime of an engineer's career?

For this reason, I think your members might enjoy a presentation I have given to several business organizations around town "10 Ways to Improve Your Technical Writing." This presentation highlights the 10 most common writing mistakes that engineers make, and gives proven strategies for self-improvement.

As the director of Plain Language, Inc., a company that specializes in technical documentation, I have worked with hundreds of engineers to help them improve their writing skills.

Does this sound like the type of presentation that might fit well into your winter program schedule? I'd be delighted to speak before your group. Please phone or write so we can set a date.

Best regards,

Request to reproduce materials

As a general guideline, it is permissible to copy and use up to 300 words or one to two percent of a work without gaining written permission from the copyright holder. Any material more than this amount requires written permission. Permission is also required for reprinting any table, figure, poetry, or song lyric (even as short as one line).

As an author, I am frequently asked for permission to reproduce articles I have written. With so many requests, I don't have time to write a letter granting this permission. That's why I much prefer that the person making the request send me a simple release I can sign and send back. I suggest you use such a release when seeking usage permission from a colleague, publisher, or other source. The first letter below is a more informal variety, primarily for your own records. The second sample letter is much more detailed and formal; this is often used when requesting permission from publishing houses.

Customize your own letter requesting permission to copy:

Letters requesting permission should offer the recipient as much information as possible. Be sure to include:

1. Letterhead stationary so the recipient knows who you are.
2. The exact material you want to copy and where you saw it. You can make things easier by attaching a copy of the material.
3. Exactly what you intend to do with the material requested. State where it will be reprinted (whether it be in a newsletter, book, article, handout flyer, or otherwise), when it will be distributed, and who it will be distributed to.
4. The credit line you will include on your reprint.
5. A place for a signature of agreement and date.
6. An easy method of return, such as a fax number or a self-addressed stamped envelope.

Letter #1:

Dear Mr. Smith:

I read your article called "Listening Skills" at the www.bizideas.com website and was quite impressed.

I will be conducting a workshop for our employees on communications skills and will have a module on listening. May I reprint your article as a handout for our training session?

We would like to distribute approximately 20 copies. If this is okay with you, please sign below and fax this letter back to me at 123-456-7890. If there are any charges, please let me know. Also, we will credit the article as bylined on the Web site, unless you have an alternate credit line that you prefer we use.

Sincerely,

APPROVED BY (signature)_____ DATE_____

Letter #2:

Date _____

To:

I am preparing a manuscript to be published by _____

Author/ tentative title _____

Estimated publication date _____ Approximate number of pages ___

    I request your permission to include the following material in this and all subsequent editions of my document, including versions made by nonprofit organizations for use of blind or physically handicapped persons, and in all foreign-language translations, and other derivative works published or prepared by the publisher or its licensees for distribution throughout the world.

Author(s) and/or editor(s)_____

Title of book or periodical_____

Title of selection _____Copyright date_____

from page ____, line _, beginning with the words_____

from page ____, line _, ending with the words _____

Figure# _____, on page _____ Table # ____,on page _____ .
(If necessary, attach continuation sheets.)

    Please indicate agreement by signing and returning the enclosed copy of this letter. In signing, you warrant that you are the sole owner of the rights granted and that your material does not infringe upon the copyright or other rights of anyone. If you do not control these rights, I would appreciate your letting me know to whom I should apply.

    Thank you.

_____

Agreed to and accepted:

By_____

        Signature   *Title*   *Date*

Credit and/or copyright notice: _____

_____

_____

Request asking someone to serve on an association committee

When you want someone to serve on a committee, the key is to make the invitation sound more like an opportunity than a favor. Focus on the benefits to the person, not only to the organization. Here is a letter you can use to invite a member to take a more proactive role in a professional or trade association.

Customize your own letter asking someone to serve on an association committee:

A letter asking someone to serve on a committee should include:

1. An upbeat tone of congratulations (don't ever imply a "sorry to do this to you" attitude).
2. A flattering reason why this person is the perfect candidate.
3. A contact person or co-member.
4. A benefit the person will personally gain from making this commitment.

Dear Roger:

It is with pleasure that I invite you to co-chair this year's Outside Speaker Committee.

Based on the great talk you gave last year, I feel speaker selection and recruitment is right up your alley. I know many of your colleagues do speaking, so here's a chance for you to showcase the best among them. As a 19-year PLT member, you know the audience's interests and needs as well as anyone.

Since we need to get started in putting together next year's programs, please let me know whether you're available to serve as co-chair. Karen Gross from Elway Technology will be your co-chair. Getting to know her well wouldn't hurt, since Elway could certainly use the types of services you offer.

Sincerely,

Letters of thanks

There are many occasions in everyday business where thank you notes are appropriate—and smart. In the rush to get ahead, we often forget to look back at what someone has done for us, and take the time to let that person know it was appreciated. This is of course, good manners, but in the push-and-shove of business, it's also the perfect way to make yourself stand out as someone who's not just a user.

Thanking a colleague for a referral

People appreciate recognition when they've given your name as a referral. Conversely, if you don't acknowledge them, they'll think you're an ingrate and give the referral to someone else next time. In fact, a second follow-up thank you a few weeks later is also a nice touch if the referral works out well for you. You might even consider enclosing a small but tasteful gift with your thank you notes—perhaps a desk calendar or a pocket diary.

Fortunately, "thank you" can be said elegantly yet simply. The first sentence of the following model letter is particularly eloquent.

Customize your own letter thanking a colleague for a referral:

Keep a copy of this letter on file in your computer. It's simple to print out and send it. Yet, this letter can reap more benefits than weeks of marketing and advertising. Be sure to include:

1. A statement that directly says "thank you."
2. The name of the person who called as a result of the referral.
3. An assurance that you will do a good job for this person (implying you will not make your correspondent regret thinking of you).

Dear Bob:

In this busy world of ours, it's gratifying when people take time to help others. It's for this reason that I'm writing to thank you.

At your suggestion, Paul Karnac recently called to contract my services. I really appreciate this referral. It looks like Paul and I will be doing a lot of business in the future. I'm sure he will be pleased with my work and will be happy you passed on my name.

Thanks again for thinking of me.

Warm regards,

Thank you for a favor

Thank people for favors in writing. Otherwise they have no way of knowing you're appreciate of, or even aware of the favor they rendered. They may even assume you are ungrateful, which will unfairly remove you from their good graces.

Customize your own letter of thanks for a favor:

A thank you for a favor is the easiest kind of letter to put aside and never write. It crosses your mind that it was nice of someone to do something for you, but you never communicate that thought. The days go by and soon it's an old idea. Put your thanks in words in three simple statements:

1. State specifically what you're thankful for.
2. Assure the recipient that he or she won't regret helping you out.
3. Offer to return the favor at any time.

Dear Jennifer:

Just a quick note to say "thank you." I spoke to Jed Hasslen today. He told me that on my recommendation you hired him to do some illustrations for your customer newsletter. I'm glad to bring new business to a talented, young artist like Jed– and I appreciate that you've given him a chance. I'm sure you'll be well pleased.

If there's ever anything I can do for you to return the favor, don't hesitate to ask. Thanks again!

Sincerely,

Here's another thank you letter in response to a generous contribution.

Dear Sol:

Your offer is very generous, and I accept! Our town school has a severe shortage of computers per student. Especially my son's third-grade class. Your old Mac is the perfect solution. I can pick up the Mac from you at your convenience and deliver it myself to Jason's classroom.

I know you said you have a lot of used computers around, but that doesn't make the act any less generous or helpful. I am grateful. Let me know how I can return the favor.

Sincerely,

---

1. Congratulate the recipient, and spell out exactly what the congratulations are for.
2. You can add humor if you like to take the edge off sounding too formal or insincere.
3. Flatter the recipient by mentioning the importance of this honor.

Dear Scott:

Congratulations! I saw in *TMI Journal* yesterday that you won yet another EGGY Award! That makes six, doesn't it?

As you know, I've only won once. So you are embarrassing me terribly. If you don't stop, I'll have no choice but to tell everyone you steal all my best ideas and the awards really belong to me, although of course it's more the opposite way around!

Seriously, congratulations again on this important honor. You are the only six-time EGGY winner I know. You should feel proud.

Sincerely,

The turn down

Unfortunately, sometimes it's necessary to say no to colleagues who ask you to do something.

Refusing a request

A polite letter goes a long way in helping people understand why you can't comply with a request. The reason is usually lack of time. The reader understands and readily accepts this because he or she also suffers the same problem.

Customize your own letter refusing a request:

When you put together a refusal be sure to include:

1. An opening compliment. Say something positive to break the ice.
2. A definite no, that leaves no doubt about your position.
3. A statement that keeps the door open to business in the future.

Congratulation Letters

The competitive environment of business can sometimes keeps us from officially recognizing the accomplishments of our colleagues. When someone in your field opens a new business, accepts a new position, or wins an honor or an award, dash off a congratulatory letter. Not only is it simple, it is also a valuable personal and business practice that reaps future benefits in both goodwill and business gains.

Congratulations to a colleague opening a new business

Whenever a colleague or anyone else you know starts a new business, send him or her a written congratulations on your letterhead. Not only does this build goodwill, but it also gives them a permanent record of your phone number and other contact information in case they ever need you. Who knows? He or she may be a potential client, vendor, or employer for you some day in the near future. If there is any possibility of this happening, hint at it in the letter, but avoid the hard sell.

Customize your own congratulation to a colleague opening a new business:

When you send a letter of congratulations to a colleague opening a new business, be sure to:

1. Say congratulations for beginning this new venture.
2. Offer a wish for success and personal pleasure.
3. Ask to be kept informed about the business.
4. Offer your help if needed.

Dear Anthony:

Congratulations on your new digital prepress business! May you derive much success and pleasure from it.

You know that I buy prepress services from time to time, so please keep in touch and maintain my name on your mailing list. I'd like to stay informed about your services. And if you never need anything from me, call anytime.

Sincerely,

Congratulations to a colleague accepting a new position

Similar to the colleague who opens her own business, congratulations are in order for a colleague who receives a promotion. You never know when a promotion may put a person in a better position to have a relationship with you as a vendor, customer, or employer.

Customize your congratulations to a colleague accepting a new position:

When you write a congratulatory letter to a colleague who has just been promoted, be sure to mention:

1. A rousing congratulations.
2. Where you heard the news.
3. Your position and how it relates to the person's new position (if appropriate).
4. That you would be glad to provide any help or advice.

Dear Cynthia:

Congratulations on your recent promotion! I read about it in the "people" column in *Technology News*. The clipped article is enclosed in case you want an extra copy.

Your new job as Vice President of Global Marketing sounds exciting and challenging. As you know, I've been involved in direct marketing of my company's software overseas for about a year. If there's any information or resources I can share with you in your expanded role, just let me know.

Sincerely,

Congratulations to a colleague who has won an honor or award

There's no real "need" to send this letter, but just do it anyway. This is a perfect way to show that your style of business does not include jealousy or backstabbing. Such a letter is also an investment in goodwill, with the potential to pay big dividends down the road.

Customize your congratulations for a colleague who has won an honor or an award:

---

4. A good luck wish for success in the venture you are refusing to join.

Dear Neil:

Thanks for the big notebook and the customer service book. Both are at your usual high level of excellence. Unfortunately, the answer to your question is, no. I'm unable to take on any additional projects right now, as I'm already too busy.

If you need further help down the line, be sure to let me know. Hopefully, my schedule will open up and allow me take on interesting work like this at a later date.

I wish you luck with the project.

Best regards,

Declining an invitation

It is very rude to ignore an invitation, even when the answer is no. The "R" in "RSVP" stands for "respond." When you simply toss an invitation without a reply it inconveniences the person making the arrangements and it annoys the person who sent the invitation. To stay on good terms with a colleague who sends you an invitation for an event you cannot attend, write a quick note explaining your situation.

Customize your own letter declining an invitation:

When you have to say no, remember:

1. Say thank you and mention exactly what the invitation was for. (Some people have more than one thing going on at a time.)
2. Mention that you value your relationship with the person.
3. Cite "prior commitment" as your reason for not attending. (Unless you choose to, there's no reason to go into the details of your refusal.)
4. Open the door to a get-together some time in the future.

Dear Gloria:

Thanks for the invitation to the Armbusters Syndicate's annual holiday bash, and for the nice words regarding my consulting services. I too enjoy and value our work together.

Unfortunately, because of prior commitments, I won't be able to make it into New York City that night to attend. Perhaps we can meet when I am in the city early in the New Year?

Thanks again for the invitation. It is very much appreciated.

Sincerely,

Letters of personal concern

Business is business, but sometimes your colleagues experience personal problems or losses that you can acknowledge through a brief note of concern. In certain circumstances, it's important to show sincere interest in colleagues as people with lives outside the office.

Letter with get-well wishes or of sympathy

In today's high tech world, many people crave the personal touch. It's totally appropriate to send a letter to a business associate regarding a personal matter, if there is an established relationship between you, no matter how small. The following sample letter voices concern over a colleague's health problem, but you can use the format to adapt a letter about any issue of personal concern.

Customize your own letter of personal concern:

When you're writing to someone who has experienced a loss whether through illness, death, or even downsizing, remember to mention:

1. Your understanding of the loss.
2. Your own experience with the same situation (if appropriate).
3. An offer of help.

Dear Sharon,

I heard from Katie that you had back surgery and are out of the hospital recuperating. From my own experiences, I know how difficult being at home for an extended period can be. I hope you are feeling better and will make a full recovery soon.

If there is anything I can do to make this time easier for you, please don't hesitate to call me. I know you would do the same for me.

Sincerely,

Here's a sympathy letter you could send if a colleague has a death in the family:

Dear Don,

I've just heard about the death of your father. I wanted you to know how sorry I am for your loss. Having lost my own father only a few years ago, I understand how difficult a time this is for you.

If there is anything I can do, don't hesitate to call me. I know it can take some time to get back on track after such an emotionally draining experience.

Best wishes,

5

CORRESPONDING WITH VENDORS

As the buyer, you probably have the upper hand over your vendors. After all, the adage states that "the customer is always right," and you're the customer. However, if you miscommunicate with or mistreat a vendor, you're the one whose bottom line is going to be affected.

Here are some tips for more effective customer-to-supplier communication:

1. Put everything in writing. If something changes after the purchase order or contract is signed, make sure to put the changes into writing.
2. Be specific and precise. Spell out the details, terms, and conditions.
3. Don't be a difficult customer. Difficult customers are often perceived as pests. Vendors may put you at the bottom of their priority list rather than the top. You won't know they've done this...until your orders take more time to arrive.
4. Don't overestimate your importance and power. Some customers delight in making vendors jump. However, they are surprised when successful vendors, who already have plenty of business, won't fill more orders for them.

Hiring vendors

You can pick up the phone and order just about any service you want. But to avoid misunderstandings and unexpected bills, you should put everything in writing. The following sample letters will help you place a quick order, request proposals and sales presentations, award a contract, notify losing bidders, and create a work for hire contract.

Placing a quick order

Sometimes, when you know exactly what you want and who you want it from, you can dash off this kind of easy order request.

Customize your own letter for a quick order:

When you send off a letter placing an order be sure to include:

1. Exactly what you need.
2. How many you need.
3. When you need it.
4. How you will pay.
5. How and when the vendor should confirm receipt of the order.

Dear Samantha:

Our publishing company is planning its annual sales meeting on June 30 in Atlanta, Georgia. Approximately 225 people will attend.

While I realize that time is short, is it possible to obtain 250 copies of your brochure "Quality Time in Quality Lives" before June 15? These can be shipped COD to my attention at the above address.

If possible, would you call my assistant, Ivan Johnson, within the next week to let him know whether these are available? Your cooperation is very much appreciated.

Sincerely,

Requesting a proposal

A request for proposal (RFP) is a formal document inviting a supplier to bid on a project and outlining the items their proposal must address. RFPs typically include a letter of transmittal, as shown in the following letter.

Customize your own letter requesting a proposal:

When you want to invite a vendor to place a bid on a project, be sure your letter of request includes:

1. The job you want to hire out.
2. Notification that a request for proposal form (RFP) is enclosed.
3. The criteria that will be used to select a proposal.
4. An invitation to call with questions or clarifications.

Dear Richard:

We have recently won a large-scale government project to produce mobile ground-based radar stations. We want to subcontract the antenna interface design and manufacture to one or more outside contractors.

Our RFP is enclosed. If you wish to bid on this project, please respond by the date indicated in the RFP. Proposals will not be accepted after the deadline date.

Price as always is an important consideration. But we are not constrained to accept the low bid. The technical solution, reliability of supply, and conformance to military specifications are also important factors in our selection of subcontractors.

If you have any questions about this, please call me at 123-456-7890.

Sincerely,

(enclosure)

Requesting a sales presentation

It's not difficult to get vendors to compete with one another to win your business. However, just because they'll come at the drop of a hat doesn't mean such presentations are productive. Tell them why you are inviting them in. Explain what they should bring and how to prepare. Be specific about the outcomes you expect. Why waste their time or yours? Make every meeting more productive!

Customize your own letter requesting a sales presentation:

When you ask someone to present their service, idea, or product, tell them in writing exactly what you're looking for:

1. Begin by complimenting their work or reputation and extending an invitation to present a sales presentation.
2. Make it clear that this is a sales presentation, not a paid consultation.
3. Emphasize that you are actively seeking to hire someone for this job.
4. Tell the vendor exactly what you're looking for and what he or she can do to prepare for the meeting.
5. Set a date and time, or ask the vendor to call to arrange a convenient appointment.

Notifying losing bidders

Every sales presentation and proposal requires a response, even when it's a negative one. Here is the form letter you can send to the firms who didn't get the business.

Customize your own letter to notify losing bidders:

This is a form letter you can keep on file in your computer and fill in the blanks when you need to send out notifications to losing bidders. It includes:

1. An assurance that the proposal has been carefully reviewed.
2. A compliment about the quality of the company's work.
3. A statement of rejection.
4. A thank you.
5. A promise to consider the company for future projects.

RE: RFP #_____.

Dear _____,

Your proposal for the _____ project has been carefully reviewed. While you are an impressive vendor, we have chosen to go with another subcontractor.

I thank you for your proposal effort. Your products might be right for some of our other contracts, and I will keep your company's name on file for consideration for future projects.

Sincerely,

Work for hire contract

A "work for hire" contract verifies that a vendor agrees to supply services for a fixed fee, and you own all rights to what you produce from this service. Here is a standard work for hire agreement you can keep on file to fill in the blanks when needed.

TO: [insert name of vendor]

[insert name of your company] requests you to prepare the following:

Description of work: _____

Due date: _____

Fee: $_____

[insert name of your company] agrees to pay you the above amount upon our acceptance of the work.

You understand that the labor performed is a "work for hire." [insert name of your company] shall own all rights to the work in its name or otherwise.

You warrant that the work will be an original work that has not been in the public domain or previously created, and that the work will be free of any unauthorized extractions from other sources. You further understand that [insert name of your company] has the privilege of referring to you as a vendor in sales and marketing presentations and materials.

Please signify your approval of this agreement by completing the form below and return one copy to us for our files.

Signed_____

TO: [insert name of your company]

I agree to perform the work listed above, and I accept the terms of this agreement as stated above.

Signature_____ SSN or Federal Tax ID #_____
                (Vendor)   (Required by IRS)

Placing and receiving orders from vendors

There are several letters you'll need when placing and receiving orders from vendors. The following sample letters include a sample purchase order, a letter to place an order, to refuse a shipment, to cancel an order, and to report damages to an insurance carrier.

Sample purchase order

Many companies use standard purchase orders to buy goods and services. If you don't already have a form for this, you can use this one or a version of it.

[insert your company name and address]	Purchase Order	
	Date:	
	Authorized by:	
Issued to:	Ship via:	
	Ship to attn.:	
Telephone Number:	Ship by (date):	

Description	Price

Purchase order number must appear on all invoices and correspondence. Please sign and return second and third copies.

Signed:	Date:

Placing an order

Small businesses that don't use purchase forms or have computerized accounting systems often use simple letters to place orders or confirm telephone orders.

Customize your own letter to place an order:

The format of an order can be anything you want it to be, but be sure to include certain vital information such as:

1. Your company name and address (presumably on your letterhead).
2. Directions on how you want the order shipped.
3. A clear, numbered list of the items you're ordering.

To whom it may concern:

Please send the following items to the above address via Fast Express Next Day Air:

Catalog No. 675-XS, toner cartridge, $80 X 4 = $320
Catalog No. 232-QP, Canary yellow card stock (case), $47 X 1 = $47
Total of order: $367.

Sincerely,

Refusing a shipment

Sometimes you will get a shipment from a vendor that needs to be returned. It may contain the wrong items, or the quality of the product may not meet your expectations. In these cases, you can either ask the company to correct the mistake, or you can cancel the order and request a refund. In either case, explain clearly why you are returning the items and what you expect the vendor to do.

Customize your own letter to refuse a shipment:

When refusing a shipment, state exactly what items you're returning. You should:

1. Give your order number and a copy of the original purchase order (if you had one).
2. Explain your reason for returning the items.
3. State what you want the vendor to do: either correct the order or refund your money.
4. Give a date by which you expect the correction or the refund.
5. End with a cordial thank you.

Dear Mr. Millington,

I am returning with this letter a recent shipment of 500 imprinted golf balls (order #3345) along with a copy of our original purchase order.

As stated, the logo should be reproduced in our corporate color, which is green. The logos on the golf balls you sent are bright blue, and therefore unacceptable.

Please make the necessary corrections and send another shipment of 500 golf balls (with the logo in our corporate green) by the 15th of this month. We need them for a company-sponsored event that starts the first of next month.

Thanks for your prompt attention to this matter.

Sincerely,

Canceling an order

There are many reasons you might cancel an order after you've placed it. You might get tired of waiting for delivery. Or, if the product was not a special order just for you, you might cancel it if you find the material for a less expensive price elsewhere or if you decide you don't need it any more. For whatever the reason, your cancellation should be made in writing. If time is of the essence, send a fax or e-mail, then follow up with a signed hard copy letter.

Customize your own letter canceling an order:

1. Give your order number.
2. State the reason you are canceling your order.
3. Make it clear that since you did not accept delivery of the items, you do not expect to receive a bill.

RE: Order #794556

Dear Mark:

After a six-week wait, we have not received the connectors we ordered from your company.

At this point, we can't wait any longer without the risk of missing our production deadlines. I am buying the connectors from a local supplier and canceling my order with you.

I do not expect to receive a bill.

Sincerely,

Day-to-day contact with vendors

When you hire out work, you will often need to keep in touch with the vendors. The following sample letters will show you how to request a status update, request changes to a job, or discontinue an order.

Requesting a status update

A fax or e-mail memo is a good way to request a status update on an order or project from your vendors. Putting the query in writing helps clarify what you're asking for and it shows the vendor you are serious and expect a timely response.

Customize your own letter requesting a status update:

Keeping track of your vendors can keep you very busy. Make it simple with a two or three-sentence request for a status update. Include:

1. The project you're inquiring about.
2. The date you expect to see the finished work.
3. Any information that will help the vendor meet your expectations.
4. A date by which you expect a status report.

Dear Sam:

How is the website coming? I know things are hectic over there, but I'm looking forward to seeing a sample of the site by Friday the 22nd. Be sure to scan in the photo I sent you last week and add the link to the publisher as we discussed. Please let me know how things are progressing by the end of this week.

Thanks,

Requesting changes to a job

Another situation in which communication with vendors should be made or at least confirmed in writing is a request for changes to a job in progress.

Customize your own letter requesting changes to a job:

It is important that this letter be very specific and each change be numbered. Be sure to include:

1. The name of the project you're talking about.
2. A positive comment to open.
3. A numbered and detailed list of the changes you want.
4. A date you will call to confirm that the changes are understood.

RE: Your invoice #_____

Dear Vendor:

Your invoice is being returned to you for the following reason(s):

☐ No purchase order number

☐ No job number

☐ No social security or federal tax ID number

☐ Amount of invoice does not match purchase order

☐ No sign-off of acceptance from customer

☐ No/incomplete receipt of goods

Please add any missing data and resolve any of the other issues indicated. Then resubmit your invoice for payment.

Letters of thanks

Sometimes a vendor is particularly good. When that happens, say so in writing. This simple communication is an excellent way to cement business relationships that benefit both the client and the vendor.

Praising a vendor

Customers are quick to complain and slow to praise. If you are happy with a vendor, tell him or her. The goodwill from such an act will make you stand out!

Customize your own letter praising a vendor:

When you have something nice to say, it's not necessary to get gushy or overdo the flattery. Simply state:

1. What you like about the service or product.
2. How it has helped your business.
3. That the vendor can expect more business from you in the future.

Dear Tiffany:

I want to tell you how much we like your video "I Don't Have Customers."

We recently used it in our seminar "Interpersonal Skills for Systems Professionals." The video clearly and forcefully gets across the point to our trainees that we all have customers—even those of us who serve internal departments. One technical professional said after the course that viewing the tape opened his eyes and changed his entire attitude for the better.

Thanks again for a great tape. I'm sure your videos will become an essential element of our interpersonal skills courses in the future.

Sincerely,

Thank you for extra effort

In today's competitive business world, many vendors bend over backwards to service, please, and retain clients. Clients know this and often demand it. The only reward for the vendor is often retention of the account.

When a vendor pulls out all the stops to serve you, the least expensive thing you can do to motivate them is to thank them sincerely. Few customers do it, so your note of appreciation stands out. If you don't think motivating suppliers should be a concern of yours, think again. Not all customers are treated equally, some are a vendor's favorites. Why not position yourself as a favorite customer, so when it counts, you will get the service and delivery you need?

Customize your own letter thanking a vendor for extra effort:

You can't send a written letter of thanks to every person you do business with all day long, but when someone goes out of the way to make things work for you, be sure to tell them with a letter that includes:

1. A loud thank you.
2. Your understanding that this was a special effort.
3. A promise of future business.

Dear Madelyn:

What a great Orlando meeting! And we have you to thank!

The problems with the hotel could not have been anticipated. When they happen, most clients come down on their meeting planners, as I did on you.

The pressure from my unhappy management made me short-tempered. But not only did you handle the situation with grace, you got things solved! Aside from the first-day mishaps, this was our smoothest conference ever.

You can be sure of our continued patronage of your meeting planning services. In fact, we should be thinking about next year soon. Give me a call after Labor Day if you don't hear from me first.

Sincerely,

Customize your own action memo:

To work efficiently, your action memo should contain the following:

1. Use a standard memo header, including the names of all recipients, your name, the date, and the subject matter.
2. State your information simply and clearly.
3. Tell the recipients what you expect them to do next.

TO: Joe Carr
          Mary Coppeyn
          Cheryl Flanart
          Donna Simps
FROM: Kathy Westerholff
RE: Training budget

We have just completed the budgeting process for next year and have established several key areas to focus on. One of those areas is skill building in customer service and communications.

In order to continue to improve the abilities of our employees to maximize customer service, we have decided to invest $5,000 per employee on training during the upcoming year. This is the biggest investment in training we have made in our eight years in business.

In January, I will meet with each of you individually to set goals, review your current skill level in a variety of areas, and to start to identify potential training sessions you should attend.

Please stop by my office sometime next week and pick up an assessment form that we'll go over in our meeting.

Spelling out simple instructions

Putting ideas and instructions in writing helps clarify them not only for the recipient, but also for the writer. Around our office, for example, we frequently write short e-mails to make clear requests of one another. Here's a sample—an e-mail I sent to my secretary concerning the preparation of the manuscript of this book for the publisher.

Customize your own memo spelling out simple instructions:

Even though they are simple, memos of instruction have an important purpose: They detail exactly what you expect and when it must be done. Giving your employees this written record of instructions increases the likelihood that it will happen the way you want it to. Use memo format, state what you want done and the date it is to be done by.

TO: PCM
FROM: Bly
RE: Letter book

Within three to four weeks, I will send you the following files for my book with Career Press: LETFM1, LETCH 1-10, LETTAPPA, LETAPPB, LETBM1.

When you get all the files I would like you to number pages in upper right corner print out, and send hard copy to Betty Shelley at her home address, one copy and disk to Jon at Career Press in Franklin Lakes, and one hard copy to me. Please do this within 48 hours of receiving the disks.

Thanks,

Announcing a change in company policy or procedure

This is a simple, straightforward communication that requires a written record. All employees must be kept up-to-date on changes and should not have to rely on the grapevine for this information.

Customize your own memo announcing a change in company policy or procedure:

This memo should get straight to the point:

1. Announce the change.
2. State when the change takes effect.
3. Provide instructions outlining how the new procedures are to be followed.

Memo of confirmation

If you are concerned that your discussion was not understood or that the other person won't meet his or her obligations, be sure to send a memo of confirmation. If it's in writing, the other person will take it more seriously. A confirmation letter is also recommended if any money is to change hands, or if important deadlines are involved.

Customize your own internal memo of confirmation:

Using correct memo format, confirm by including:

1. A positive note.
2. Details of the facts you wish to confirm.
3. An invitation to contact you for clarification.

TO: Jennifer Croocens
FROM: Jane Seey
RE: Project confirmation

Thanks for spending some time with me this morning to go over the WatchWord project. As we agreed:

1. To complete this project on time, you can hire a consultant for a fee of $1,000.
2. The deadline remains May 14th.
3. We will meet again to check progress on May 1st.

In the meantime, please call me with any questions.

Encouraging employee usage of company perks

Many companies, especially large corporations, give a variety of benefits and perks that many employees don't fully use and some don't even know about.

Benefits and perks are part of the employee's total compensation package, and most employees today look at perks and not just the base salary when evaluating how well you take care of them and whether they should look elsewhere for a better deal. Therefore, encouraging employees to use company services and perks not only builds goodwill, but it also aids in employee retention.

Customize your own letter encouraging employee usage of company perks:

This letter should serve as a detailed announcement and a reminder. Include:

1. The perk you want to focus on.
2. The facts such as time, place, and benefit to employees.
3. Further explanation of the advantages (if appropriate).
4. A note about this perk being "special" for your employees only.

TO: All Beldicite Technologies Employees
FROM: Ron Matthews
RE: Lobby discount sale

Just a reminder: Once a month we offer our own closed-out and damaged merchandise to Beldicite employees at incredible discounts, often up to 70 percent off list price.

I encourage you to stop by and look over the merchandise displayed in the lobby at lunch hour on the last Friday of the month. You can get some incredible bargains if you're looking for a VCR, stereo, CD player, tape deck, and other Beldicite electronics products. The closeouts are current models about to be replaced by next year's model; usually the difference in features is minimal. The "damaged" goods may be slightly scuffed from shipping but are otherwise new and in perfect working order. All merchandise is covered by the standard Beldicite one-year warranty (although if you work in service, you may end up repairing it yourself while at work!).

This is a great deal that is available only to Beldicite employees.

Offering new benefits to employees

It is a pleasurable task to inform employees of new benefits. Your letter should explain the benefit, encourage its usage, and build goodwill by showing the value of what you are offering.

Customize your own letter offering new benefits to employees:

A memo announcing new benefits can get lost in the paper shuffle if it looks like any of the other hundred memos your employees receive each day. The sample above presents the benefit with an attention-grabbing headline. It then goes on to state:

1. A lead that engages the reader's interest.

2. A statement of the added benefit.
3. A few details about the benefit.
4. Directions how to obtain more information.
5. The inclusion of a brochure with more details.

**As you go through life, your housing needs change.
Now the Employee Mortgage Program can make sure
you get the cash you need to make those changes happen.**

Dear Employee,

Buying a home? Refinancing a home? Don't have a clue where to begin?

Well, easy home financing starts here...with the Employee Mortgage Program from Southwest Mortgage.

Through this value-added program, Beldicite employees have preferred-status access to the mortgage services of Southwest Mortgage. With more than 20 years of home-financing experience...and 1 million satisfied borrowers nationwide...Southwest Mortgage has helped more corporate employees land the home of their dreams than any other mortgage company in the region.

If you are curious about whether you qualify for a mortgage, call Southwest Mortgage Monday through Friday, 8 a.m. to midnight at 800-123-4567. Experienced Mortgage Advisors can tell you just how big a mortgage you can get.

The attached brochure shows you the many ways Southwest Mortgage can help you come out ahead in the housing game.

Sincerely,

Announcing a change in health benefits coverage

When you change health benefit coverage, the change may not be universally seen as an improvement. Employees tend to feel unjustly ripped off and need an explanation about why this is happening and how it will affect them. This kind of major change should be presented on paper—not by e-mail.

Customize your own letter announcing changes in health benefits coverage:

This kind of change that directly affects each employee should be stated directly and clearly so there is no misunderstanding. Include:

1. An immediate statement that there is going to be a change.
2. A reason for the change.
3. The details of the change.
4. The benefits of this change to the employee (there must be something!).
5. An offer to explain further or answer questions.

TO: All employees
FROM: Rachel Bronkson, Employee Benefits Manager
RE: Change in major medical coverage

As of May 14, there will be a change in our employee health coverage.

Each year our insurance broker, Senders & Johnson, performs an audit of all our policies to help control corporate health care expenses. As the result of this year's audit, we will be keeping Guardian General as carrier but switching to one of their alternative plans to prevent health costs from spiraling out of control.

The coverage is nearly identical to the current plan, with one major exception: The deductible per illness has been raised from $50 to $250.

Although having a higher deductible is not a positive change, there are other aspects of the change that compensate. We can afford to keep our private major medical plan with Guardian, enabling our employees to continue to be reimbursed while choosing the physicians and other health care providers they prefer. Without this plan readjustment, we probably would have been forced into an HMO or PPO, which in our recent employee survey the majority of you said you did not want. The new plan permits you to keep seeing your regular doctors and have the visits paid for.

The modified coverage will be in force effective May 14. If you have any questions, call me at X5567 or e-mail me via company mail at RCHLBRON.

Communication with your employer

Request for training

In my second corporate job, I had to handle the management of trade show displays—an area in which I had little experience. Unfortunately, my boss was not a fan of training or spending money he didn't have to. Here is the letter I sent that convinced him to spend $450 to have me attend a two-day local seminar on trade show management.

Customize your own letter requesting training:

The trick here is to show that the time and cost of training will increase profits and productivity. Include:

1. A clear statement of what training program you want to attend.
2. An acknowledgment of the cost and a statement explaining how this cost will be recouped in improved sales, profits, productivity, and the like.
3. The reason why you need the training.
4. A direct request for the go-ahead.

TO: Mike Olson
FROM: Bob Bly
RE: Training Program

Dear Mike:

Enclosed is a brochure I received on a seminar called "Trade Show University." I'd like to take this program.

I realize the tuition of $450 is not cheap. But we will spend $100,000 this year redoing our displays and exhibiting at shows. If the seminar can help me cut these costs even five percent, it will pay for itself more than 10 times over.

My previous experience is in booth design only. I have not managed the exhibit from start to finish. The more knowledge I have, the smarter the buying decisions I can make.

Can I go ahead and register, and have Ken in accounting cut a $450 check to Trade Show University? Please let me know. Thanks.

Request to attend a trade show

Trade shows offer unique opportunities to learn, network, or just visit a nice venue for a day or so. If you want to go but aren't on the approved list, send a request to your manager.

Customize your own letter requesting to attend a trade show:

Trade shows take you away from work and cost money. Show your boss that it's worth it by mentioning:

1. Your company position and a problem in your area that needs to be solved.
2. How attending a trade show will help you fix a problem in the company.
3. The cost of the show and how this money is an investment in future progress or profits.
4. A direct request to make all necessary arrangements and file receipts on an expense report.

TO: Bob Norman
FROM: Fred Bulsara
RE: Control and Instrumentation Expo

Dear Bob:

As you know, you recently reassigned me to process management. Part of the immediate task Larry has set for me is control optimization. My initial review indicates that current equipment, some of it 10 years old, can't handle the requirements we have.

Rather than visit control manufacturers individually to demo new models, I'd like to attend the upcoming Control and Instrumentation Expo. The vendors I'm interested in are all exhibiting at the show, and four of them have live demonstrations at their booths. This will enable me to evaluate four potential systems in one visit and compare them side by side.

Several manufacturers have sent me complimentary passes. My only expenses would be round trip travel for a day to and from Pittsburgh which is around $500. I feel this is a good investment considering that the control system we select will have an expected lifetime of eight to 10 years.

Can I make travel reservations and then file the receipts with my expense report? Please let me know.

Creating a new position

Usually you cannot create a new position without the approval of your boss or human resources, or both. Write a memo that explains the need and makes clear the necessity. Speak as the authority in the needs of your department.

Customize your own letter asking for permission to create a new position:

This request asks for a major change and investment. Be convincing in your approach. Include:

1. A hook to the employer's own feelings about progress in the company.
2. The name of the position you want to create and what purpose it would serve.
3. Evidence that you have researched the idea with other employees who would be affected positively by the creation of this position.
4. A recommendation of person from within the company who could fill the position and the details why this person is best. If no one from within is qualified, propose that a new employee be hired and state the qualifications that this person should possess.
5. An enclosed job description that shows you have thoroughly investigated and planned the new position.
6. A direct request for approval.

TO: Ruth Marker
FROM: Ted Strykar
RE: Creating a position for an in-house Web designer

Dear Ruth:

At our meeting last week, you agreed that we need to increase the power of our on-line presence. I believe one step toward meeting this need would be to create the position of an in-house Web designer.

I investigated the matter and talked with supervisors in both graphics and IT. They agree that this would be a wise move, and we all feel that Dick Young could handle the position very capably.

Dick has been with our firm in IT for only six months, but has very strong technical skills in new technologies including HTML and Java. In addition, he is a Web junkie, and knows the Internet inside and out. Right now he is doing Y2K Cobol conversion and, quite frankly, is bored. In this new position, he would become our in-house expert in Web design—something for which he is unabashedly enthusiastic.

Attached is a job description for the Web designer position. If this meets with your approval, I'd like to begin the process with Human Resources so we could create the position, establish the salary, and offer Dick the job. What do you think?

Sincerely,

Asking for a pay raise

This is always a tough letter to write. You have to blow your own horn without sounding conceited, and at the same time be convincing about your value and worth to the company. Adapt the following letter to boost your chances of getting what you deserve.

Customize your own letter asking for a pay raise:

You cannot write this letter unless you have some indication that your supervisor is satisfied (in fact, highly impressed) with your work. That's what unscheduled raises are based on. Use that information to plead your case:

1. Identify yourself and your position in the company.
2. Right up front, state the raise you are seeking.
3. Remind the reader of his or her approval and/or satisfaction with your work.
4. State your exceptional skills, work habits, results.
5. Repeat your request.

Dear Ms. Whitehouse:

As a CAD/CAM operator in your automotive aftermarket group, I would like to request a raise of $3,000 per year effective January 1. This would bring my annual salary up to $34,000.

You have mentioned to me that you are highly satisfied with the quality of my work and my commitment to FitForm Parts. I have been a conscientious employee and have always finished tasks in an accurate and timely manner. I'm sure you have noticed that because I treat the design teams as if they were customers, they often ask to work with me in preference to other CAD/CAM operators.

You have often noted that I am a great asset to our team and have frequently complimented my professional, service-oriented manner. Although I have been with FitForm only eight months, I am asking that my salary be increased and that my compensation be reviewed again in 12 months.

Sincerely,

Recommending a pay raise

If you are a manager or a supervisor you may be in a position to request a raise for someone who works under you. The quality of this letter will determine if this person gets the raise or not, so it must be carefully planned. It should include all the details you would put in a letter requesting a raise for yourself (see the letter on page 105).

Customize your own letter recommending a raise:

This letter is upbeat, positive, and strong. Make sure it includes:

1. An identification of the employee and his or her position in the company.
2. Right up front, state the raise you are seeking for this employee.
3. State your approval and/or satisfaction with the employee's work.
4. State his or her exceptional skills, work habits, results.
5. Repeat your request.

Dear Ms. Spadafora:

I recommend that we offer Bill Dickey, a CAD/CAM operator in our automotive aftermarket group, a raise of $3,000 per year effective January 1. This would bring his annual salary up to $34,000.

I am highly satisfied with the quality of work he produces and his commitment to FitForm Parts. He is a conscientious employee, finishing tasks in an accurate and timely manner. In addition, he treats the design teams as if they were customers; they often ask to work with Bill in preference to other CAD/CAM operators.

Although Bill has been with FitForm only eight months, I am recommending that his salary be increased and that his compensation again be reviewed in 12 months. He is a great asset to our team and should be rewarded for the quality of his work and his professional, service-oriented manner.

Sincerely,

Spreading good news

Stay on the lookout for pieces of good news that you can share with your employees. These good-news memos and letters are a great way to keep up morale and give public credit when credit is due.

Congratulations on a work anniversary

In today's information-overloaded work environment, everybody has too much to read and not enough time to read it. Yet the volume of cordial correspondence has diminished to near nothingness. Therefore, the thank-you note still stands out.

Customize your own letter of congratulations on a work anniversary:

This letter shouldn't be too heavy in job-performance evaluation. Keep it simple, upbeat, and congratulatory. Include:

1. The details of the anniversary (number of years in current position or total years as an employee).
2. A personal note about their first days (if you were there and remember).
3. An overview of the recipiant's accomplishments since taking the position.
4. A toast for many more years of continued excellence.

Dear Mary,

This week marks your fifth year of employment with Westway Pharmaceuticals. Congratulations on this important anniversary.

I can hardly believe it's been half a decade since you walked into my office for an interview...and I spilled coffee all over your resume!

Despite the awkward start, I was fortunate to make the right decision and hire you for the position. Aside from your excellent performance record, you are truly a pleasure to work with.

Here's to another rewarding and profitable five years for Westway...and the two of us!

Sincerely,

Congratulations on a job well done

Don't pass up an opportunity to motivate employees and build morale. When someone has done a good job, take a few minutes to acknowledge that effort. You'll be paid back in increased loyalty and commitment.

Customize your own letter of congratulations on a job well done:

It's not necessary to go overboard and gush all over a person. Simply state your congratulations and appreciation. Include:

1. What it is you're pleased about.
2. Why this project/service/contribution is especially valued.
3. A word about future work.
4. A thank you.

Dear Lou:

I just finished reading the first draft of the Syntron manual and am very pleased with it.

What amazed me was how quickly you were able to take a mass of unorganized tech specs, memos, and assorted gibberish and edit it into a strong, cohesive introductory product guide.

I'm circulating the manual to the design team for comments now. As you know from experience, when writing about a product still under development, specs change from day to day, so I anticipate a lot of little edits and corrections, which should be easy for you to make. But the basic organization, style, and content of the document are right on target.

Thanks again for the excellent work. I value your contributions to Syntron's success.

Sincerely,

Congratulations on an extraordinary effort

You know instinctively when you have pushed your employees to deliver service and effort above the norm. When they rise to the challenge, thank them. A letter is a good start; a small token of appreciation is also a good idea (and a comp day is even better).

Customize your own letter of congratulations for extraordinary effort:

This letter is the "pat on the back" that an employee has earned with effort that goes beyond the call of duty. Make it express sincere thanks by including the following:

1. State exactly what the employee did (he or she will probably put this in a file for future career use).

2. Acknowledge the personal sacrifices that were required.
3. Offer apologies for undue hardships (if appropriate).
4. Say thank you.

Dear Jeff:

Thanks for your extraordinary efforts on the GoldSeek version 2.0 beta release. Without the dedication of you and other members of the team, we would never have made this impossibly tight deadline.

You clearly went above and beyond the call of duty, without letting the long hours and steady diet of late-night pizza affect your effort. In addition, I know there are a lot of family and school events around the holiday season, and that you have kids. I hope the project didn't interfere unduly, though I suspect it did. And for that, you have my apologies and thanks.

Now, as the holidays approach, you can take the well-deserved rest you need.

Sincerely,

Announcing a promotion

A friend of mine went into the office of an employee to criticize her handling of a project. She argued back vehemently—too vehemently, he felt, for a subordinate. He reminded her that *she* worked for him. However, he got a big surprise: *He* in fact worked for *her!* She had been promoted, and the lines of reporting reversed. Embarrassed and upset, he left her office, hoping his new boss would not hold his tirade against him. That's why all employees in a department or workgroup should be told when one of them is promoted.

Customize your own letter announcing a promotion:

This kind of correspondence is usually distributed in a memo or an e-mail. Make it short and simple:

1. State the person's full name, the old and new positions, and the date the promotion takes effect.
2. Detail how that promotion affects other employees and the chain of command.
3. You may add a note of congratulations if you like.

TO: All department personnel
FROM: Joy Robbins
RE: Promotion

Effective June 1, Sheila Anderson is being promoted from shipping clerk to director of shipping operations. She will report directly to me, and all employees designated as shipping clerks, service desk representatives, or order handlers will report directly to Sheila.

I'm sure we all join in congratulating Sheila on this well-deserved promotion.

Announcing a retirement

This announcement is routine for you but not for the person retiring, who may have strong emotional attachment to his job, workplace, coworkers, customers, or vendors. Personalizing this letter with an anecdote or observation makes it more memorable and pleasurable for everyone reading it.

Customize your own letter announcing a retirement:

This letter serves two purposes: It notifies all employees of the retirement, and it praises the retiree for his or her years of dutiful service. It should include:

1. An announcement of the retirement and effective date. State the person's name and position for employees who may not personally know him or her.
2. Give a short background history on the retiree, such as when he or she began and the positions they've held.
3. A personal anecdote about a positive experience with this person is a nice touch.
4. If you know the person's retirement plans and are sure they won't mind having them announced, you can give a brief description.
5. If you plan any kind of retirement celebration, you can add the details to this memo.
6. End with a verbal toast, noting that the person will be missed by all.

TO: Newsroom staff
FROM: Theresa Colace, City Desk Editor
RE: Stu Gruben is retiring!

Stu Gruben is retiring from his position as managing editor effective April 1st.

Stu started with the *Herald* in the 1960s as a reporter, eventually working his way up to managing editor. When I first started here in the 1980s, I handed in an article in which I referred to a politician having "a surgical procedure." Stu circled it and wrote in the margin, "Why not just say 'operation'?" I'm sure we've all learned similar lessons from Stu about how to be better journalists.

In retirement, Stu plans to move to Minneapolis to be closer to his children and grandchildren. He told me yesterday he also plans to pursue the novel he has wanted to write. We wish him well.

We are having a retirement party at lunch this coming Friday to honor Stu Gruben as he retires from our staff. A buffet lunch will be served and we'll all toast to a wonderful and productive retirement for a top editor whom we will all miss.

Appreciation for a suggestion

I was green with envy when a friend of mine, employed by a large computer company, told me he was paid a bonus of $100,000 for a simple suggestion he put into a suggestion box. Your reader isn't expecting $100,000 from you, but a simple letter of appreciation is a nice idea.

Customize your own letter of appreciation for a suggestion:

It's the thought that counts. Make your letter convey your support of employee input. Include:

1. An upfront thank you for the suggestion. (State the suggestion specifically in case the employee has submitted several and needs to know which one you're talking about.)
2. State why you like the idea.
3. If you cannot implement it right away, explain why.
4. Invite the employee to continue to be involved in the implementation of the suggested idea. Or, if that is not

appropriate, encourage him or her to continue to share thoughts and ideas in the future.

Dear Rhagu,

Thank you for your great suggestion on how to restructure the Artech Web site to give international customers access to pricing and product information specific to their country.

It's something we discussed for this year but didn't implement because of its complexity and our limited budget. Our goal was just to get basic product descriptions up on the site to create an Internet presence for Artech, which we did.

For this year, doing country-specific pages or sites is again on the agenda. We were thinking of picking one country or region as a test site. Do you have a preference of which we do?

Sincerely,

Sending out bad news

If you're in a position of authority, it will often be your job to be the bearer of bad news. The letters that convey this news should be well crafted so you never appear to be uncertain or weak.

Announcing a layoff

A layoff is never a happy occasion. If there is realistic hope of a quick solution to the problem, say so in your letter, but do not promise. Encourage supervisors to discuss each employee's situation with him or her separately. The more notification you can give, the better. A sudden loss of employment is always traumatic; be sure to convey that you are sensitive to this.

Customize your own letter announcing a layoff:

This letter must be many things at one time: It should be firm, informational, sympathetic, and hopeful. Be sure it includes:

1. An explanation of the negative financial circumstances that have recently affected the company.
2. The announcement that these circumstances (which are beyond your control) require (or may require) employee layoffs.
3. The details, if known, about who will be laid off and when.

4. Assurances that further information regarding all employee status will be forthcoming.

5. A request for continued hard work on remaining projects with the explanation that this is the way to reduce the need for further layoffs.

TO: Long Island Plant employees, Virtuen Industries
FROM: Sol Bier, Personnel Director
RE: Employee layoffs

Unfortunately and unexpectedly, Virtuen was not awarded the contract for the EWACS inertial navigational system for which, until recently, we thought wc were a shoe-in. The customer preferred the new E-5 technology from Allied Corporation because of its compatibility with GPS-7. We could not certify such compatibility and lost the contract on that basis.

Because EWACS was projected to be a significant part of our total revenue over the next two to three years, we are enforcing a hiring freeze effective immediately and may be looking at layoffs for up to 10 percent of the plant staff within the coming months. At this time, we do not know for certain how many and which employees will be affected by the layoff. However, we want employees to be aware of this potential problem and to plan accordingly.

Supervisors will be kept informed and will communicate the status of the Long Island plant to employees on a regular basis. Employees having concerns about employment status should see me or their supervisors.

In the meantime, we must double our efforts to implement the new GPS-7 compatible upgrades and to prepare bids for other opportunities now on the table including ElGIN and EAGLE. Even a partial win on just one of these would retain jobs potentially lost due to the EWACS disappointment.

Warning memo to employees about poor attendance

Employees have many legal rights on the job, and the law today seems stacked against the employer. For this reason, every major incident of discipline should be documented and communicated to the employee in writing, with a copy for the employee's personnel file.

Customize your own warning for an employee's poor attendance:

If you ever have to fire an employee due to excessive absenteeism, this memo will become an invaluable document. Craft if carefully to cover all your bases:

1. Refer to a company rule regarding absenteeism (if one exists).
2. State that there is a problem with the employee's absentee rate.
3. Give absentee dates and times and details of previous warnings.
4. State that you are very concerned about this problem.
5. Tell the employee what you expect in the future.
6. Outline exactly how all future absences must be handled (doctor notes, advanced approval, and so forth).
7. Give a warning that a copy of the memo will be placed in his or her file.
8. State what will happen if the problem continues.
9. Instruct the employee to sign on the space provided to verify that he or she has read the letter.

TO: Bob Brook

FROM: Danielle Mosely, Manager

RE: Company Rule Nine which states: "Employees will be disciplined for excessive absenteeism."

The following documents a problem with excessive absenteeism:

On December 7, 14, and 21, you were absent from work. Each of these absences was on a day before your scheduled day off. On December 27, I counseled you about your attendance on the job. You were absent again on January 5 and 16. On January 29, I again counseled you about your attendance on the job and cautioned you that further absences would lead to formal disciplinary action.

On February 1, you called in sick. This was the day before your weekend off. When you returned to work on February 4, you told Bob Sharpe, your supervisor, that you had gone dirt bike riding in the desert. On February 7, I met with you to discuss your attendance. During this meeting, I gave you a verbal warning about your poor attendance record.

I want to be sure you understand that I am seriously concerned about your attendance record. I expect you to be at work, on time, every day you are scheduled to work unless you have a legitimate medical emergency that prevents you from coming to work or are authorized in advance to take time off.

If you are unable to come to work, you must contact Sam Rodriguez in advance. If you miss work for medical reasons, you must submit a doctor's note indicating that you are medically able to return to work before you may begin working. If you want to use some of your accumulated vacation days for time off, you should submit a request at least two days in advance.

A copy of this memo will be placed in your file. Unless you follow this directive, you will be subject to further serious disciplinary action. Please sign below and return to my office before you leave work today.

I have received a copy of this memo:

_____

Bruce Black/Date

Warning letter to employees about attitude problems

Here is another discipline letter, this one documenting a poor attitude. Note how the writer took an arguably vague topic, "poor attitude," and proved it with detailed specifics.

Customize your own letter warning an employee about attitude problems:

Like other letters of warning, this letter may become the ammunition you will need if you ever need to fire the employee. It is important to show a paper trail of warnings and efforts to help the employee improve. This letter must contain:

1. An immediate statement of disapproval for a specific act. Give the date and time and details.

2. Detail all previous training, counseling, mentoring experiences given to the employee to teach what is expected.

3. State exactly what you expect the employee to do from now on.

4. Offer another opportunity for further training, counseling, or mentoring.

5. Advise the employee that this letter will be placed in his or her file.

6. Explain what will happen if the problem continues.

7. Instruct the employee to sign on the space provided by a certain designated time to verify that he or she has read the letter.

TO: Jim Shipman, Customer Service Representative
FROM: Kathy Flanders, Customer Service Manager
RE: Written Warning—Work Performance

Your behavior and attitude toward customers that I witnessed yesterday are completely unacceptable. As you were assisting a customer at noontime, I walked into the showroom and heard you say, "I am sick of listening to you complain about our products. Did you ever think it doesn't work because you didn't read the manual?" When I asked the customer what had happened, she said she had asked several questions about the Owner's Manual. She said you were impatient and rude. She said that you had talked loudly to her, almost to the point of shouting. When I asked you what had happened, you told me, "I am tired of dealing with customers who are too lazy to read the manual." This behavior and attitude is unacceptable.

When you joined our company on November 1st, you attended two weeks of customer service training. Our training program emphasizes the importance of working with our customers to meet their needs. Several of the exercises involved role-playing to show you how to work with customers under various conditions. Then, you worked beside Neil Villalos, Senior Customer Service Representative, to learn from him during your first two weeks in the department.

After all this training, you must realize that your primary job is to help customers. When you talk to customers, I expect you to listen carefully to their comments. I expect you to confirm what the customer says by using statements such as, "I believe you are asking...," or "That is a good question. Let's look in the manual for the answer." When you have a problem communicating with a customer, I expect you to ask another Customer Service Representative to help you.

The Training Department is offering a new course on stress management beginning on the 15th of this month. If you would like to take the course, please see Pat Cooper to sign up for it. (I strongly suggest that you do.)

This is a written warning. It will be placed in your personnel file. You must meet or exceed the objectives outlined in the third paragraph. If you do not meet or exceed them, you will be subject to disciplinary action, up to and including termination. Please sign below and return to my office before you leave work today.

I have received a copy of this memo:

_____
Jim Shipman /Date

Termination with regret

When you have to fire someone, do it face-to-face in a private meeting. The letter is merely a confirmation. (The primary circumstance under which you might terminate someone via letter is for a distant employee in a branch or remote office.) The following letter is a sample of what you can say when the employee is fired due to various company circumstances, rather than poor performance, attendance, or attitude.

Customize your own letter of termination with regret:

This letter is the official notification after you have discussed the news with your employee. Be sure to use official company letterhead paper and write a formal letter—not a memo, fax, or e-mail. It should contain all the details about the termination, benefits, and company assistance:

1. Begin with a note of regret.
2. Note that this letter confirms a previous conversation regarding termination.
3. Give the details of why the employee is being let go.
4. State the terms of termination, which include any severance pay, profit sharing, retirement benefits, and medical coverage.
5. Explain what the company will do to help this person find new employment.
6. A thank you note for good work and a wish of good luck in finding new employment.

Dear Joe,

This is my least favorite letter to write. But here it is....

As we discussed on Tuesday, the severe setbacks in our corporate earnings have put a hold on our acquisitions activities. As a result, your position of Business Development Manager has unfortunately been eliminated.

To confirm our conversation, your employment will end effective July 22. You will receive severance pay equal to four months' salary. In lieu of profit sharing for the year, you have agreed to accept a one-time payment of $6,000. Your retirement benefits will be retained by the company until we receive instructions from you. Your medical benefits coverage will continue until you find new coverage for up to a period of one year.

We will assist you in your search for a new job. I have provided a letter of recommendation (copy attached), and you may use me as a reference. You can continue to use your office during your job search. And, you will be receiving consulting assistance from Black & Change, a leading outplacement firm we have retained to help you and other employees during our current downsizing transition.

Thank you for all your many contributions to this company, and good luck in your job search.

Sincerely,

Termination with just cause

Sometimes an employee just cannot do the job he or she was hired to do. This situation requires a sometimes-lengthy process of verbal warnings, meetings, counseling, and warning letters. But eventually you may have to lower the ax. Firing someone should always be done in person; the letter is sent to confirm the termination and outline the details.

Customize your own letter of termination with just cause:

This letter is a confirmation of terms of termination already discussed. It's important to get them down in writing so there can be no misunderstanding. Be sure to use official company letterhead paper and write a formal letter, not a memo, fax, or e-mail. Include:

1. An opening that states clearly that the person is fired effective by a certain date.

2. State the reasons for the termination with mention of any previous warnings.

3. Impress upon the recipient that this is a logical course of action because you obviously need employees who can do the job they are hired to do.

4. Give the facts about any severance pay, noting when and how it will be paid.

Dear Bob:

As we discussed in my office this morning, your employment with Current Sales has been terminated effective March 5. You have received verbal and written warnings about your excessive absenteeism and each time you gave me assurances that you would shape up and correct the problem. Yet last Friday, you once again were absent without prior approval or notification. I'm sorry Bob, but that was your last chance. I'm sure you can understand why we need an employee who is on the job during scheduled hours.

You will of course receive the standard two weeks' severance pay. I have already requisitioned a check for you, which will be mailed to your home within the next week.

Sincerely,

Interoffice e-mail messages

Many of the memos and letters cited above can be sent by e-mail, but generally interoffice e-mail messages are different from those sent on paper. The messages are shorter, quicker, and pertain to rather routine, daily events. The language, while still always grammatically correct, is more curt and to the point. The style is less formal. Often they are messages that are sent to many employees at once. (That's one of the great things about e-mail: one click of the button and your message is routed to many people instantaneously.) The following examples will give you an idea of the kind and style of correspondance that are routinely sent by e-mail.

Meeting announcement

```
Subject: Change of date for weekly team meeting
From: Allen Cvelic
To: Alpha Team Members


The meeting has been rescheduled for Friday 10 a.m. instead of the
usual time on Thursday. Please let me know if you have a conflict.
```

Holiday schedules

```
Subject: Holiday schedule
From: Timothy Casey
To: Capselle Employees


This year City plant will be open December 26 and 27, but closed
from December 28 to January 2. These days are scheduled for plant
maintenance, so only maintenance supervisors and their crews will
be working. The building will not be accessible to other
employees.
```

Office holiday party

```
Subject: Office holiday party
From: Kevin Hancock
To: Newsroom and pressroom staff

This year's holiday office party will be held at O'Sullehbhain's
Pub on December 23 starting at noon. As most of you already know,
the pub is on the corner of 61st and Madison. Please remember to
bring a grab-bag gift worth $15 or less.
```

Summer hours

Subject: Summer hours
From: Kara Richardson
To: Agency staff

From June 22 to September 4, we will be operating under summer hours.
During summer hours, we will close at 3 p.m. instead of 5 p.m. on
Fridays. On all other days, we will be open from 9 a.m. to 5 p.m.

Expense reports

Subject: Expense reports
From: June Barrel, CFO
To: Sales staff

Expense reports must be filed on or before the last day of the
month. Filing your expense report after that deadline my delay
reimbursement up to 30 days. For your convenience, your expense
reports may now be filed electronically. Just send your completed
Expense Report form to Andy Devin in accounting at andyde@it.org.
This speeds communication and helps assure our receipt on or
before the end-of-month deadline.

Company car policy

Subject: Company car, maintenance of
From: Ed Flannery, Fleet Manager
To: Company car users

As our fleet of company cars ages, users have been experiencing some
car problems. Checking our records, I find that 70 percent of
company vehicles are not brought into the garage for maintenance
according to the schedule that fleet management requires.
The Maintenance Schedule for company cars is posted on our intranet
at http://www.goa.com/fleet. Please make sure you bring your company
car in for all scheduled maintenance checks and tune-ups.

7

LETTERS TO GET, KEEP, AND SATISFY CUSTOMERS

It's true: The more contact you have with customers, the more likely they are to place their next order with you instead of with your competitor. The reason for this is that customers are bombarded with messages from vendors looking for an order. The more recent your last communication, the more likely they are to think of you first when a need arises.

Therefore, frequent contact with your customers, whether it be by phone, mail, or in person, contributes to your bottom line. This chapter gives you model letters you can use to boost the quality and frequency of customer communication. The samples cover a wide range of situations—from announcing a product upgrade to getting buyers to renew a subscription, policy, or service agreement.

Getting business

At its root, all the business letters you write are for the purpose of getting and retaining business. The following samples are ones you can use to directly market yourself, gain new accounts, and retain the customers you have.

Reporting results and quoting prices

This kind of letter pulls double duty: It tells prospective customers why they need your product or service and then how much it will cost them.

Customize your own letter reporting results and quoting prices:

The letter that reports results and quotes prices has four parts:

1. It explains the results of industry research, or of a requested estimate, a consultation, an inquiry, or any other professional information that shows the product or service is necessary.

2. It presents recommendations based on the results.
3. It states an estimate of the cost of those goods or services.
4. It asks the recipient to contact you to proceed.

Dear Mr. And Mrs. Magin:

My dental exam of your son, Andy, shows a 1.5 mm space between the upper central incisors, as well as some crowding of the lower front teeth.

I recommend the use of a removable plastic and wire appliance to take the upper right central incisor out of crossbite.

The fee for this treatment, including the previously taken diagnostic information and also including subsequent future visits until additional diagnostic data or treatment are needed, would be $600. This can be paid in the following manner: $300 initially, and the $300 balance by five monthly payments of $60 each.

Please call my office and we will answer any questions you may have. If you'd like, we'll make an appointment to fit the appliance.

I look forward to hearing from you.

Sincerely,
John Trackman, D.D.S.

Requesting referrals

You should ask satisfied customers to refer friends and colleagues to you. Referrals from satisfied customers are just about the best leads you'll ever get.

If your clients aren't giving you as many referrals as you want, here's a letter you can use to ask for more:

Customize your own letter requesting referrals:

This letter should be short and sweet and include:

1. A reminder of something the customer liked about your product or service.
2. A request for a favor.
3. Simple instructions to give you the names of people who might benefit from your product or service.
4. A self-addressed stamped envelope. (This makes it very easy for the customer to respond.)
5. A thank you.

Dear Joan:

I'm glad you liked the spring catalog I recently sent you. Like you, I'm always on the lookout for new business. So I have a favor to ask. Could you jot down, on the back of this letter, the names, addresses, and phone numbers of a few of your colleagues who might benefit from knowing more about my services?

(Naturally, I don't want anyone whose product line is in direct competion with your own.)

Then, just mail the letter back to me in the enclosed reply envelope.

I may want to mention your name when contacting these people. Let me know if there's any problem with that.

Once again, thanks for the favor!

Regards,

Letter for soliciting testimonials from clients

After completing a job successfully, you can use this letter to solicit a testimonial from the client. A page filled with testimonials is a very powerful addition to a promotional package and convinces prospects that you are good at what you do. I always send a self-addressed stamped envelope and two copies of the letter. This way the recipient doesn't have to make a copy of the letter or address or stamp his own envelope.

Whenever a supplier you like asks you to give a testimonial or act as a reference, do it! As one of their reference accounts, you are guaranteed superior service. Once your testimonial or name appears in their marketing materials, the vendor will go to great pains to ensure your ongoing satisfaction.

Customize your own letter soliciting testimonials:

This letter asks for a favor which may, or may not, be granted. Give it your best shot by including:

1. An explanation that you are compiling a list of testimonials from satisfied customers.

2. A request for the customer's opinion.

3. Instructions on how to do this easily by writing on the back of the letter and using the enclosed self-addressed stamped envelope.

4. A form at the bottom for the customer to sign giving his or her permission to use the testimonial for marketing purposes.

Dear Andrew:

I have a favor to ask of you.

I'm in the process of putting together a list of testimonials about my services from satisfied clients like you.

Would you take a few minutes to give me your opinion of my writing services? No need to dictate a letter; just jot your comments on the back of this letter, sign below, and return it to me in the enclosed envelope. (The second copy is for your files.) I look forward to learning what you like about my service…but I welcome any suggestions or criticisms.

Many thanks.

Regards,

_____

YOU HAVE MY PERMISSION TO QUOTE FROM MY COMMENTS AND USE THESE QUOTATIONS IN ADS, BROCHURES, MAIL, AND OTHER PROMOTIONS USED TO MARKET YOUR FREELANCE WRITING SERVICES.

Signature_____ Date _____

Letter for getting permission to use unsolicited testimonials

Some clients will send you unsolicited and glowing testimonial letters. Before you use them in your promotions, get the client's permission in writing. You can use the following form letter as your base. This is good practice for preventing customer problems. If a customer gets an irate call from his boss asking, "Why are we quoted in XYZ Supplier's brochure?" and you included a testimonial from her without permission, rest assured it will damage your relationship.

Customize your own permission letter to use unsolicited testimonials:

It's rare that customers put compliments in writing without being asked to. So when they do, grab hold of it and ask to use it to promote your business. Your letter should include:

1. A thank you for the kind letter.
2. A request to use it to promote your business (try to state specifically how and where you would use it).
3. Instructions to sign and date the bottom of your letter.

4. Include a copy of the testimonial letter and a self-addressed stamped envelope.

Dear Ms. Hernandez:

Thank you so much for your letter of February 15 (copy attached). It's always nice to hear when things are going right!

You've said such positive things about us that I'd like to quote from this letter in the ads, brochures, direct mail packages, and other promotions I use to market my writing services...with your permission, of course. If this is okay with you, would you please sign the bottom of this letter and send it back to me in the enclosed envelope? (The second copy is for your files.) Thank you once again!

Regards,

_____

YOU HAVE MY PERMISSION TO QUOTE FROM THE ATTACHED LETTER IN ADS, BROCHURES, MAIL, AND OTHER PROMOTIONS USED TO MARKET YOUR FREELANCE WRITING SERVICES.

Signature_____   Date_____

Explaining monthly retainer arrangements

Some customers may want to establish a regular relationship with you by hiring you on a monthly retainer. Customers who request such a relationship may have no idea of what is involved or how it works, so you must spell it out for them in writing before you both enter into an agreement.

Customize your own letter outlining monthly retainer arrangements:

Of course the details of your retainer agreements will vary from this sample, but the letter should always include:

1. Acknowledgment that the recipient either has asked for information about this arrangement or might be interested due to the amount of on-going work you do together.
2. The monthly fee.
3. Exactly what that fee buys the customer: how much time, what result, any priority advantages.
4. Work that would not be covered by the retainer.
5. The payment schedule.

Dear Mr. Glicksman:

You recently mentioned that you are interested in hiring me on a monthly retainer to handle your company's ongoing copywriting and consulting requirements for small projects that need quick turnaround.

My standard arrangement is a monthly retainer that covers one full day's work at our current rate of $1,600. We find that that's a sufficient amount of time to handle requirements of this type. Larger stand-alone projects (such as our two upcoming mailings) are quoted separately.

Retainer clients get 24- to 48-hour turnaround with priority in handling their assignments and no rush charges. If I spend more than a full day in a given month on your work, you do *not* get charged extra, as long as my time on your account averages a day a month. If you regularly require more or less service, we can talk about setting the monthly fee upward or downward accordingly.

There is no advance payment required. At the end of each month, you will be billed the month's fee net 30 days. You can cancel at any time, and you just have to pay for the time spent to date that month.

Does this sound like what you had in mind? I look forward to continuing this conversation.

Sincerely,

Offering renewal at birth

The next time you order something from an infommercial or mail order ad, notice what happens when you call. After taking your payment information, the operator tells you there is a special, and if you order two instead of one, you get a discount. This is called "upselling," and it is extremely effective.

One version of upselling that can be done profitably by letter is called "renewal at birth." This is essentially a brief renewal sent at the time of order. It asks the customer to order more units or a second year of service while paying for the first year or units. Eliot Schein, a direct mail expert, says that, on average, three to five percent or more of customers will respond positively to the renewal at birth offer.

Customize your own letter offering renewal at birth:

You have an opportunity to sell more products or services every time you send out an invoice by adding this cover letter. Include:

1. A statement that an invoice is enclosed for a particular order.

2. A discounted offer for more units, upgraded services, new product, or extended service.
3. Instructions how to take advantage of the offer.

Dear Mr. Whitman:

Thanks for ordering MediCare Data Online. Your invoice is enclosed.

If you regularly consult Medicare data in your work, here's a chance for immediate savings. Check the box on the invoice for extended service and pay the amount indicated. You'll get an updated disk every six months for two years instead of one year. That's four disks instead of two. And you'll save $59 off the regular rate.

When you return payment of this bill, just check the box in the lower right-hand corner to take advantage of this special discount. You'll be glad you did.

Sincerely,

Renewal series

When a contract, subscription, or agreement is about to expire, a series of renewal letters can be used to get customers to continue service. This series of letters can contain as many letters as you'd like to keep sending. The four sample letters below give you an idea of how they progress in content.

Renewal letter #1

The first letter is typically sent four to six months in advance of the expiration date of the service or publication. It is called an "early bird" because, even though you're asking the customer to renew, he or she still has plenty of time to do so. In exchange for renewing early, offer a reward such as a discount, free bonus gift, or extra service.

Customize your own renewal letter #1:

This is your first contact with a customers whose contract is not going to expire soon. There is no need to be too pushy. The letter should read like you're offering a favor. Include:

1. The announcement of an early bird discount.
2. The name of your company or product and an invitation to continue being a customer.
3. The special benefit of renewing now rather than later.
4. A review of why your service or product is the best.

5. A final request to encourage the customer to take advantage of your discount offer.

Dear Mr. Smith:

SPECIAL EARLY BIRD DISCOUNT OFFER

Renew now and save $55!

If you are enjoying your subscription to *The Journal of Financial Management*, **now** is the best time to renew. Here's why:

Accept this early bird renewal now, and you will continue to receive *The Journal of Financial Management* at our lowest rate available. Renew for two years and you save $55. Renew for one year, and save $25. Either way, you win!

Importantly, this is only a one-time offer. It will not be repeated. To get these savings, you must forward us your renewal instructions right away.

In today's complex markets, it's more important than ever to get the expert analytical insights, clear explanations, effective strategies, and proven techniques only *The Journal of Financial Management* provides. Now you can get it <u>cheaper than ever</u>...maximizing the return on your subscription investment.

Please take advantage of these savings today! Thank you.

Sincerely,

P.S. Remember, you can save up to $55 by sending us your renewal instructions **now**. The subscription price on subsequent renewal notices <u>will be higher</u>.

Renewal letter #2

The second letter is sent a month or so after the early bird. It reminds the customer that it's time to renew so your service doesn't accidentally lapse. This approach works well for insurance, subscriptions, support contracts, and health plans.

Customize your own renewal letter #2:

This letter is still offering a gentle reminder and a financial incentive to renew the contract. Include:

1. An attention-grabbing opening line.

2. The benefit from the service or product you provide.
3. A request for a renewal order.
4. A reminder that this service or product will keep the recipient on top.

ACT NOW...BEFORE IT'S TOO LATE.

Dear Mr. Smith:

It's true. In institutional investing, financial managers who have access to the <u>best information</u> are the ones most likely to generate the highest risk-adjusted returns—month after month, year after year.

That's why it makes sense to renew your subscription to *The Journal of Financial Management* now instead of later.

Each issue lets you pick the brains of the top experts in institutional investment management. Practical applications, innovative methods, and illustrated case studies help you maximize profits, stay way ahead of the competition, and deliver even greater value to your clients all year long.

Even better, renew now and lock in our current lowest rate on a one-year subscription, or get a discount of $35 on a two-year subscription (see the attached Subscription Renewal Form for details). Act now and save!

Sincerely,

P.S. *The Journal of Financial Management* publishes the most relevant, challenging, practical, and significant institutional investment ideas in practice today. No institutional financial manager should be without it. Don't delay. Reply today.

Renewal letter #3

The third letter is sent about a month prior to expiration. It reminds the customer that he or she is in the last month of service, and if the contract is not renewed now, service will stop shortly.

Customize your own renewal letter #3:

This letter says "time's up." It allows your customer a last chance to renew the contract before it expires. It should include:

1. A boldface statement of "expiration notice."

2. An opening of regret and surprise that the contract has not yet been renewed.

3. A statement of concern that as a valued customer they may miss out on valuable service.

4. A review of the quality and benefit of your service or product.

5. Instructions how to avoid missing out on continued service.

6. A reminder that the renewal must be done immediately.

SUBSCRIPTION EXPIRATION NOTICE

Dear Mr. Smith:

The other day, I got some rather unexpected **bad** news.

My circulation manager handed me a list of *The Journal of Financial Management* readers whose subscriptions are about to expire. Despite the fact that we've sent several renewal notices, **your** name was on it!

I'm concerned that you may not have gotten our previous letters. Whatever the situation, your subscription ends with your next issue...and you should complete and return the attached renewal form **now** to continue receiving the *Journal* uninterrupted.

As you know, *The Journal of Financial Management* is written by top practitioners in the field *for* top practitioners. Our authors deliver the tools you need to explore the latest theories...test your own concepts...approach traditional investment practices with a fresh perspective...and take advantage of breakthroughs in strategic financial management.

In today's complex markets, the *Journal's* "inside information" can give you a competitive edge to help you outperform your competitors month after month.

Is this an edge you really want to do without? To ensure uninterrupted service of your subscription to *The Journal of Financial Management* and prevent any missed issues, complete and mail the attached form today.

Thanks,

P.S. To ensure on-time delivery of your next issue of *The Journal of Financial Management*, please give us your renewal instructions today.

Renewal letter #4

The fourth letter is sent at expiration. It is notification that the agreement has expired. It tells the customer that if he or she acts immediately, service can continue on the same terms as if the agreement had never lapsed.

Customize your own renewal letter #4:

This is your last pitch to retain this customer. You've done your best to push a renewal; now you can make one last offer and then it's time to let go. Your letter should include:

1. A "Final Notice" announcement up top.
2. A one-time courtesy offer to reactivate the expired contract.
3. An explanation that after this time the rate for signing up for your service or product will be higher.
4. One last plea to renew now and a promise that no further renewal offers will be sent.
5. A postscript, repeating that this is a final offer before the customer's name is deleted from active files.

FINAL NOTICE

Dear Mr. Smith:

I would like to extend the following one-time courtesy offer to you:

Re-activate your expired subscription **now** to continue uninterrupted service and delivery of *The Journal of Financial Management*. Lock in our low renewal rate. Avoid higher prices that new subscribers will be forced to pay due to increases in printing and postage costs.

Technically, because your subscription has expired, we would normally charge you our regular rate for new subscribers.

Because your subscription lapsed only a few weeks ago, I can offer you renewal at the current rate, on a one-time-only basis.

Please take a moment and mail your completed Subscription Reactivation Form today. Your subscription will continue, as if it had never expired.

But I urge you to act **now**. This is your last chance. After this letter, no further renewal offers will be sent. This is the last one you will receive.

Sincerely,

P.S. This is your final notice. Your name has been deleted from our active subscriber files. No further issues of *The Journal of Financial Management* will be sent unless you mail the Subscription Reactivation Form.

Request to reactivate an inactive account

Experience shows that it costs five to 10 times more to acquire a first order from a new customer than to solicit and get a reorder from an existing account. Don't let customers drop out of sight without making an effort to either get them back or find out why they left (so it doesn't happen again).

When making your request, you might want to enclose a reply form (questionnaire or survey) the customer can complete and return to indicate the reasons why they stopped buying from you. In some cases, you will be able to overcome these objections and get the business back. But your chances of reactivating a dissatisfied account are slim unless the customer tells you what's wrong.

You may also consider giving a bribe. One technique I have used with success in the past is to use the phrase, "INSIDE: A shameless bribe to get you back" on the front of the envelope. Then, I offer a discount certificate or a free gift to the customer if they order.

Customize your own letter to reactive an inactive account:

You don't want to be too pushy in this situation, but a polite request for an explanation is good business. Your letter should include:

1. The fact that you haven't heard from this valued customer in a certain period of time.
2. An assurance that his or her business is important to you and valued.
3. The simple question, "May we still call you a 'customer'?"
4. Instructions to jot a response on the back of the letter and return it in the enclosed self-addressed stamped envelope.

"We miss you...and we want you back!"
Dear Mr. Smith,

It's been more than 18 months since you last favored us with an order. Did we do something wrong?

Your business is important to us, so we would like to know why we haven't been in touch. Could you take a moment to let us know whether we can still call you a customer?

There is no need to dictate a letter. Simply jot your reply on the back of this letter and return it to me in the postage-paid envelope enclosed.

Thank you for your time and effort.

Sincerely,

Daily business transactions

Every day your business success requires communication with your customers. Most rather routine correspondence is offered in this section. You can use these letters as guides in helping you with all the occasions you need to say something important to the people who keep you in business.

Following up a sales discussion

After an in-person or telephone discussion with a prospect concerning his or her needs, reiterate your strengths and methods in a follow-up note.

Customize your own letter following up a sales discussion:

This is a letter that says: "You told me what you needed, here's how I can help." It should include:

1. A reminder of your sales discussion and the topic discussed.
2. Agreement that the person's needs are vital and that your company can meet them.
3. The details of what you can do for this customer.
4. What they can expect to receive from you in the next day or two (if appropriate).
5. An offer to answer any further questions.
6. End on a positive note stating your pleasure in working together in the future.

Dear Ms. Nagel:

I enjoyed chatting with you today about your plans for a new employee benefits program. It sounds exciting!

Proper selection of the right insurance carrier and coverage, of course, is **critical** to maximizing coverage while minimizing the premium.

That's why, as you requested, I've told ABC Insurance's regional manager in your area to put together a free, no-obligation Competitive Policy Analysis for your review.

Based on a thorough analysis of the various plans offered by the 25 major insurance carriers covering your area, our Competitive Policy Analysis will identify those companies and plans that give you the best value for your premium dollar.

And, with our large volume and decades of experience, we are often able to design plans with "tiered" levels of coverage. This allows you to pay for basic coverage for employees, while giving them the option of buying additional insurance for themselves if they so choose.

You'll have our Competitive Policy Analysis on your desk shortly. In the meantime, if you have any questions or need additional information, you can reach me at 123-456-7890.

We look forward to providing your employees with affordable health benefits, as we have for hundreds of companies and millions of employees (and their families) throughout the tri-state area.

Sincerely,

Giving prices to a current customer

When giving price estimates to existing customers, you can opt for a short letter or memo instead of a more formal form or proposal.

Customize your own letter giving prices to a current customer:

Current customers know your work and the value of your service. They simply need to know prices for other projects. Make it simple and include:

1. A cordial greeting.
2. A quote of your prices or fees.
3. An alternate service or product if you think the client might like a choice.
4. An estimate of the time required for the job.
5. A request for a response.

6. If appropriate, add a note indicating that you are sending an enclosure with additional information.

Dear Rich:

Thanks for coming by. I enjoyed seeing you, as always.

I normally charge $10,000 to $12,000 or more for a traditional annual report. The reports typically run 25 to 40 pages with art and photos reproduced in four colors.

For $5,000 to $7,500, I can design a shorter, two-color annual report similar in style and complexity to the one you did last year.

I will need approximately 30 days for comps and camera-ready art on disk.

Let me know what you think.

Thanks,

P.S. We are sending you separately the two-color samples and my list of recommended printers.

Making a recommendation to a specific customer

While serving an account, you may encounter situations that suggest the customer needs to improve its procedures, whether internally or through the use of more outside vendors. Regardless of whether there is money in it for you or not, you can build goodwill by putting the idea in a letter or memo and passing it on to the client.

Customize your own recommendation to a specific customer:

This is a letter that can lead to increased orders for you either directly through your recommendations or through the goodwill you will create by taking the time to offer helpful ideas. Your letter should include:

1. A mention of the work you currently are doing for this customer.
2. A suggestion on additional ways to improve their business (if appropriate).
3. A suggestion how the customer might fix the problem.
4. A closing that makes it clear you're just trying to be of help to a valued customer and that your door is always open.

Dear Tom:

I just spoke with Steve about the fulfillment letter and will have a draft for you next week.

Steve mentioned that we get a large number of leads from the ad but many are not qualified and most don't result in business.

Based on this, I feel you need some inexpensive means to keep in touch with this database of prospects on a regular basis.

Steve mentioned doing a follow-up telemarketing script to reactivate and requalify old leads, which is a good idea. We can definitely take care of this.

In addition, I think it might help your response if you also have some sort of mailing going to this prospect database, ideally once a quarter. This could be as elaborate as a newsletter or a simple as a series of postcards. Or, it could be brief letters accompanying the latest reviews and press clippings on the product. But you need something to remind interested parties that a solution to their needs exists.

Just thought these ideas might help. Let me know if you want to discuss this further.

Sincerely,

Declining to bid or provide service

Turning down jobs from existing customers can potentially offend or even anger them. The trick of the "letter declining to bid" is to say "no" in a way that makes customers think you are serving their best interests rather than refusing to serve them.

Although you may not be able to help your customer, suggest a vendor who may be better qualified than you to do the job or fill the order in your letter. Or if there is a way you can fulfill part of the order or at least satisfy part of the need, suggest it and say you would be happy to do so.

Customize your own letter declining to bid or provide service:

This letter should include:

1. A thank you for offering the opportunity to bid or provide a service.
2. A brief summary of what your company provides and what the customer is looking for.
3. Your refusal to bid or provide services with regret. The reason will be either that the job does not fall in line with your company's

capabilities, or that you are simply too busy right now to do the job up to the high standards you know the customer deserves. Note that taking the job under these circumstances would be very costly for the customer.

4. An alternative the customer should consider and how you can help them do that.

5. If appropriate, an offer to bid or provide the service if the customer insists and is willing to pay the price.

Dear Kay,

Thanks for allowing us to quote on the "Networking Sales & Marketing Guide." I appreciate the opportunities you give us, including this one.

As you know, our specialty is marketing and promotional materials that stress persuasive selling, marketing strategy, powerful graphics, and arresting design.

Your current format for the Sales & Marketing Guides leans more toward a training manual and technical information document, rather than a promotional piece.

The bottom line is that while we can do this for you, it's not our strength. Consequently, we probably wouldn't do as good a job as a firm that specializes in documentation and manuals. Besides, our charges would not be competitive.

We're thinking you'd be better doing this job with your in-house technical publications department or through a freelance technical writer/desktop publisher. If you need a recommendation on a freelancer, let me know and we can ask around for you. Or, if you still want us to quote on this job, let me know and we will prepare an estimate.

Sincerely,

Letter requesting extension of deadline

Missing a deadline is bad business. It can cost you untold losses, not only because it may cost you the job or the next one, but it also hurts your reputation as a reliable businessperson. If you can see that you will not meet an agreed-upon deadline, don't let the day come and go without saying anything. Well in advance of the deadline, write a letter requesting an extension.

My advice concerning deadlines is simple and straightforward:

1. Don't miss deadlines.

2. Don't promise what you can't deliver.

3. Negotiate a reasonable deadline before you accept the order, job, or assignment. Don't forget to factor in weekends and holidays.

4. If you need a deadline extension, request it sooner rather than later. Speak up early. People hate surprises.

5. When setting a deadline, specify not only a date, but also a time of day as well as method of delivery ("November 23, 1999, by 3 p.m. or sooner via e-mail," for example).

6. Request the deadline in writing but follow up to confirm acceptance. Since it's an urgent request and time is of the essence, send your communication via e-mail or fax rather than interoffice or postal mail.

7. If the need for an extension is due to factors beyond your control (for example, if someone else in the workflow chain failed to deliver and that affected your ability to meet a deadline), point it out, but don't lay blame or make excuses. Simply state the facts.

8. If there is a way you can make up time later to adjust for the current lateness, offer it. For instance, if you are late handing in a layout for a promotional flier, perhaps you can send it to a different printer who can treat the job as a rush priority, and therefore get the printed pieces delivered on schedule.

Customize your own letter requesting an extension of deadline:

Don't let this letter sound like you're pointing fingers. State the facts:

1. State the name of the project and the original deadline.
2. State your reasons for needing more time.
3. Offer an alternate deadline.
4. Leave the door open to other possible solutions to the problem.
5. Ask for a response.

Dear Cheryl:

We originally set a deadline of October 10 for delivery of the XTH budget and forecast. To date, we haven't received the figures from sales or accounting. Since normal turnaround time for the analysis is five to seven days, we need to rethink the October 10 deadline. I've asked Sherry in sales and Larry in accounting about data status, and they promise raw data to me by tomorrow at noon. If they do this, we can work over the weekend and have the report no later than October 12, and quite possibly by October 11, assuming we hit no weekend computer glitches or missing figures.

Please let me know if this is acceptable to you. If it isn't, let's discuss alternative solutions.

Sincerely,

Annual account review letter

Many organizations, such as banks, credit unions, insurance carriers, phone companies, utilities, raw materials suppliers—send customers monthly or annual statements of their accounts. If you do it annually, use this annual letter to resell your organization and its value to the customer. If you do it monthly, the monthly notices are an ideal place to highlight news, new products, changes in service policies, and other items of importance.

Customize your own annual account review letter:

There's no end to the kind of information you can get to your customers through this kind of notice. Typically, the letter will include:

1. Notification that the annual statement is enclosed.
2. A brief summary of why your company is tops in the field and the kind of advantages you offer your clients.
3. An invitation to the client to review the information and talk with a representative to review the policy and discuss any possible changes.
4. A thank you.

Dear Policyowner:

Your annual Crest benefit statement is enclosed for your review. It details your policy's current financial growth and status.

Your Crest life insurance policy is one of your most valuable and affordable assets. It is designed to serve your financial and protection needs throughout your lifetime. The guaranteed cash value will increase over time and, more importantly, so will your ability to earn dividends that can greatly reduce your out-of-pocket cost of insurance. For 75 years, Crest policyowners have shared in our outstanding performance and prudent leadership.

Please take this opportunity to review and assess your insurance benefits with your Crest representative in light of how your financial needs and circumstances have changed over the past year.

Thank you for choosing Crest. We will strive in continuing to earn your trust and confidence.

Sincerely,

Announcing a new product or service to customers and prospects

When you have a new product or service, all current customers, inactive customers, and prospects should be notified by mail or e-mail.

Customize your own announcement of a new product or service to customers and prospects:

This is both a piece of sales literature as well as a courtesy call. Make it simple and to the point, but cordial. Include:

1. A statement of a customer's needs.
2. An offer to meet those needs with a new product or service.
3. A clear listing of exactly what you are now offering to clients.
4. An acknowledgment of what is not included (if appropriate).
5. The cost or fee.
6. An invitation to call for more information or to order.

To all of my clients:

Many of you have asked for assistance in putting together or enhancing your Web pages on the Internet. I am now offering this service to individual clients. It is something I have already done for more than half a dozen corporations, including AT&T and IBM.

The primary services I'm offering include:

- Content creation and copywriting.
- Web site organization, design, and logical link recommendations.
- Editing, rewriting, and writing of Web site content (pages).
- Web site promotion—getting prospects to visit your home page.

With most clients, Web pages can be built by scanning and modifying printed literature, so all that is required is organization, design, a home page, linkages, and some interactive functionality.

I do not do programming or graphics, but I have available resources to help you with these aspects of your Web site.

The fee is simple: I charge the hourly or daily rate you are currently paying me, multiplied by the amount of time we agree I should spend to help you.

Call me today at 123-456-7890 for a cost estimate on your project.

Thanks once again,

Announcing a company name change

The announcement of a company name change must catch the reader's attention. This is not junk mail; it is contains one of the most valuable things your company owns—name recognition.

Customize your own letter announcing a company name change:

This letter must show your best side. Using quality letterhead paper (with the new name) and perfect writing format and form. Include:

1. An exclamatory opening that announces a name change with enthusiasm and excitement.
2. The old name and the new name.
3. The reason for the change.
4. Assurances that quality service/product will continue.
5. Any changes the customer can expect.
6. A final reminder of the old and new names.

Dear Philp Pottsen:

Important news! You're about to get the same great delivery service you're accustomed to under a new name!

Associated Delivery Service, a leader in transportation, distribution, and logistics since 1953, is now changing its name...to Global Systems...to better symbolize our expanding range of worldwide capabilities.

This means you get the same on-time delivery, the same fast, responsive service, the same dedication to excellence...you've come to rely on from Associated.

But you also get an enhanced system...a one-stop resource with expanded capabilities...for meeting your total shipping and logistics requirements—both domestic and international.

You'll notice our name change soon on all our mailings, packaging, invoices, and promotional materials. It's still the same company, just a new name.

Remember: Associated Delivery Service is now Global Systems.

Sincerely,

Announcing an acquisition

Acquisitions are generally seen by customers as an advantage since they offer expanded size, economy of scale, and product or service line. Be sure to announce this good news.

Customize your own letter announcing an acquisition:

This letter needs to give certain important pieces of information. Include:

1. The announcement of the acquisition. Name your company and the company you are acquiring.
2. A brief statement about why this acquisition has been made.
3. An introduction to the acquired company to help your customers better recognize who they are.
4. The advantage of this acquisition to the customer.
5. An invitation to ask questions or gather more information.

Dear Customer:

Industrial Gases is pleased to announce its recent acquisition of all the assets of Becton Industries, a leading manufacturer of valves, manifolds, and other corrosion-resistant gas distribution equipment.

For the past seven years, our corporate mission has been to become the leading supplier of gas solutions for corrosive applications. Our acquisition of Becton brings us one step closer to accomplishment of that goal.

As you may know, Industrial Gases has already been distributing Becton valves in its catalogs. Not only will the acquisition reduce our pricing on these components, but Becton will begin offering custom skid-mounted solutions for Industrial Gases customers. Becton components will continue to be sold under their current model names but through the Industrial Gases sales organization.

If you have any questions or comments, please contact your sales representative.

Sincerely,

Confidentiality agreement

If you have to learn confidential facts about a customer's business to render service or customize products, you gain access to competitive intelligence about their operations. An important part of customer service is taking precautions to make sure this information does not fall into the wrong hands.

Some clients may ask you to sign a confidentiality agreement saying you won't share their proprietary information with other people. If the client wants you to make such a promise but doesn't have a formalized confidentiality agreement, you can perform a valuable service by providing such an agreement. You can use the simple confidentiality memo shown below as a model.

TO: Sue Simpon, XYZ Systems

FROM: Bob Bly

RE: Nondisclosure agreement

To render service to XYZ System, I agree to the following:

1. "Confidential information" means any information given to me by XYZ Systems.

2. I agree not to use, disseminate, or share any confidential information with my employees, vendors, clients, or anyone else.

3. I will use reasonable care to protect your confidential information, treating it as securely as if it were my own.

4. I won't publish, copy, or disclose any of your confidential information to any third party and will use my best efforts to prevent inadvertent disclosure of such information to any third party.

5. The copy I do for you shall be considered "work for hire." XYZ Systems will own all rights to everything I produce for you, including the copyright. I will execute any additional documents needed to verify your ownership of these rights.

Agreed: _____ Date _____

Taking care of business

The letters in this section will help you stand out from the crowd. They are letters that are optional, but smart. They keep you in touch with your customers and let them know you care about their needs and not just your own welfare.

Client satisfaction survey (post-assignment)

A good way to please and retain customers is to ask them if they have any problems with your service or product that you can solve. Try Surveying your customers to see if they are pleased. If they respond, thank them and pledge to remedy their complaints. Then make sure you do so.

Customize your own customer satisfaction survey:

This survey should give you information you need to better service your customers in ways that may be unique to your business. Areas of concern you might possibly survey include:

1. A rating for the quality of a specific product or service.
2. A rating for the overall quality of your company's service.
3. A rating to compare the quality of the product or service with the fee.
4. An opportunity to comment on the good things about your product or service.
5. An opportunity to comment on the negative things about your product or service.
6. A space for the person's name (this is optional).
7. Instructions on where to send the form.

Dear Valued Client:

Would you please take a minute to complete and return this brief questionnaire to me? (Doing so is optional, of course.) It would help me serve you better—and ensure that you get the level of quality and service you want on every job. Thanks!

1. How would you rate the quality of the copy I wrote for you?

☐ Excellent ☐ Very good ☐ Good ☐ Fair ☐ Poor

2. What overall rating would you give my copywriting services?

☐ Excellent ☐ Very good ☐ Good ☐ Fair ☐ Poor

3. How would you rate the value received compared with the fee you paid?

☐ Excellent ☐ Very good ☐ Good ☐ Fair ☐ Poor

4. What did you like best about my service?_____

5. What would you like see improved?_____

Your name (optional):_____

Company_____

Please return this form to:

48 Cooper Road Suite #2
Oak Ridge, NJ 07438

Referring a lead to a client or colleague

When you get a request you can't handle, don't just turn the prospect away. Instead, figure out who in your network can help the person. Then put the two of them together. Here's a sample letter referring an opportunity.

Customize your own letter referring a lead to a client or colleague:

When you offer a client or colleague a referral, try to be very clear about the details so the person can judge if this is an opportunity he or she has the time and knowledge to take on. Include:

1. An explanation of what the project is, where the work is coming from, and the offer to pass it on.
2. The reasons why you thought this person or company would be right for the job.
3. More details on the job or the source of the project (if desired).
4. Instructions on what to do next.

Dear Tom:

Harry Nerburg, the largest independent publisher of telecommunications magazines, has recently asked me to write a book about wireless voice and data applications. I cannot take on this project right now, but I thought it might be something you'd be interested in.

This could be an excellent way to further solidify your company's leadership position in the industry ("the people who wrote the book") and educate both service providers and end users on the variety and benefits of wireless voice and data applications.

Harry Nerburg is a reputable company that can offer you many opportunities down the line as well. They publish *Computer Connections* and founded *WireCom Magazine*. He is also the number-one publisher of telecommunications books (Telecom Books).

If you're interested, give me a call and I'll hook you up with the publisher over there.

Sincerely,

Suggesting a substitute product

When a customer orders a product you have, the easiest thing to do is ship it. But what if another product would better meet his or her needs?

Taking the time to suggest the substitute, rather than automatically fulfilling the original order, is a value-added service your customers will appreciate. Because this communication can delay delivery of the order, it's best to send it by fax or e-mail.

Customize your own letter suggesting a substitute product:

This letter must have a friendly and helpful tone, not one reminiscent of a bait-and-switch sales pitch. It should include:

1. An acknowledgment of the original order and its availability.
2. The suggestion that another product might better meet the customer's needs.
3. A description of the substitute product.
4. A comparison of the substitute product to the ordered product in price, quality, and function.
5. A request for further instruction about the order.
6. Mention of a guarantee, if there is one available.

Dear Bob:

We do have the book you ordered, *Career Planning Guide*, in stock, and I'd be happy to send you 12 copies immediately for your outplacement program.

However, we've recently introduced a product that might be a better value for your program: *Career Planner 1.0.*

This software package is an interactive version of the *Guide*. It includes spreadsheets for all the exercises in the book as well as a database for the job-seeker to enter contact information for potential employers and networking leads. The software, which runs on Windows 95 or higher, comes with a companion book that is essentially an updated version of *Career Planning Guide.*

Career Planning Guide sells for $29.95 per copy, and *Career Planner 1.0* is $49.95 for the book and diskette. But as the enclosed order form shows, our volume discount for software is higher than for books. So, for 12 units, your cost for *Career Planner 1.0* is only $37.95 per copy.

Let me know whether you want to order the book or the updated software-and-book package. Your order is covered by our usual 90-day money-back guarantee, so there is no risk of any kind.

Sincerely,

Advising clients of a vacation schedule

Customers depend on their vendors to be available to help them. When going on vacation, send a notice advising customers. Send it at least two to three weeks in advance. Customers hate surprises.

Customize your own memo advising clients of your vacation schedule:

This memo needs to be very specific about the dates of your vacation how business will be conducted in your absence. Include:

1. The dates of your absence.
2. Your plans for keeping in touch with the office (if any).
3. How customers or clients can get in touch with you if necessary.
4. An invitation to talk before the scheduled departure.

TO: Clients

FROM: Bob Bly

RE: April schedule

I will be traveling and out of the office April 21 to 25. I will be in touch with the office via voice mail. The office will be open during this period, and if you need anything, you can leave a voice mail for me at 123-456-7899, or call me directly at 123-456-7890. Let me know if you have any questions or need additional information before I leave.

Notifying customers of a new account representative

Whenever customer service personnel change, notify customers immediately of the change. Be aware that in some industries customers tend to stick with a vendor regardless of who is their representative, while in other businesses (stock brokerages and so forth), customers commonly follow the person they're dealing with and move their business to his or her new company. In the latter case, an immediate phone call to follow up the letter (which can be sent via fax or e-mail if the change will take place immediately) can help reduce customer movement and loss.

Customize your own notice of a new account representative:

This letter must have a very positive and reassuring tone. If the replacement is due to any internal problems, keep this information to yourself. The letter should include:

1. The announcement that the account representative has left (you can state the reasons if they are positive).

2. Introduce the new account manager and give his or her credentials in brief.

3. Assure the customer that the high level of service they have come to expect will continue uninterrupted.

4. If possible, suggest a time when you can introduce the new representative in person.

Dear Mr. White:

Joe Carr has left our account management team to become a regional manager at our California office. John Newcomb will be your new account manager.

John has worked with us for 11 years in a variety of production-related positions and has a keen grasp of the technical aspects of our product line. We are pleased to assign him to your account, and I'm sure he'll do an exceptional job in serving your needs, especially when it comes to training operators and handling support matters. I have been working with John for several weeks to train him in your procedures and to bring him up to date on your account.

I notice you are signed up for our Advanced Process Management seminar for next month in the Hilton. I will attend and bring John with me. Perhaps we can talk and you can meet John in person over coffee in the morning or at the lunch break.

Sincerely,

Keep in touch

The more frequently and recently customers hear from you, the more likely they are to think of you when they have a need for your type of product or service.

Therefore, keeping in touch is not only a sales tactic for you—but also a service to the customer. A good example is the postcard your dentist sends that says "It's time to schedule an appointment!" The patients are reminded to get routine dental care to catch any problems early while maintaining good dental health. The dentist gets more appointments.

Periodic letters to customers help keep your name before them. This keep-in-touch letter gets response by offering these customers a chance to update their literature files. This is the kind of letter that can be sent in any form you like: snail-mail, fax, or e-mail.

Customize your own keep-in-touch letter:

This is not a sales letter; try to make it sound friendly and helpful:

1. Open with a cordial greeting that states the purpose of this letter: to keep in touch.
2. Offer the customer something new: an updated catalog, product information, an industry news clipping, a business newsletter, and the like.
3. Give the customer an opportunity to ask for your product or service or information.
4. If desired, you can also give the customer an opportunity to be removed from your customer list.

TO: My valued clients
FROM: Bob Bly, Copywriter/Consultant
RE: FREE reprints and tapes on improving marketing
        communications

This is just a cordial note to keep in touch and offer you a chance to update your files. I'd like to send you, absolutely free, a selection of recent article reprints, audiotapes, and copywriting samples. To get any or all of these items, just call me. Or, if you prefer, you can complete and mail this form, or fax it to 123-456-7890.

Thanks,

Bob Bly

P.S. To discuss a potential copywriting assignment, call me at 123-456-7899. There's no charge for a cost estimate, and no obligation of any kind.

BOB, please send me the following *free* items:

Articles

☐ "29 Articles You Can Use in Your Company Newsletter"

☐ "Getting More Pick-Up of Your Press Releases"

NEW Audio Tapes

☐ 815—"How to Create Great Collateral"

☐ 816—"What's Working in Direct Mail Today"

RECENT Copywriting Samples

☐ Direct mail packages—business-to-business newsletters, loose-leaf services, directories

☐ Direct mail packages, consumer newsletters

___Call me to discuss a potential assignment.

___Please remove my name from your valued client list.

Name_____

Title_____

Company_____

Address_____

City_____ State_____

Zip_____

Phone_____. _____

Fax_____ _____

Being courteous

It's always smart business to be courteous to your customers. Take the time to write any one of the following letters this week and watch what happens to your relationship with your customers!

Welcome letter to a new customer

A growing (although still not widely used) practice in business is to send a "Welcome Kit" to new customers. The benefits include increased customer goodwill and an opportunity to clearly communicate terms, conditions, ordering information, and other important information.

The kit can include standard documents (brochures, catalogs, labels, air-bills) as well as documents written specifically for the kit. The first of these is usually a cover letter as shown below.

Customize your own letter to welcome a new customer:

This letter is not a sales letter; it is a welcome letter that supplies information. It should include:

1. A thank you for the order or business.
2. A referral to enclosed company literature.
3. An introduction to the area sales manager (if appropriate).
4. An open invitation to call for information or service.

Dear Mr. Singer:

Thank you for your order last week. We're delighted to be doing business with you.

To give you a better feel for who we are and what we do, I've enclosed our corporate capabilities brochure and latest purchasing catalog. On page two of the catalog, you'll find our terms, conditions, shipping, and return policies.

Our sales representative serving your region, Joe Young, will contact you to set up an appointment. He can explain our product line more to your liking and answer any questions you may have.

In the meantime, if there's anything I can do to help serve you better, please call me directly at 123-456-7890.

Sincerely,

Thanking a customer for a referral

I can tell you from my own personal experience that not thanking some-one for a referral irks them. However, most people don't even acknowledge the referrals you give them! When that happens, I myself assume the referral is not appreciated, and I am more likely to refer someone else the next time if an alternative vendor comes along whom I like and trust. To avoid this from happening when you get referrals, use the simple letter below.

Enclose a small but tasteful gift as a thank you for the referral. When I thank someone for a referral to a writing assignment, I enclose an autographed copy of one of my books. You should send the thank you and the gift regardless of whether the referral results in an order. It's the thought that counts, not the result.

Customize your own letter thanking a customer for a referral:

This is short and sweet, but it packs a strong message:

1. Open with the details of the job you have been contacted about.
2. Acknowledge that you know the work was referred by the person you're writing to.
3. Explain why this referral is so pleasing to you.
4. Give your sincere appreciation.

Dear Ilise:

Yesterday I received a big assignment from BWJ Advertising and was told by the creative director, Gale Krashner, that you were responsible for my getting the business.

I was pleased to get the project, Ilise, but even more pleased that you thought well enough of me to recommend me to Gale. Considering the source, it's an endorsement of the highest caliber, and I appreciate it sincerely. Thank you.

Cordially,

Thanking customers for their business

A.L. Williams, the life insurance tycoon, once observed that "you beat 90 percent of the competition just by being competent." Sales trainer Paul Karasik agrees: "Success means doing the little things exceedingly well." One thing businesses don't do nearly enough of is thank customers for their patronage.

It's a small thing, but if neglected, it can cause a slow-burning resentment among good customers. Done properly and frequently, it can help you beat the 90 percent of competitors who don't pay attention to these little details. The best time to thank someone for their business is immediately after they've given it to you. The recent communication makes the message seem fresher and more relevant.

Customize your own letter thanking customers for their business:

This letter can serve two purposes: It says sincere thanks, and it also reminds the customer of your special services or features. Include:

1. An upfront thank you for a recent order or patronage.
2. An acknowledgment of past business dealings.
3. Things you've done to ensure top quality service or product.
4. A wish for future success.

Dear Ms. Camico:

I want to thank you again for choosing the Atlantic Reef as your headquarters during the five days of the Manager's Conference. It's people like you who make the hotel business rewarding and satisfying.

Of course, I know you didn't choose the Atlantic just because it was the site of the exhibit hall. You have regularly booked the Atlantic whenever you have an event in our region, and of course we are delighted to have you do business any time you visit the coast.

To make each stay the best it can be, we strive to provide you with total support for all your event management needs. For instance, we didn't add our new videoconference center just for your group's executive board, but we were thinking about your need for videoconferencing when we made the decision to build it. I'm glad you found it so helpful in linking with your Swiss office on this trip.

I hope you had a good trip back to California and were satisfied with the tape duplicates of your breakout sessions made by Sound Enterprises.

Sincerely,

Cover letter accompanying an article sent to a customer

Regularly clipping and sending articles of interest to customers, along with a short cover note, is a great customer communication strategy. Your customers will appreciate the fact that you're thinking of them. In addition, people like getting articles on topics related to their business. I have had many prospects and customers tell me that my article clippings are appreciated and made them think of me when they needed to buy what I was selling. The best articles to send are those by or about you. But any article related to the reader's business, products, markets, or industry will be of interest. Try clipping and sending articles. It works!

Customize your own letter to accompany an article you send to a customer:

This is neither a sales letter nor a request for business, nor is it an opportunity to pitch a new product. Rather, it is a random act of kindness that shows you are thinking about your customers and what they are interested in. Make it simple and include:

1. A statement that says you saw this article and thought the reader might be interested.
2. A comment about why you know this is a subject of interest.
3. A wrap-up wishing the reader well.

Dear Mr. Martin:

I saw the attached article in this month's Business Magazine and I thought it was something you'd be interested in reading. We've talked in the past about the difficulty resellers have when choosing a leasing company. This article gives a few very helpful tips. I hope you find it useful.

Best regards,

Cover letter accompanying a gift to a customer

You want to make your customers happy. People like to get presents. By sending an occasional inexpensive and tasteful gift, you go a long way toward building goodwill—and your customers will fondly remember your name. A simple cover letter that accompanies the free gift is all that is necessary.

Customize your own letter to accompany a gift to a customer:

There's not much to say here besides:

1. The gift is to say thank you.
2. We look forward to working together more in the future.

Dear Ms. Roth:

The enclosed gift is our way of saying "thanks" for the business you gave Jane Edleman Associates last year. We look forward to servicing your needs in the future. Enjoy!

Sincerely,

Personal congratulations

Although this is a book of business letters, not every letter a businessperson writes is about business. Addressing the personal side of a customer's life on appropriate occasions is an effective technique for strengthening the bonds between you. Here is a letter you can use to congratulate a customer on a non-work related achievement.

Customize your own letter of personal congratulations:

This has nothing to do with business, so don't use it as an occasion to sell. Simply include:

1. The event warranting congratulations.
2. The fact that you're impressed, happy, pleased, or proud.

Dear John,

I read in this morning's *Record* that John Jr.'s soccer team, the Screaming Eagles, won the East Division Title in Sunday's game.

Congratulations to John Jr. I'm sure he must be thrilled!

And congratulations to you too. I know how dedicated you are to being a team coach and the late hours you put in to accommodate this time-consuming activity around your busy work schedule. Although it's an effort I do not duplicate, I admire it immensely.

Sincerely,

Customer survey: cover letter and form

One of the best ways to find out what your customers need is simply to ask them. The customer survey form is a good idea when you're looking to add products or services to your line. When you send a survey to customers, you need to include a cover letter indicating what you are sending and its purpose. You can use the following letter to accompany your survey. In addition, you can improve the odds of getting a response to a survey if you offer a free gift in return.

Customize your own cover letter to a customer survey:

You're asking someone to give you their time, so ask nicely:

1. Acknowledge that you're asking a favor.
2. Give the details about why you're interested in the customer's opinion.
3. Give instructions about how the attached survey should be completed and returned.
4. Flatter the reader by explaining why his or her opinion is so valuable to you.

Dear Direct Marketer:

Would you do me a favor? Tell me about your wish list.

Right now, I'm planning a special half-day executive briefing called "Database and Direct Marketing: How to Double Your Response Rates This Year." I'll be inviting you and a select few other direct marketing professionals to attend this informative seminar without charge.

Before I finalize the program, I want to gauge your interest and find out which topics are most important to you.

So, if you could please take a moment to complete the attached reply form, it would be gratly appreciated. Please fax it back to me at 123-456-7890. You are one of the best in this business, so I value your opinion. Your response will help me offer the topics that will be most beneficial to you and other direct-marketing professionals.

Sincerely,

P.S. If it's easier, you can also respond by phone. Call 800-223-2194 and ask to speak to my assistant Philip Paine at extension 1234.

A sample survey

The following short-form customer survey will give you an idea of the format to use in your own survey.

Complete and return this form today:

1. Would you be interested in attending a special FREE half-day executive briefing, "Database and Direct Marketing: How to Double Your Response Rates This Year"?

☐ Yes ☐ No ☐ Possibly

2. Which of the following topics would you be most interested in discussing at the seminar? (1 = low interest, 5 = highest interest)

Choosing mailing list brokers   ____

List selection   ____

Testing   ____

Saving money with net-name arrangements   ____

Merge/purge   ____

NCOA processing   ____

Database marketing   ____

3. Other Comments:_____

Name_____

Title_____

Company_____ Phone_____

Address_____

City_____ State_____ Zip_____

Dealing with problems

If you have customers, you're going to have problems. Dealing with these problems in writing is a good way to get down the facts and offer possible solutions. The following samples will give you a guide.

Negative commentary letter

Sometimes a client or customer will ask your opinion, and your answer won't be what he or she wants to hear. A letter or fax is a nonconfrontational way of presenting your response, without the awkwardness of a face-to-face confrontation. It also gives the person being criticized time to think about your comments and a response, rather than responding on the spot in a way that may be defensive.

Customize your own negative commentary letter:

This letter needs to sound helpful not critical. Include:

1. A positive statement to open.
2. A statement about what's wrong.
3. A detailed explanation (or list) of problems you see.
4. A suggestion for solutions and next steps.

TO: Harry Mostly
Via: Fax
FROM: Bob Bly
RE: New A&B-Shield letter

Dear Harry:

While your A&B-Shield letter is very well-written, I do not think it will work. Here's why:

1. You are selling two separate things in one mailing: a Windows upgrade to A&B-Shield, and a support program. You should sell one thing in one mailing. These offers should be promoted in two separate mailings.

2. The Windows version should be positioned as an upgrade of the DOS product, and should therefore be offered via mail order at a fixed price that represents some discount off the list price. That is, existing A&B-Shield users should get it at a deep discount of 50% or more.

3. The new Windows version and the new partnership program are totally unrelated. I should be able to buy the Windows upgrade for a fixed price, just as I bought my DOS version, by mail, without committing to a monthly partnership fee.

The partnership might work as a more formalized support program. However, that's a separate mailing, and we would have to give much more value and benefits than outlined here.

Letter to a customer when you do not get the order

A good practice is to send a short letter to customers and prospects when you do *not* get the order. Your letter should thank them for their consideration and then praise, rather than criticize, the decision they made.

This has several benefits. For one, it creates a professional image and is contrary to the sour grapes the customer might get from other suppliers (your competitors) who also didn't get the order. At the same time, you can correct wrong impressions that may have led to your not getting the job. Even though you lost this sale, you can set the stage for repeat inquiries (and eventually, a new order) from this customer.

Also, if you know who the customer has chosen, be sure to say something good about that firm. If there was a selection factor the customer overlooked or did not know about, let him or her know about it. Perhaps you'll get called if the first supplier doesn't deliver.

Customize your own letter to a customer when you do not get the order:

Don't sound too disappointed—sound optimistic! Include:

1. A thank you for the opportunity to bid (or give a sales presentation or proposal).
2. A statement saying you're happy they found someone qualified to do the job.
3. Add a piece of additional information that would be interesting to this client.
4. Request to be given the chance to bid on another project.
5. A small piece of flattery.

Dear Karen:

Thanks for the opportunity to bid on the Fergeson job. I'm glad you could find someone who can meet your requirements so quickly, especially given your tight deadline.

In the future, please keep in mind that we just became a dealer for a new supplier that manufactures a midrange product ideal for your work. It isn't the premium brand like the Insu-Range we normally use, but it fits your specifications and is 20 percent cheaper.

Please keep us in mind for your next job. We are always glad for the opportunity to send a bid to a quality company like yours.

Best wishes,

Announcing a store closing

Announcing the closing of a business is more than a formal courtesy. Often there is inventory, office equipment, real estate, or other assets that need to be disposed of. By selling them, the owner can pocket a handsome sum and avoid large losses.

The notification of closure letter can be used to promote the going out of business sale. An effective offer is to sell the remaining inventory and assets at a discount given to past customers and shoppers.

Customize your own letter announcing a store closing:

Whether you're happy or sad about closing your business, this letter should convey good news to the reader. Make sure it includes:

1. The announcement that you're going out of business.
2. If desired the reason for closing.
3. The savings you're offering to your customers.
4. Dates of sale and store hours.
5. Final closing day.

Dear Preferred Customer and Friend:

Al's Men's Store is quitting business. And that means a sale with our best prices ever!

After 30 years, I am retiring, and we are having an absolutely incredible "going-out-of-business" sale. Our entire inventory of men's clothing is on sale during this huge discount sale. Even the store fixtures and equipment are for sale.

Unfortunately for me (but fortunately for you) our vendors could *not* cancel our last orders after we notified them of our closing. This new merchandise has been shipped, and we have to unload it—fast! You will probably never have a chance to buy quality clothing in these brands and styles at these incredible low prices anywhere else, ever again!

You should not miss this event! Beat the rush and shop **now**! As a preferred customer, you have first choice of all merchandise at rock-bottom liquidation prices. If you have a friend or relative you want to share this opportunity with, simply bring them (and this letter) with you when you come to the store.

Our going-out-of business hours are Monday through Saturday, 10 a.m. to 7 p.m. This is a wonderful opportunity to save money. We're ready to move merchandise. Everything must go (so I can go fishing in Florida). Come now. This sale ends January 21, and then we close our doors forever!

Sincerely yours,

Responding to customer complaints

One essential technique for ensuring customer satisfaction is to respond to complaints promptly and with genuine interest in solving the problem. This is a fax I sent to a client who wasn't happy with an ad that I wrote for him and who wanted me to adjust the bill downward. As you can see, I complied, but I also addressed the issue more broadly to prevent recurrence.

Customize your own letter responding to customer complaints:

When you write to a customer in response to a complaint, you must walk the fine line between keeping the customer happy and being walked all over. Make sure your letter includes:

1. An acknowledgment of the complaint and a statement about valuing your business relationship.
2. An explanation of how you perceive your obligation to the customer in this circumstance.
3. An explanation of how you perceive the customer's obligation.
4. A request for agreement to avoid similar situations in the future.
5. A request for a response.

Dear Mike:

Thanks for your memo. Obviously, I value our long-term relationship, and if you want to discuss an adjustment to this bill, I'm happy to do so.

I do want to be clear about the conditions under which I work for clients. When you ask me to do an ad, letter, or other piece of copy, I guarantee your satisfaction. I do this by offering unlimited rewrites at no extra charge—something almost no other writer does. I can't guarantee anyone's satisfaction with the first draft, of course. But I can and do guarantee your satisfaction with the rewritten copy. It is my responsibility to listen and polish until you're happy.

At the same time, it's the client's responsibility to let me know if he's unhappy, and to tell me where the copy didn't meet his expectations. If a client doesn't take advantage of my free rewrite service, they are then billed for the agreed-upon amount. If they later decide to have me revise, there is generally no charge, provided the request is made within a reasonable period of time.

Does this sound like a reasonable way for the two of us to work together? It would require that you let me know when you're unhappy with something. In return, I will correct any defects in a timely manner to ensure your total satisfaction. Fair enough? Let me know your thoughts.

Sincerely,

Letter responding to complaints about price increases

The best way to avoid complaints about price increases is not to raise them too frequently (once a year is enough for business products and services) or too much at one time (no more than 10 percent per increase).

You may still get complaints because no one wants to pay more. At the same time, your customers know that prices on everything go up. Most will eventually accept this if it is patiently explained. Some will not, and with every price increase, you may lose the bottom percentile of your customer base to lower-priced vendors.

Customize your own letter that responding to price increases:

When you raise prices, you're bound to hear complaints. Don't just ignore them, use them as an opportunity to communicate with your customers and build goodwill. Make sure your letter includes:

1. A note of appreciation for taking the time to complain.
2. An agreement that no one likes to pay more.
3. An explanation of why prices must go up occasionally.
4. An assurance that you work hard to keep prices affordable.
5. An offer to work with this person to find a way he or she can continue to afford your product or services.

Dear Annette:

I appreciate hearing from good customers like you about our recent price increases on components and subassemblies.

No one likes paying more, and we do not raise our prices at a whim. But when the manufacturers whose products we stock and distribute raise their prices to us, we have to pass on at least part of that cost increase to you.

Our price increases are a result of Tension Tools and other major suppliers raising their prices across the board—from 10 to 20 percent or more, depending on the item. This reflects higher production costs they incur due to increased materials prices and higher standards

If you compare our prices with other distributors, you'll find we are right in line, and usually lower for the brand names listed above. Some of the biggest distributors can beat some of our prices on some orders. But as you know, our Total Supply Management Solution keeps your overall cost of goods lower when you buy from us in volume.

Our price per unit on Tension and other major brands is as low as it can be. If you need to cut component costs further, give me a call. Perhaps we can substitute compatible components from alternative manufacturers.

Sincerely,

Sample virus protection policy

I once nearly lost a client who felt she had received a computer virus from an e-mail I sent. Since that time, I give every client a copy of my company's virus protection policy.

Computer viruses can cause customers significant headaches and expense. By helping to keep their computers free of viruses, you are performing a valuable customer service.

If you perform a customer service that's valuable to your customers, make sure they know about it. Explain to new and existing clients in a memo the steps you take to prevent the files you send them from being contaminated with viruses. Here is a sample anti-virus protection policy.

TO: All clients and potential clients

FROM: Bob Bly

RE: Our anti-virus policy

Because I know we are all concerned about computer viruses infecting our online business relationships, my company has outlined a virus protection policy that I wanted you to know about so you can feel more comfortable doing online business with me. Take a moment to read the policy and then be sure to give me a call if you have any further questions or concerns.

ANTI-VIRUS POLICY

1. We make every effort to ensure that files sent to our clients via e-mail or floppy disk are virus-free, but we *cannot* guarantee it.

2. We run Carumen 3.5 VirusScan, which is the most widely used anti-virus program worldwide. It is used by 50 million people, 90 percent of the Fortune 1000, and 400,000 organizations.

3. According to Carumen, VirusScan technology has been shown in lab tests to detect virtually every virus. These include boot, file, multiparties, stealth, mutating, encrypted, and polymorphic viruses.

4. Because new viruses crop up all the time, we routinely upgrade our VirusScan program by downloading the latest versions from the Carumen BBS (bulletin board). We recommend that clients running VirusScan do likewise.

5. Even running the latest anti-virus software cannot guarantee a virus-free file with absolute certainty, because of the new viruses that are constantly launched. Clients should run the most recent version of whatever anti-virus software they use.

---

6. If you open a file we send you via e-mail and it contains a virus, that does *not* mean it had a virus when we sent it from our end: Files sent via the Internet can pick up viruses in transit.

7. The only 100-percent foolproof protection against receiving a virus is to request that documents be faxed instead of e-mailed. You can't pick up a computer virus from hard copy.

8. If you have any problems with a virus in a file we send you, please notify us immediately. If you are having a virus problem in general, we can refer you to computer consultants who may be able to help.

8

BUSINESS AND CONSUMER COMPLAINTS AND REQUESTS

According to the White House Office of Consumer Affairs, 68 percent of customers who leave a business (and never go back) do so because a manager, owner, or employee has treated them with indifference.

In addition, 96 percent of dissatisfied customers don't bother to complain; they simply stop buying. Even worse, the average dissatisfied customer tells eight to 10 people about his or her negative experience with you.

In this chapter, you will find model letters for making and handling complaints and requests as both a businessperson and a consumer.

Business letters that handle requests

In an ideal situation, a person makes a request and you oblige. Everybody's happy. But in the real world, you simply can't do what everyone asks you to do. When this happens, it's a good idea to put your refusal into writing so there can be no misunderstandings. The following sample letters will give you a good idea how to say no and yet remain on good terms.

Turning down unrealistic requests from customers

Sometimes we cannot do (or are unwilling to do) everything a customer asks us. But even when customers are at fault or their expectations are unrealistic, they may be irritated by our refusal. That's why the refusal should be made in a firm but polite letter that explains your reasoning and, when possible, offers alternative solutions.

Customize your own letter turning down a request from a customer:

This letter can be written when someone returns merchandise by mail or makes a refund request over the phone. The details of your letter, of course, will be different depending on your product and the customer's request, but it should include:

1. An acknowledgment of the request and an apology for the dissatisfaction the customer feels.
2. A firm statement of your policy regarding the topic of complaint.
3. The details of why the request is unrealistic.
4. If appropriate, a compromise solution.
5. An offer to talk further.

Dear Mr. Kane:

I received the wildlife prints you returned and your request for a refund. I'm sorry you are unhappy with this merchandise.

However, we offer a refund only on merchandise returned within 30 days in good condition. According to our sale records, you bought these prints over 14 months ago. They are a discontinued series, and we no longer stock them.

In addition, the prints are wrinkled and discolored, as if they had been exposed to bright sunlight or moisture over an extended period. Therefore, even if we did still carry them, these particular prints could not be resold.

Based on the condition of the merchandise and the expiration of our guarantee period, we would not normally grant a refund. But we do value you as a customer. What I can do, based on your preferred customer status with us, is to give you a credit for 50 percent of the purchase price of these prints, which comes to $125.

I hope you find this solution satisfactory and fair. If you have any questions or concerns, call me at 123-456-7890 and we can talk further.

Sincerely,

Refusing a business request

The following model can be easily adapted to your needs. In this situation, a potential client asked us to prepare, on speculation, a memo for which we typically charge a fee. His logic was that it offered us opportunity to get new business; he did not realize that we already have more than enough business and therefore do not need to do speculative work. Here is the reply we sent in response to his e-mail:

Customize your own letter refusing a request:

Refusing a request is a sensitive area. It should be dealt with honestly, succinctly, and directly. Doing so via mail, fax, or e-mail is better than via telephone or in person, because it lets the recipient understand your reasoning before reacting. The letter should include:

1. A direct "no" (cushioned with an "I'm sorry"). Make refusals firm. Don't be ambiguous. Don't hint that you're flexible if you aren't.

2. A short explanation of your reasons (nothing too detailed; no time or no budget are usually good enough). However, don't just say what you won't do, also say what you would be willing to do to help. For example, if you can't sponsor a fundraiser, maybe you could donate some of your products as a door prize.

3. An offer to do something else (less costly or time consuming) to help.

4. A wish of good luck.

Dear Richard:

Sorry, I can't help you on this one. Right now, I'm just not interested in convincing anyone to do direct mail. I'd rather work with clients who are already convinced. Also, my schedule does not allow me to write a proposal on spec for something that is so uncertain at this point.

To support your meeting in Denver, you are welcome to use any of my materials. Often my book on direct mail helps people decide to enter the business. If you'd like another copy, I'll be happy to send you one. Just let me know what materials you'd like and I'll send them to you via express mail.

Good luck on this project.

Sincerely,

Turning down a request to advertise

Frequently, companies are asked to advertise in media that would support a local community cause, but would not be a cost-effective use of the firm's advertising dollars. You can use this short note to politely decline to participate without offending the person who extended the invitation.

Customize your own letter turning down a request to advertise:

A simple "no" won't do here. It can cause ill feelings and hurt business down the road. Take the time to explain your reasons and maintain a cordial relationship. Include:

1. Appreciation for the offer.
2. A regretful decline to advertise.
3. The reasons you will not be buying an ad (budget restraints or target market problems are acceptable the reasons).
4. If desired, a helpful referral to more appropriate business types (best not to name a particular business).
5. A thank you and wishes for success.

Dear Brett:

I appreciate your invitation to purchase an advertisement in Smalltown Annual. Thank you.

Unfortunately, we will not be able to contribute an ad this year. Many thousands of service club books are published each year, and it is impossible for us to purchase advertising in all of them. National advertisers like us are forced to spend their money where the message gets into the hands of purchasing managers, office managers, principals, and others who buy in large quantities. Your market doesn't match these needs.

I expect that you will have to rely mainly on local community businesses to purchase space in the Annual. Many businesses feel a strong obligation to support worthy community activities; just having their names associated with your Annual is a strong incentive. Indeed, we feel the same way about Central City, which is our home base.

Thank you for thinking of us, Brett, and best wishes for the most successful Annual that has ever been published.

Cordially yours,

Declining a request for a donation

When saying no to a fundraiser, the important thing to remember is that your refusal to donate does not mean you don't support the cause. If you point out that there are limitless fundraisers competing for a limited amount of your company resources, your refusal will seem reasonable and acceptable.

Customize your own letter declining a request for a donation:

Keep the door open to good will by including:

1. A thank you for the invitation to donate.
2. An acknowledgment of the good work the organization does.
3. A statement of decline, with regret.
4. A statement keeping the door open to possible donations in the future.
5. A wish for success.

Dear Mrs. Mintzer

We carefully study all requests for contributions we receive and we thank you for inviting us to donate to donate to the Anytown Symphony Orchestra.

Although we all unanimously agree that the Anytown Symphony Orchestra contributes much to the community—as well as to the performers themselves—we can't, unfortunately, provide financial support at this time.

I do hope that in the future we will be in a position to provide some funds for the Symphony. In the meantime, we wish you success with your efforts on behalf of this excellent organization.

Sincerely,

Business complaint letters

As a businessperson, you not only get complaints from customers, you may often find yourself in a position to be making a complaint. The following letters will help you find the words you need when things aren't going right and you want to tell someone about it.

Business-to-business complaint

Here's a complaint letter from one business to another.

Customize your own business-to-business complaint:

There are a thousand reasons you might write to complain to another businessperson. Use this sample as a guide to make sure you include:

1. A direct statement of your complaint.
2. Specific details of the problem (don't give a vague or general complaint).
3. An acknowledgment of the fact that you value your business relationship with this person and want to work out the problem.
4. A course of action you would like the recipient to take to resolve the problem.
5. A cordial and upbeat ending.

Dear Richard:

I am writing because I feel that communication between us is deteriorating and will soon affect my ability to continue doing business with your firm. I have found that in the past month I cannot discuss our company sales policies without feeling very defensive, faced with your immediate negative responses.

The example that comes quickest to my mind occurred last Friday. If you remember, I simply wanted to ask if it was possible to transfer your discount credit to next month's order, but ended up arguing the value of the discount policy in general.

I value our relationship very much and I think you have a terrific service to offer. But our ability to do business suffers when our communication breaks down and we don't understand each other.

If you have complaints about our overall business arrangement, please let me know so we can get the problem out in the open. Otherwise, I need you to listen before you start arguing when I call with a question. Let's try this one again: "Is it possible to transfer your discount credit to next month's order?"

I look forward to continuing our business relationship in a positive and cordial manner.

Sincerely,

Intraoffice complaint

It is only within the last 10 years or so that I have heard businesspeople use the term "client" to refer to people *within their own company!* But that's how line managers (managers with profit and loss responsibility) view service departments within their companies as vendors (information systems, marketing communications, technical publications, shipping and logistics, and so forth).

This view is more accurate than ever before: With downsizing, service departments are usually the first to be cut; line managers are more likely to retain their jobs. The rising popularity of outsourcing gives managers more flexibility than ever in "farming out" computer programming, package design, technical writing, and other functions previously performed in-house. Therefore, the "clients" really do have a choice. Accordingly, the service department needs to treat them as clients, not as burdens or annoyances.

This customer-focused orientation toward internal clients will only become more critical as time goes on. Look for people who you formerly thought of as "co-workers" to treat you as "vendors" and think of themselves as "customers" as in the memo below:

Customize your own intraoffice complaint:

This letter shouldn't burn any bridges or kill working relationships, but it should get right to the point. Any intraoffice complaint should include:

1. A concise statement of the problem.

2. Any history of correspondence about this problem.

3. How this problem affects others in the company.

4. An acknowledgment of the difficulties surrounding this problem.

5. If appropriate, a statement acknowledging that the client has other options and is willing to exercise them.

6. A statement of exactly what you expect the recipient to do to remedy the problem.

7. A request for a reply.

TO: Steve Mahal, GT Services Manager
FROM: Kim Kohad, Sales Manager
RE: New sales automation system

Dear Steve:

When we last spoke, you promised me that "90 percent" of the first pass on the new sales automation system would be ready last week. I counted on that deadline because I know you realize how much these dates affect the entire line of production.

Unfortunately, last week has come and gone, and I have not heard from you.

The delayed arrival of the system is seriously compromising the performance of our field sales force, which in turn has a direct negative impact on the bottom line. In addition, I'm taking considerable heat from my vice president for the late delivery of the software.

I know how busy you are. But this is a deadline you promised you could make. If you had told me you were too busy to take this job on at the beginning, I would have chosen an alternative supplier. That is still an open option.

If you can't delivery a system by the end of the month, we will turn this project over to a third-party vendor. Using you as our in-house source is an option, not a mandate.

I'd prefer to have you finish what you started, but I am running out of time and options. Can you get the work done by June 30—yes or no?

I await your reply.

Complaint to management from an employee

The key to complaining to a manager or supervisor is to frame your communication as a request rather than a complaint or demand. The key is to show not how you are personally inconvenienced, but how the problem adversely affects either the company as a whole or the area under the recipient's direct management.

Customize a complaint to management:

Whether you're complaining about your parking space or the latest executive dictate, remember that the written word is mightier than the sword (and can be almost as deadly). Choose your words carefully so they don't come back to stab you. Your complaint should include:

1. The topic of your complaint.
2. The exact reasons for your complaint.
3. An acknowledgment of the manager's point of view.
4. A request for a compromise solution (give the details).
5. A request for a response.

TO: Jim Burke, Group Product Marketing Director
FROM: Alex Freeman
RE: Ad agency services purchasing procedure

Dear Jim:

I just received the Approved Agency list. According to the memo, we may purchase creative and production services only from a list of six approved agencies.

I think this is counterproductive for several reasons:

1. These agencies are among the highest-priced vendors we use. They already charge fees that our limited budgets cannot accommodate.
2. When they learn they have a semi-monopoly on our business, they'll charge even more.
3. The freelancers and graphic design studies I currently use are familiar with our technology; they do as good or better job than the agencies on the list, and their fees are reasonable.
4. The turnaround from freelancers is much faster.

I agree that reducing the number of agencies helps create a consistent look and strategy. But can we amend the new policy so that marketing communications can continue to buy certain creative services (mainly copy, design, photography, and illustration) on an a la carte basis? What do you think about this?

Sincerely,

Complaining of late delivery for a product

The key to writing an effective complaint letter concerning a late delivery is not merely to restate that the delivery is late, as the recipient already knows that. Instead, you want to make him or her aware of the inconvenience you may be suffering as a result of their lateness.

Customize your own letter complaining of late delivery:

If tardy delivery is costing your business time, money, or goodwill, let the recipient know that. Make sure your letter includes:

1. The details of the problem shipment: the merchandise and the purchase order number.
2. The promised date of delivery and the actual date of delivery.
3. The internal problems this delayed shipment has cost your company.
4. The problems the delayed shipment has caused you with your customers (both in reputation and finances).
5. A positive statement about the quality of the company's products and your desire to continue ordering from them.
6. What you need in order to continue doing business with this company (a promise of future promptness, a written agreement for late penalty fees, and so forth).
7. A request for an immediate response.

Dear Mr. Travis:

We received the three linear amplifier circuits we ordered today on PO # 3456. As you know, this is six days past the promised delivery date.

As a result, we have had to delay shipment of a base station to one of our most important network accounts. We also had to log considerable overtime in our shop to make up for the delay your late delivery caused.

We now have a major customer complaining about our service, not to mention a substantial loss of profit margin on this particular sale. Obviously, my management is not happy.

Zarcon makes excellent amplifier circuits, which is why we favor you with substantial business. But now my boss is asking for technical bids from other companies.

I would like to continuing placing our orders with you if you can assure me that the delivery problem will be corrected on all future orders. In addition, we may want to write a cash penalty for late delivery into future contracts.

Please call me as soon as possible to discuss these terms and arrangements.

Sincerely,

Complaining of missed deadline for a service

When one person misses a deadline, the whole chain of business production falls behind. Make sure you keep a paper trail of all the dates missed and your complaints about each one.

Customize your own letter complaining of a missed deadline:

Your letter should include:

1. The name of the project you're writing about.
2. The dates involved (original due date, any extension dates, and the overdue date).
3. The names of people who have been involved in setting or extending deadlines.
4. The reason the delay is not acceptable.
5. The current deadline with the details of exactly what's due.
6. A reassuring note that the recipient won't let you down.
7. An offer to answer any questions.

Dear Sheldon:

This letter will confirm our correspondence regarding the deadline for the *Handbook of Telecommunications Acronyms and Standards.* As I noted in our conversation, we expect to receive the complete manuscript, including revisions and any new text, in hard copy and on disk by December 28. This deadline is an extension of the December 10 deadline that was set with Betsy Shephard on November 19.

We cannot extend the deadlines any further nor can we delay this publication any longer. Therefore, the above submission deadlines need to be met so we can meet our publication schedule.

I look forward to receiving your manuscript and disk on December 28. If you have any questions, please contact me at 123-456-7890.

Sincerely,

Letters that handle customer complaints

When someone complains to your company, don't shrug it off. This is a great opportunity for some good public relations work. Respond quickly, offer apologies, and turn a disgruntled consumer into a loyal customer.

Resolving a product complaint

In this example, a woman purchased a particular flavor of ice cream and found that it did not have the usual amount of chocolate chips in it. Disappointed, she wrote the manufacturer to complain. Here is the letter she received in reply:

Customize your own letter resolving a product complaint:

In most cases, your job is to assure the complainant that the customer is always right. Your letter should include the following points:

1. Thank the customer for contacting you.
2. Rather than evading the issue, address it directly and apologize.
3. Offer an explanation. An excuse is not necessary, but let the customer know if the problem is an exception to your normal practice.
4. Assure the customer that the problem is in the process of being resolved, and that he or she could count on you in the future.
5. Offer restitution in some the form (such as a gift certificate, replacement product, or credit on future orders) to replace the original purchase.

Dear Ms. Poivre,

Thank you for your telephone call regarding your recent purchase of MochaCocoa Chip Ice Cream. We are sorry to hear that the ice cream lacked the quality you have come to expect from us.

During our manufacturing process, added ingredients are mixed into the ice cream using a special feeder. In the case of your carton, it appears that we were the victims of human or mechanical error, in that the feeder failed to add the appropriate quantity of chocolate pieces to the mix. Please be assured that we have reported this incident to our quality assurance department and that they are implementing measures to ensure that this situation does not recur.

We are sorry that you were unable to enjoy your ice cream as a result. Please accept the enclosed gift certificate for one quart of our premium ice cream to replace your purchase. We hope that you will give us another chance to provide you with the quality ice cream you deserve and that all your future encounters with our ice cream bring you nothing but pleasure.

Warm regards,

Enclosure: Certificate—One Quart

Rectifying a problem

When a customer has a problem, fix it. When you resolve a problem promptly and fully, your relationship with that customer can actually strengthen. Part of gaining that benefit is to let the customer know what you have done for him or her, which of course, can be communicated in writing.

Customize your own letter rectifying a problem:

Effective problem resolution letters contain the following points:

1. Apologize for the problem.

2. Take responsibility. Use personal pronouns and the active voice rather than the passive corporate voice (for example, "We made a mistake" and not "The wrong unit was inadvertently sent by the shipping clerk").

3. Show how the situation has been corrected now and will be prevented in the future.

4. Don't make excuses. For instance, I heard a cook in a luncheonette tell a customer who complained about his hamburger being too rare, "That's because we use thick patties." That's absurd reasoning—the cook should grill the burger as ordered. As Ben Franklin once observed, "People who are good at making excuses are seldom good at anything else."

Dear Danielle:

I apologize for sending a Custom F-5 Module that was not produced according to your specifications.

We have shipped a replacement unit that fits your specifications, via overnight freight, at our expense. It has been reviewed against your written specifications by Lanes Milstead, our senior application engineer.

We'll arrange for someone to pick up the other unit—at our cost and your convenience, of course.

Again, my apologies. We made a mistake, and I've alerted our production department to ensure that it is not repeated.

Sincerely,

Consumer letters for making requests

When you need something from a business, not as a businessperson but rather as a consumer, your letter of request should still be professional and concise. The following two samples will serve as your guide.

Consumer request letter

Many consumer requests are made by phone, but it's always a good idea to back up any conversation with a written request. This documents your need and the date of your request.

Customize your own consumer request letter:

Whether you're requesting reservations, information, a change in policy, free samples, or whatever, letters of consumer request should include:

1. An opening statement of exactly what you want.
2. The details such as time, date, product number, size, color, and so forth.
3. If not included in letterhead, your address and phone for the response.
4. A thank you.

Dear Alicia:

To confirm our phone conversation, I would like to reserve five round-trip seats from Newark to Orlando on ABC Airline. We will leave Newark at 3 p.m. on Saturday, April 19 (arriving in Orlando 5:45 p.m.) and returning Saturday, April 26 from Orlando at 3 p.m. (arriving in Newark at 5:40 p.m.). I understand you also are requesting seats as far toward the front as possible with three and two behind (window and middle) configuration.

I've enclosed a deposit of $500 and will send the balance on April 1st.

Thank you!

Sincerely,

Requesting a refund

Refund requests should be made in writing. Enclose a copy of the receipt, bill of sale, or any other proof of purchase. If the product is defective and small, enclose it with the letter. If it is large, ask in your letter how the seller wants the product returned and where it should be sent. Also ask them to pay for the shipping.

Customize your own letter requesting a refund:

When you ask for a refund, give all the details. Include:

1. An opening that states what product you're writing about.
2. The problem with the item.
3. The reason you do not want a replacement or credit.
4. A request for a refund, stating the exact amount.

Dear Mr. Smathglatter:

On August 8th, I purchased an NCA Dual Line Digital Phone from you over the phone. The person I spoke with was Shelley Dougan.

Today I hooked up the phone, and found it doesn't work. There are two major problems:

1. The phone can receive calls but not dial out. After I get a dial tone and dial, I hear silence for a few seconds, then a click, then get the dial tone again.
2. The LED displays random characters. It does not display the correct information for caller ID or any of the other messaging features.

I needed a phone right away, and could not wait for a replacement from your company. In its stead, I have purchased a new digital phone from a local electronics superstore.

The defective NCA phone, along with a copy of the bill of sale, is enclosed. Please send me a refund for the purchase price of $149.50 plus $4.95 for shipping the phone back to your distribution center. Thank you.

Sincerely,

Request for service or repair

Your request for service or repair should be detailed so the provider knows exactly what you need, when and why. The style of your request will change depending on the circumstances and the level of cooperation from the provider. The following three letters will show you how your request can grow from simple asking, to demanding, to verging on threatening.

Customize your own letters requesting service or repair:

Whether you are sending your first letter requesting service or repair or your tenth one to the same company, every letter should include:

1. The item needing repair or service and the date of purchase.
2. The problem that requires attention.
3. Exactly what you want done.
4. The date by which the service or repair should be complete.
5. A copy of or reference to all previous correspondences.
6. Notice of copies sent to the Department of Consumer Affairs (if appropriate).

Letter #1: Cordial Request

Customer Service:

On May 1st I purchased a [name of car] from your dealership. Despite repeated phone calls, there are still a few lose ends that need to be tied up:

1. I am still waiting for a copy of the bumper-to-bumper warrantee.

2. I have not yet received an itemized list of registration costs, and the exact amount of credit I received from the Department of Motor Vehicles for the canceled plates voucher.

3. I have asked for a new bill of sale that includes the payments for the alarm system and extended warrantee.

I have an appointment to have the car serviced on June 30th. I would like to have these details taken care of before that time.

Thank you.

Sincerely,

Letter #2: Forceful Demand

Notice that in the second letter the writer now has the name of person to correspond with and has forwarded a copy to the Department of Consumer Affairs.

Dear Richard,

Attached is a copy of my June 8th letter to Customer Service. After having my car serviced on June 30th, the list of problems has grown. These matters need your immediate attention:

1. Although I did finally receive my copy of the warranty after waiting two months, it is not bumper-to-bumper as Mr. Schecht promised. It also requires service at your facility unless the warranty administrator waives that requirement. I purchased the car from you at a premium price with the expectation that I would have a bumper-to-bumper warranty that I could use at any dealer. I never would have bought this car from you if I knew about these limitations. I expect two things: A written waiver from the warranty administrator that allows me to have warranty service performed at any dealer, and a wrap-around warranty, provided at your cost, that turns this limited warranty into the promised "bumper-to-bumper" warranty.

2. I expect an itemized list of registration costs, and the exact amount of credit I received from the Department of Motor Vehicles for the canceled plates voucher I gave to Mr. Schecht. If there is a refund due, I expect it within 15 days.

3. I expect a proper bill of sale that itemizes and describes the payments for the alarm system and the extended warranty, and includes all the items on the original bill of sale.

4. Your mechanic was unable to locate a cause for the burning smell. The smell persists. I expect your written assurance that if and when the cause for this smell becomes known, you will repair the problem at your cost.

5. The mechanic did *not* repair the left front marker light, although he promised he would. Enclosed is a copy of your invoice for this repair, which wasn't made, as well as an invoice from another dealer who actually made the repair. I expect reimbursement for $22.90.

Sincerely yours,

cc: Joe Smith, Department of Consumer Affairs

Letter #3: Forceful Complaint

The previous demanding letter did get results. The consumer had all his demands met except for one very important one. To prompt the dealership to send the documents requested, the consumer mailed a complaint letter that looked like a legal notice. It worked. Within days, this consumer received the warranty requested.

TO: Dave Cenoso, Manager, Anothertown Auto

FROM: David Afterwards

**Notice of demand
in the matter of failure to deliver vehicle services agreement**

Whereas, A vehicle service agreement was purchased and paid for by David Afterwards, residing at 00-00 Mockingbird Lane, Anytown, USA on May 1, 0000, bearing the application number HH3104.

And whereas, Paperwork for said vehicle service agreement has not been completed, and the manufacturer has no record of entry of the information for this agreement into its computer system.

Therefore Demand is made that: Paperwork must be completed and a validated Vehicle Service Agreement must be delivered to above-named plaintiff by the close of business on August 30.

Signed this _____ day of _____ by:_____

Witnessed by: _____

Consumer complaint letters

When writing complaint letters, don't rant and rave. Be direct and to the point. Spell out the action you want the company to take. To make sure the recipient gets your letter, and to gain his or her attention, you can send it certified mail, return receipt requested.

Complaining of inferior product quality

The key to writing an effective letter of complaint about a product you have purchased is to detail specific flaws and then state what you expect to be done about the problem.

Much less effective is to vent anger, lay blame, insult the seller, or make vague claims of general dissatisfaction that are not backed by specifics. Be specific, be controlled, and stick to your complaint—don't veer off into tangents.

Customize your own letter complaining of inferior product quality:

When you purchase a product that does not meet your expectations, you should contact the manufacturer with a letter that states:

1. What the product is and when you purchased it.
2. State the problem.
3. Express your disappointment with the product.
4. If you'd like to try your luck with this company again, you can ask for a credit or a replacement product.

TO: Tele Toys, Customer Service
FROM: Nicholas DeLorenzo
RE: "Action Robot" construction set

For Christmas my nine-year-old son received the Action Robot construction set.

Although he looked forward to building the robot, this didn't happen, for several reasons.

The main problem is your instructions, which are incomplete, vague, and extremely difficult to follow. The box states "Ages eight and up," but as an adult (certainly over the age of eight) I found the instructions almost impossible to follow.

Also, many of the joints do not connect easily; some, not at all. None of the wheel joint caps will stay firmly on the axle, so the wheels always fall off.

Perhaps the connectors are faulty. I have enclosed a parts list for our model where I have circled the connectors that do not work so that you are aware of the problem.

I am very disappointed in the quality of this product (not to mention the disappointment of my son). What do you propose to do to restore my satisfaction and faith in TeleToys?

Sincerely,

Complaining of poor service

Complaining of poor service is a good example of how the written word still maintains its power in today's age of images. Try this experiment: complain over the phone. Often the person on the phone will sound sympathetic, but no action will be taken. Then try complaining in writing. You'll find written complains resolved more completely and quickly.

Customize your own letter complaining of poor service:

When you complain about service, you must mention:

1. The location, date of the occurrence, and the person(s) involved.
2. Detail exactly what happened.
3. Something to indicate that you are a desirable customer.
4. An expression of disappointment.
5. You can ask for restitution of some sort, if you like.

Manager
Viva Olé Restaurant
Anytown, USA

Dear Manager:

On October 21, my wife and I had lunch at your restaurant. I had a ground beef taco.

While chewing, I bit down on something hard and sharp. In the ground beef I found a piece of twisted metal! Fortunately, I didn't cut my mouth, or even worse, swallow the sharp metal, which would have no doubt landed me in the emergency room.

We called the waiter (whose name tag said "Jonathan") and explained what happened. He said, "I'm sorry," and that was it! There was no genuine concern. There was no offer to replace my lunch. There was no restitution. What we did get was a bill charging me full price for my meal!

When I objected, he pointed out that I had eaten it, which was true, and there was nothing he could do. When I asked to see the manager, he said the manager was out. You can only imagine my upset and displeasure.

My wife and I have been frequent patrons of your restaurant and have come to enjoy the excellent service. This experience has left both of us disappointed.

Sincerely,

P.S. A copy of our paid check for the lunch is enclosed.

Complaining of noncompliance with a service agreement

Why are so many consumers with service contracts so unhappy? It's both the customer's and the vendor's fault. The vendor promises a lot in its sales pitch and promotional materials, but the service contract contains not enough specifics and too many loopholes and exceptions.

The customer, in turn, doesn't read the fine print in the contract. When service rendered doesn't meet expectations and the customer complains, the vendor points to the contract they signed. The customer says, "I don't care about the contract; I'm holding you to what your ad (or commercial or sales rep) promised." Often, a letter citing these specifics is an effective way to persuade the vendor to resolve the problems in your favor.

Customize your own complaint with a service agreement:

Service agreements are notoriously difficult to understand. But when you're not getting the service you believe you are entitled to speak up. When writing this letter:

1. Open with a statement that acknowledges there is a problem with servicing.
2. State the product and the service contract you have.
3. Detail the problem: list dates, times, and names.
4. State exactly what you want the company to do.
5. Request an answer.

Ralph Edwards
Acme Network Services
RE: Service Contract #29956
Dear Mr. Edwards:

I'm writing to resolve a conflict we're having in Acme's servicing of our account.

As you know, we are three months into a one-year network support contract. Although the quality of your support personnel is excellent, the response time to network outages is not what we expected.

When we signed with your firm, Tom Nevins told us that you provide response "in under four hours." Indeed, the promotional brochure he gave us makes the same statement: "Our network technicians will respond within four hours of your call for service—and often faster."

Unfortunately, "often faster" has become "usually slower." Response time continually takes the better part of a business day. Tom tells us that this promise is superseded by your contract, which he pulled out at our last meeting. He pointed to the language that said, "Best effort will be made to respond to support calls as conditions allow." He then pointed out that I had signed and read the contract.

Yes, I signed your contract, but I believe promises that vendors make to me, and I expect them to abide by them. We are your customer, and we expect you to be our partner in network support and not our adversary.

My question is simple. Are you going to deliver the fast four-hour response you promised when you sold us the contract?

Sincerely,

Complaining of misrepresentation

Complaints of misrepresentation should always be made in writing and copies of these letters retained, in case the matter escalates to the point where legal actions are needed.

Customize your own letter complaining of misrepresentation:

If someone has taken advantage of you by misrepresenting a service or product, you should immediately write to complain and demand restitution if it is due:

1. Give the details of the time, place and person(s).

2. Explain what you understood to be the case.

3. Detail how this understanding has been twisted or misrepresented.

4. Firmly state what you want the company to do next to rectify the problem.

Jack Frome, Vice President
Big Life Insurance Company
Big City, USA
RE: Whole Life Policy #699959

Dear Mr. Frome:

Sometime last October, two of your independent representatives visited our home to make a presentation about whole life insurance for my spouse.

At the time we were undecided, so they invited us to fill out the application except for signature. We filled it out, but we never heard from them again. (The application is attached.)

Last week, my new bookkeeper pointed out that, for the past two months, Big Life Insurance Company has been deducting $224 monthly premium for a Whole Life Policy for my wife. This is $448 for insurance we do not want and did not agree to purchase. We already have low-cost term life insurance that meets all of our combined estate planning needs.

Effective immediately, I have instructed my bank not to make any further payments to Big Life. I will expect a refund check for $448 from your company within 10 days. The policy is null and void, and I do not consider my wife to be an insured of your firm.

Sincerely,

Complaining about a billing error

When the billing error is not simple or routine, send a letter to explain your position. Keep copies of all letters until the problem is resolved.

Customize your own letter complaining of a billing error:

Billing department representatives don't want to hear a song and dance; just give them the facts:

1. Provide the details right up front: note the product or service, the date in question, the order or customer number.
2. Note that a copy of the bill in question is attached.
3. Concisely explain why the figures on the bill are incorrect.
4. State what you want the company to do.
5. Offer to provide further information if needed.

Dear Mr. Finagle,

I recently received a second notice for lab charges my insurance company tells me I am not responsible for paying. (Copies of your letters and the insurance company's response to me are attached.)

As a preferred provider, your medical lab has agreed to provide services for those covered by my plan for "usual and customary rates." The insurance company has explained to me that I am not responsible for fees above the "usual customer rates," to which you have agreed and which they have already paid.

Please remove these charges from my account immediately and stop sending me these insulting letters.

I hope this letter clears up this matter, but if I can provide more information, please call me at 123-456-7890.

Sincerely,

Complaining about a bank error

Another common complaint which can be handled by letter is a potential error in your business bank account.

Customize your own letter complaining about a bank error:

Bank statements are not infallible. Your best defense is by keeping records of all your banking transactions combined with a letter documenting the problem:

1. State that you believe there is an error in your back statement. Note the date of the error and your account number.
2. Detail what should have been recorded as compared to what the statement says.
3. Explain what you would like the bank to do about this problem.
4. Offer to provide further information if needed.

Dear Ms. Jensen:

I believe I may have discovered an error in our February checking account statement. Could you please look into this and help us reconcile the discrepancy?

Our statement shows deposit of a client check (Morgan Jewelry, check #551) on February 26 for $350.

Then on February 27, a check we wrote to a vendor (TheftProof Electronics, our check #1106) for $872 was returned for insufficient funds, and we were assessed a $25 overdraft fee.

According to my records, however, the February 26 deposit was actually $3,500, not $350 as the statement shows. And that amount would have more than covered our February 27 check.

Attached are copies of the check we deposited on February 26 along with the deposit slip. Perhaps the teller misread my handwriting on the deposit form.

Please call me with your assessment of this situation. Our office number is 123-456-7890. I am at extension X242.

Thanks for your helping me resolve this situation as promptly as possible. I look forward to hearing from you within the next few days.

Sincerely,

Complaint about incomplete or inadequate work

When the contractor or vendor is finished with a job but the work does not meet your expectations, you gain nothing by insulting or talking down to the vendor. Write a letter that maps out the problem along with a requested course of action. A subject line is a good way of quickly identifying the project as a redo or revision rather than a request for new fee-paid services.

Customize your own complaint about incomplete or inadequate work:

Don't rant, rave, and holler—get to the point quickly:

1. Give the details of the work that you are dissatisfied with.
2. Explain exactly what you want done to complete the job.
3. Be clear about whether you expect a further charge to complete or fix the work done so far.
4. Make sure the vendor understands that no further charge will be accepted without your prior approval.

5. Thank the vendor for his or her understanding.
6. State when you expect the work completed.
7. Enclose copies of paperwork relevant to your complaint (contract, agreement, invoice, canceled check, warranty, and so forth).

RE: Watch repair

Dear Mr. Lane:

I'm returning the watch you repaired for me last month because it is still not keeping accurate time. The watch kept accurate time for about a week after I got it. Since then, it's been losing 15 to 20 minutes every day.

This seems to be the original defect I paid you to repair, and since I've already paid you, I assume you will fix the problem without further charge. If that's not the case, let me know. I've enclosed a copy of the receipt you sent me for the original repair. It states that all repairs are guaranteed for 90 days, so as far as I can see, I am still covered by your guarantee.

If you have further questions about my watch, or need to speak with me about this matter, my daytime number is 123-456-7890.

Thank you for your understanding and service. Unless I hear otherwise from you, I'll expect to receive my repaired watch from you on Friday the 23rd.

Sincerely,

Thanks for resolving a complaint

Whether you are a businessperson or consumer, if your complaint is addressed and resolved you should extend the courtesy of a thank-you note. The key message in this letter is that the strategy worked; by resolving the problem as I requested, you retained me as a customer.

Customize your own letter of thanks:

Well-written thank you notes carry a strong message. They give the recipient motivation to continue to please you in the future:

1. Say "thank you" and explain why.
2. Acknowledge that your problem/complaint was addressed to your satisfaction.
3. Assure the recipient of future business.

Dear Ms. Lieb:

Just a short note to say "thanks" for your courteous letter and for sending a replacement amplifier cover so promptly.

In today's pressured world, many customers (including myself) are quick to criticize and slow to praise. This is a letter of praise.

Your response was fair and exactly was what I wanted. You have resolved my problem, transformed dissatisfaction into satisfaction, and assured continued future orders from me. Both of us got what we want. Thank you.

Sincerely,

9

Credit and Collection Letters

Credit and collection are sensitive topics—on many levels. Denying or limiting a buyer's credit, or reminding her that she owes money, is potentially an emotional powder keg. Your goal is to remain professional and neutral, and get or protect your money, while retaining customer goodwill.

Letters regarding credit

These letters will give you the words you need to ask for credit, check on your own credit, offer or deny credit to others, and make changes to your existing credit policy.

Requesting credit

Credit is part of the American way of life today. For example, when I went shopping for a mini-van for our family recently, salespeople in the auto showrooms were shocked that I wanted to pay cash for a new vehicle, rather than financing or leasing it.

According to Studebaker Worthington, a leasing company, more than 35 percent of cars, 30 percent of computers, and 40 percent of copiers and office equipment are sold through leasing. More and more sellers these days are prepared to grant credit, making the process faster and easier.

Customize your own letter requesting credit:

Different sellers will need different information to grant credit approval, but you can expedite the process by including the basics in your initial request. Your letter should include:

1. What you want to purchase and the total price of it.
2. The terms of credit you would like.
3. Very brief background information about your company.
4. A list of two or three credit references (companies you regularly buy from on credit).
5. An offer to provide further information if needed.
6. Banking information, including your bank's name, address, phone number, and account number.

Dear Mr. Hale:

We are looking for a supplier of quality dyestuffs for our dyehouse operations. After seeing your ad in *Textile World*, we sent for your catalog and were impressed with the breadth of your line.

We would like to purchase an initial inventory of one unit each of #1055, 1058, and 1070. At $800 each, this would be an initial order of $2,400. We would like to purchase these materials on net 90-day terms

XYA was established seven years ago and since that time we have grown very rapidly. Our practice is to favor a limited number of suppliers with the majority of our orders. In turn, we look for volume discounts, favorable terms, and the kind of first-rate service others have told me you supply.

Other vendors and credit references include:

VelTech, 8496 Stave Avenue, El Paso, TX 56049, ATT: Jim Pascal

FabelCorp, 584 Fourth Street, Middletown, NJ 07410, ATT: Nancy Watson

Chemical Supply, 670 Bergen Avenue, Vernon, NH, ATT: Dave George

If you need additional financial information, I will be glad to supply it. Or you can contact our bank directly: First Local Bank, Washington Avenue, Anytown, USA, phone 123-456-7890, account #15886798. You can talk to the branch manager, John Sullivan.

Sincerely,

Requesting a credit report

One of the most basic credit communications is a request for your own credit report. Here is a form letter you can send to credit agencies to get that information.

To get a copy of your credit report, write to the credit agencies listed below:

Equifax Information Service
Customer Correspondence
PO Box 105873
Atlanta, GA 30348
800-685-1111

Experian
PO Box 2106
Allen, TX 75013
800-392-1122

TransUnion
PO Box 390
Springfield, PA 19064
800-916-8800

To Customer Service:

I would like a copy of my credit report. Please send my report to the following address:

[Your full name (include middle initial and any Jr. or Sr.)]
[Your address]
[Your Social Security number]
[Your year of birth]

You will also find enclosed documentation verifying my identity. Thank you for your cooperation.

Sincerely,

Contesting a credit report

If your credit report contains errors, you must notify the credit-reporting agency in writing. Don't rant and rave and spend ink explaining how their error has cost you time and money.

Customize your own letter contesting a credit report:

Be sure to provide all the information the credit bureau will need to make the change quickly. Include:

1. A statement that there has been an error that needs to be corrected.
2. What that error is.
3. What the correct information is.
4. How this information can be verified.
5. A request for the correction to be made within 10 days.
6. A request for a copy of the corrected version.
7. Include your phone number and Social Security number at the end of the letter.

Dear Customer Service:

Please correct the following error in my credit report:

The loan account number listed for Citizens Bank on the report reads: "137547899." This is incorrect. The correct account number is 137557899.

To verify this information call my branch manager, Len Dane, at 123-456-7890.

This correction should change the report by deleting the erroneous statement that says I have twice been 60 days late in making payments.

Please update my credit report and send me the corrected, clean copy within the next 10 days.

Yours Truly,

Requesting credit information from a potential customer

Another routine credit correspondence is requesting information from a potential credit account so you can perform a credit check.

Customize your own letter requesting credit information from a potential customer:

You want to keep the order, but you also want to protect yourself. Be sure your letter includes:

1. An opening "thank you" for the customer's interest in your company or product.
2. A request for the information you need to process the credit application. This may include credit references, bank account numbers, bank statements, statements of ownership, and so forth.

3. A promise to expedite the order as soon as the requested information is received and the credit application is processed.

Dear Ms. Porter:

Thank you very much for your interest in our SP-500 digital writer. This instrument was designed with the needs of the small to midsize photofinisher in mind, and your choice of this model makes good sense.

I also appreciate your request to lease. The credit references you supplied to our sales rep on your order form will be very helpful. Thank you.

Would you please send me a copy of your most recent statements of ownership and results of operations? We also need a copy of your latest business bank statement.

As soon as we have the information we need, we'll process your request for financing. We're eager to help increase your profitability with the SP-500 digital writer. We'll do our best to expedite credit approval, shipment, and installation.

Sincerely,

Credit referral check on a potential customer

Credit and collections take less time and are more efficient when you develop a library of routine correspondence for handling the most frequent communications. The letter below can be sent to any credit references given to you by a potential customer on whom you are running a credit check.

Dear Ms. Macadam:

We have received a request for credit from Greta Freytag at XYA Company in Anytown, USA. Your company was listed as a credit reference. I would be grateful if you would supply the following information about this customer:

1. Credit terms extended to the customer, including limits.
2. A brief statement about the customer's promptness in meeting obligations.
3. Your reservations, if any, about the customer's financial condition and general reliability.

A reply envelope is enclosed for your convenience. I assure you that the information supplied will be treated as confidential.

Cordially yours,

Granting credit

When you accept or reject a request for credit, do it in writing. Here's an example of a letter granting it. To customize this letter, put this letter on file in your computer and use it exactly as is, changing only the addressee each time you need it.

Customize your own letter granting credit:

This letter has four simple parts:

1. State that the customer's application for financing has been approved.
2. State the product or service you are now happy to provide.
3. Briefly review the terms of the credit agreement.
4. Close by stating that you are looking forward to a continued business relationship in the future.

Dear Ms. Porter:

Your application for financing on the acquisition of your new SP-500 digital writer has been approved. Your order for one SP-500 with continuous sheet feeder will be shipped within five days by truck.

As the enclosed lease documents indicate, your monthly lease payment is $1,870. Since your lease covers the entire purchase, including "soft" costs, installation and training are completely covered, with no additional fee or payment required.

We look forward to serving you and hope you will call upon us for service, support, and supplies. Please keep in touch and let us know how the SP-500 is working to improve sales and customer service in your shop.

Sincerely,

Denying credit

On occasion you will have the unpleasant task of denying credit to a potential buyer. This refusal should be handled with tact and diplomacy.

Customize your own letter denying credit:

This letter should include:

1. A thank you for wanting to do business.
2. A positive word about the company, their products or services.
3. A regretful denial of credit and the reason.
4. An open invitation to talk further to create a gradually increasing credit line (if this is reasonable).
5. A reminder that cash purchases are always welcome.
6. A positive ending wishing the customer well.

Dear Mr. Colson:

Thank you for your application for credit at Barrow's. We appreciate your interest.

Your personal references are exceptionally good, and your record of hard work indicates that your business prospects are good for the near future. Unfortunately, at the present, your financial condition only partially meets Barrow's requirements. We cannot extend the $5,000 open credit you requested.

Please call me at your convenience. I am sure we can set up a program of gradually increasing credit that will benefit both of us. Meanwhile, remember that deliveries on cash purchases are made within two days.

Let me hear from you soon. We are interested in your business venture.

Sincerely,

Extending limited credit

Another situation that must be handled sensitively is granting credit, but not in the amount the customer wants.

Customize your own letter extending limited credit:

Make this letter short and to the point. Include:

1. A thank you for the order.
2. A statement of the line of credit you are able to offer.
3. An explanation of the balance required to deliver the entire order.
4. An invitation to further discuss extending the credit limit (if appropriate).
5. An ending that assures the customer you value your business relationship and are appreciative of the opportunity to work together.

Dear Mr. Smith,

We appreciate receiving your order for 1,000 XTM-500 linear circuit amplifiers.

Our credit department has approved your firm for a credit line of $10,000. Because the total on your current order exceeds this limit, we need at least partial payment (half up front) to ship the goods to your factory.

If you anticipate more purchases of this size, call me and we'll see what we can do about extending your limit.

We value your business, hope this is a satisfactory solution, and we thank you for the opportunity to be of service to you.

Sincerely,

Putting an account on credit hold

One of the toughest business decisions is whether to put an account on hold, especially a large volume customer. The best course is to establish a firm credit policy, stick with it, and suspend credit for buyers who fail to meet criteria for receiving credit. Do not criticize, insult, or blame the customer in any way. Do not request payments due; this should be done in a separate collection letter as outlined later in this chapter.

Customize your own letter putting an account on credit hold:

The letter should explain why the decision to put credit on hold was made and what the customer can do to restore credit status. Include:

1. An opening that says you value this customer.
2. An explanation how late payments affect your company.
3. An assurance that you want to continue doing business.
4. An explanation that you require payment with future orders until past debts are paid.
5. An invitation to open a credit card account (if appropriate).
6. An assurance that the customer will return to the original credit status when the account becomes current.
7. An invitation to talk further about this problem.

RE: Your account #58589922

Dear Ms. Jones:

We value you as a customer. But for us to offer you quality goods at competitive prices, we depend on on-time payments from our accounts. And lately, your payments have been late and your account seriously past due.

We still want to provide you with the connectors and fasteners your business needs. And we won't cut off shipments. But until your account is made current, we require payment with future orders.

A review of your account shows frequent purchases with an average order of $250. For your convenience, you may pay by credit card. Just call our Credit Department 123-456-7890. Ask for Sheila or Sam and give us your credit card number and expiration date. We'll immediately set you up as a credit card account.

You may go off credit card status and return to a billing arrangement as soon as your account is current. If you prefer another arrangement, please call us and we will work with you to find an alternative payment method that works for you.

Sincerely,

Restoring credit

This letter not only notifies the customer that credit has been restored, but offers thanks and praise to the customer for improving the payment record. If there is a perk you can tie to the restored credit status, such as an extended credit line, do it in this letter.

Customize your own letter restoring credit:

Don't assume your customers know that credit terms are restored after a required payment. Notify them in writing (they may need this for their records). Include:

1. A thank you for payment.
2. The announcement that their credit line is now restored.
3. A positive change in the terms of credit (if appropriate and desired).
4. A final closing mentioning your appreciation.

RE: Your account #58589922

Dear Ms. Jones:

Thanks for your recent prompt payments. Our records reflect your account is now current.

Given these circumstances, I am happy to restore your full credit line. In fact, your recent payment record enables me to *extend* your credit line from the previous $5,000 to $8,000. This will enable you to stock the added inventory you need to accommodate the growing demands of your customers.

On a personal note, I admire your cooperation and appreciate your sincere efforts. You have made my job easier, and I appreciate it.

Sincerely,

Collection letters

It's one thing to give your customers credit—they like "free money." However, it's another to actually collect the money due. These collection letters need to be firm, yet understanding (to a point) to convince your credit customers to write out the check today.

Model invoice

Firms that extend credit must bill customers. You should have a standard form invoice you use to bill credit customers. But if not, here's a format you can use:

Invoice # _____

Reference: Purchase order #_____

From: _____

[name, address, phone]

To: _____

[person's name, company name, address, phone]

For: _____

[product or service you are billing for]

Amount: $_____

Terms: _____

 [for example: net 30 days]

Notification of credit terms and conditions

A bill should never be a surprise to a customer. If you attach financial penalties to your business terms, such as a doctor's office charging patients for missed appointments, these conditions must be communicated to the client in advance. Written communication is the best way to do this.

Customize your own letter changing credit terms or conditions:

This letter should state the changes you are implementing and reasons for the change. It should include:

1. A positive statement about appreciating the customer's business.
2. An explanation of why you find it necessary to change the terms of your credit policy.
3. A direct statement of the change.
4. The benefit to the customer of this change.
5. An invitation to discuss the change further.

To All Clients:

Each account is of utmost importance to me. I strive to fill all orders quickly and efficiently and to extend to qualified customers satisfactory terms of credit.

However, due to an excessive backlog of overdue accounts, I find it necessary to make the following change in the terms of my credit policy effective May 1:

1. All accounts 30 days overdue will be assessed a two percent late fee.
2. All accounts 60 days overdue will be assessed a three percent late fee.
3. All accounts 90 days overdue will be referred to a collection agency.

The only way I can continue to offer reasonable rates to each of you is if I am assured payment for the products I supply. I'm sure you can understand the necessity for these changes in credit terms.

If you would like to discuss these terms, please feel free to contact me.

Thank you,

Refusing a partial payment plan

When a customer offers a partial or monthly payment plan, it's generally a good idea to accept. Not doing so causes ill feelings and often results in no payment at all. However, there are cases where the customer's proposition is simply not acceptable. Your job is to say no politely but firmly.

Customize your own letter refusing a partial payment plan:

This is a letter of compromise. It should include:

1. An acknowledgment of the customer's interest in making payment.
2. A review of the customer's account.
3. An explanation of why you must refuse the suggested payment plan.
4. An offer of an alternative compromise plan.
5. An invitation to discuss the terms further.

Dear Mr. West:

Thanks for your letter. We appreciate your sincere attention to your account balance.

Given your balance of $1,600, we feel $50 a month is too long for us to bring this account current. Let me suggest an alternative: $100 a month, with you having the option to skip one month per year without penalty if you need to.

To discuss this further, you can reach me at 123-456-7890.

Sincerely,

Collection letter series

It's a sad fact of business life: Many customers won't pay their bills on time. Some won't pay them at all.

Milt Pierce, author of How to Collect Overdue Bills, says that for the typical small business, 10 to 70 percent of assets are typically tied up in accounts receivables at any given time.

Here is a collection series that you can use to collect past-due bills. All of these letters can be stored on your computer as is and used as form letters when you need them. Just fill in the blanks. After the fifth letter, consider using a collection agency to shake the payment loose. See "Collection Tips" on pages 210-214 for the details.

Collection letter #1

The first collection letter is the softest in tone. It is a reminder, and nothing more:

Dear _____:

Just a reminder that payment of Invoice # _____ for [insert name of product or service] is now past [number of days/weeks] due. (See copy of invoice attached.)

Would you please send me a check today? A self-addressed stamped reply envelope is enclosed for your convenience.

Regards,

Collection letter #2

The second collection letter is just as polite as the first, but it is a little firmer in requesting payment. It also sets a time frame for responding.

Dear _____:

I haven't received payment for Invoice # _____ yet. Did you receive my original bill and follow-up letter?

Is something the matter? Is there some special reason why you have not paid? Did you receive our earlier invoice?

If you should need more time, don't hesitate to ask.

Otherwise, please send me a check for $____ within five business days.

Thanks,

Collection letter #3

The third letter is more insistent in tone. It says you either need payment or a good reason why payment hasn't been sent.

Dear _____:

This is the third notice I've sent about Invoice # _____ (attached), which is now [number] weeks past due.

Let me assure you that this bill will not be forgotten.

Please, for the sake of your good credit rating, make every effort to clear up this problem right now. If payment cannot be delivered within five business days, call to discuss extending the terms.

Sincerely,

Collection letter #4

From this point on, the letters you send should become increasingly more insistent and urgent. Be firm. Do not make payment seem optional; make clear it is mandatory. This letter should be sent by certified mail.

Dear _____:

Despite three previous notices about Invoice #_____ (attached), it remains unpaid. I haven't heard from you, and you haven't responded to my letters.

Unless you act within the next five days, your invoice will be referred to an outside collection agency. I have made every effort to collect payment, and still you have ignored every opportunity to pay this bill.

You now have only five days to clear up this matter before more drastic action is taken.

I do not like turning accounts over to a collection agency but you are leaving me little choice.

Sincerely,

Collection letter #5

The final letter makes clear that the grace period is over and you expect to be paid. You have to strike a balance between sounding serious and not being overly threatening. After five days, it's time to give this final notice:

**YOU HAVE LEFT US NO CHOICE. WE MUST NOW PROCEED
WITH EVERY LEGAL MEANS OF COLLECTION.**

THERE IS ONLY ONE WAY THAT YOU CAN PUT

A HALT TO OUR NEXT LEGAL ACTION...

Dear [Name]:

If there is some good reason that you would like to discuss regarding your unpaid bill, you have only one final opportunity to put a halt to the legal action that we plan to take in your area.

YOU CAN TELEPHONE ME—RIGHT NOW

AT THIS NUMBER: 123-456-7890

Unless I hear from you within *the next 48 hours,* I shall institute every legal means for the collection of the amount of money that you owe.

You must act immediately. This is a serious problem.

Very truly yours,

Collection courtesy

When a customer responds to your request for payment for an overdue bill, it's a good idea to send a follow-up thank you note. You should also respond in writing if you have made an accounting error and wrongly sought to collect money not owed.

Thanking customer for payment

When a customer makes a payment, thank him or her. In your letter, stress the thank you, not the fact that they have been late payers. Compliment and praise rather than criticize or condemn.

Customize your own letter thanking a customer for payment:

Although it's about time your customer paid, be gracious with your thanks. Write a letter that includes:

1. A thank you for the payment.
2. An acknowledgment that the customer's business is important to you.
3. A reminder of the present credit status.
4. A gentle reminder of the next payment due to motivate the customer to keep up with the payments and not be delinquent again.

Dear Mr. Jordan,

Thank you for your payment of $1,500. We appreciate your attention to your account status with us. Your patronage is important to us, and we thank you for responding to our payment queries.

Just to bring you up to date: Your current balance is $5,000, your credit limit. A payment of $750 is due May 1. If there's any problem or question, call me at 123-456-7890. Thanks.

Sincerely,

Apologizing for an accounting error

The danger of being too tough when chasing late payments is the possibility that the payment may really not be late. Your letter and the customer's check may have crossed in the mail. Or your accounting department may have misplaced or not credited a recent payment. Clear up these mistakes at once in writing. Apologize sincerely to defuse customer annoyance and anger.

Keep in mind, that if you made the error, the customer suffers the additional damage of having his or her time wasted trying to resolve a problem that was your fault. Consider compensating the customer for it. A discount on a future order is the best compensation, since it not only gives the customer real value, but also encourages more purchase of your product or service.

Customize your own letter apologizing for an accounting error:

This letter will reflect the particular error you have made. But the basics should include:

1. Thanks for your customer's patience, and an apology for the mistake.
2. An assurance that the problem has been corrected on the customer's records.
3. Any adjustments to or the elimiation of any penalties that were implemented.
4. Compensation you will give the client to rectify the inconvenience caused (optional).
5. Repeat the thank you for patience and the apology.

Dear Mr. Bindleglass:

Thank you for your patience and understanding. Let me apologize for the error we made in your account statement.

When you called last Friday, I said we had not yet received your last payment. It turns out we had your check but it had not yet been posted to our system. I have credited your account $850.

Our policy states that 2.5 percent interest is accrued on the last business day of the month for all credit accounts. However, we are waiving this policy from January 1 through today. This will remove late-payment interest charges of $65.78 from your balance.

To offset any inconvenience you have had in reconciling your account, we will give you a 20 percent discount on your next order. This should be automatically reflected in the invoice for that order. If not, let me know and I will personally handle it.

Thank you again for your patience. We value your business. Please accept my apology.

Sincerely,

Collection tips

The following collection tips will help you use your collection letters (also called dunning letters) to gain the most positive response. The goal is to get the money owed to you and at the same time keep the customer—not an easy tasks.

A change in letterhead lifts response

Experience proves that a change in letterhead in a dunning letter series will lift responses virtually every time.

One situation where such a letter works well is as a replacement for the third or fourth effort in your internal cycle—typically after you have sent a bill and two notices and have suspended shipment of further orders.

Response boosting tips

Here are some techniques that can successfully boost response:

- Vary the dunning cycle. To extend the billing series and increase net recovery rates, progressive agencies vary the timing between efforts, typically from 14 to 28 days. This is a proven response-booster.
- Vary the text of each letter in the series. Tone should increase from soft or mild to more severe and insistent.
- Change the color of the paper the letter is printed on as well as the outer envelope. Switching from white to red or blue changes the entire tone of the effort—and can significantly increase recoveries.
- Vary the size, shape, and appearance of the outer envelope.

The key is to keep each mailing fresh so the subscriber does not think it's the same notice he or she received before. Remember, even the most powerfully written collection effort will get no response if the envelope is not opened.

Bring the collection agency in early

How long should you try to collect the money yourself? For merchandise, the internal dunning cycle (collection letters sent directly from the company) should consist of at least four efforts sent at 30-day intervals. (See sample collection series earlier in this chapter.)

At that point, it's time to refer the account to an outside agency. As you know, the older a bill gets, the more difficult it is to collect.

Getting a third party involved creates a greater sense of obligation and urgency. When the collection letters suddenly start appearing on the official-looking letterhead of a third party, instead of your organization's letterhead, the bill suddenly becomes a "real" debt to the customer—one he perceives he is obligated to pay.

Choose the right agency for the job

Finally, here are some things you need to look into when evaluating outside collection agencies:

- How many years has the agency has been in business?
- Check references. Find out what clients say about the agency. Is the agency successful? Are the agents easy to work with?
- Look at sample credit reports; are they clear and easy to read? Do they provide the information you need?
- Is the agency bonded? Is it a member of the American Collectors Association, or the American Commercial Collectors?
- Are the agency's IT systems compatible with yours?
- Fees are important, but beware: The lowest-priced agency may actually cost you more if they don't perform. By the same token, the agency generating the highest gross recovery rates may not make you the most money if its fee is too high. You want the agency that can generate the highest net recovery rates.

Third party or contingency arrangement?

Collection agencies typically work on two different fee arrangements: third-party letters and contingency.

In a third-party arrangement, you pay a fixed fee per collection letter mailed. This is typically $400 to $600 per each thousand collected, but can be more or less depending on volume. Keep in mind that there may be minimum volume requirements for the agency to work on such a fixed-fee basis. The third-party arrangement offers you a low, fixed cost per letter, enabling you to budget accurately and to predict returns based on projected response rates.

In a contingency arrangement, the agency's compensation is a percentage of the money recovered. This is typically 40 to 50 percent. You pay only for results, not for pieces mailed. With the contingency method, there is no initial investment, no risk, and no out-of-pocket cost. You can initiate this type of program at any time because it does not require you to have a budget for back-end collections. The agency assumes all cost risks, and the program generates the agency's fee.

Whether it is better for you to use third party or contingency collections on your first effort depends on your situation. The contingency arrangement reduces risk, because there's no out-of-pocket exposure. It also allows you to test a new collection agency for free.

On the other hand, if you have reason to think that response to the first external effort will be high, the third-party arrangement can net you more cash. You can determine the return on investment at different response rates through a simple break-even analysis based on the agency's fee and the average dollar balance of the accounts. Traditionally, the first external effort generates the highest recovery rate in the series, so it's where you are most likely to recoup your investment in a third-party mailing.

Approve collection letter copy

Review all agency letters before they are mailed. Question any language you find inappropriate for any reason.

The tone of your collection letters should be consistent with the philosophical or customer service approach of your company. Because most businesses are concerned with image, your collection letters shape your customers' perception of your organization as much as your service or product does. What works for the phone company in a billing series may not necessarily work for a landscaper.

At the same time, don't err on the side of being too soft or conservative in tone. Remember, your customer placed an order and then did not pay for it, despite repeated requests to do so. Firmness is required. Remember that the first effort in the external dunning cycle must be at least as firm as the last effort of your internal cycle.

Many businesspeople worry that the external collection cycle will upset or "turn off" unpaid accounts, alienating them from making future purchases. Experience shows this fear is largely unwarranted. Author Milt Pierce notes, "A customer who owes you money and is not responding to dunning will not place another order with you." To have a good business relationship, bills must be paid.

Any level of customer sensitivity can be dealt with, and if the agency carefully tailors the collection letters to your product, offer, company and readership in a professional manner, complaints will be few and far between. Properly written external collection letters are never offensive. And they always protect the customer's right to dispute the invoice.

Have your agency share information with you

Make sure that information gathered by your agency's customer service and special correspondence response departments is shared with you. This information alerts you to problems.

For example, are there shipping delays? Do your sales reps make the terms unclear or mislead prospects about their obligation? Are your collection efforts evoking any ill will? In the external dunning cycle, your agency gets this information first-hand from dealing with your no-pay subscribers. Make sure they share it with you.

Find out the reason why buyers are not paying. Some will tell your agency they never received your product or received it but wrote "cancel" on the bill and returned the goods. Other excuses range from "I paid already" to "I don't like your product." Be sure to discuss with your agency how you want them to react to these kinds of responses.

Keep on top of collection results

An external collection cycle proceeds quickly, with only two to four weeks between efforts. So it's important to keep on top of results on a timely basis.

Your agency should provide statistical reports on external collection recoveries in an easy-to-read format. The agency should also have the ability to check the status of any account on an online basis. The purpose of the report is to track external collection results and monitor agency performance.

A collection agency report should show, for each month's referrals, the following information:

- Number of accounts referred to the agency.
- Beginning total amount to be collected for these accounts.
- Average dollar balance.
- Payments made both directly to you and to the collection agency, both full and partial.
- Number and percentage of bad addresses (nixes) and "skips" (customers who have moved without leaving a forwarding address).
- Credits and adjustments.
- Remaining number of accounts to be collected and total dollars owed.

Ideally, your agency should also be able to provide not only a summary of the above information for each month but also a detailed report showing the activity for each account, sorted by ZIP code, source, or any other variable you desire.

Don't give up too early

Many outside collection agencies use only one or two letters to collect past-due accounts. But they may be giving up too early.

You want an agency that isn't just content to collect the "easy" receivables, but also goes after those hard-to-collect delinquent accounts. Testing by the agency may suggest that additional efforts are beneficial. For instance, although a one- or two-letter external series is common, some progressive agencies are achieving profitable recoveries with an extended letter series. Ask for these details before you hire a collection agency.

Practice customer retention, not just collection

The goal of your dunning cycle is not just to collect the money owed you, but to retain the customer—and her goodwill. You are not just a collector but a customer service representative as well. The by-product of good service is payment.

Here are some ideas on how your collection agency can help you improve customer service:

1. The external letter copy must acknowledge that not every customer the agency duns actually owes you money (for instance, it's possible a customer is being billed in error). Letters should not only seek payment, but also encourage customers to call or write and explain why they have not paid or feel they do not owe the money.
2. Once the customer pays, it's your responsibility to start shipping his orders to him again promptly. Make sure your agency or accounting department can transfer payment information to your shipping department on a timely basis and in a convenient format so pay-ups can be quickly fulfilled.
3. Promptly acknowledge and resolve every nonpayment and partial payment response. Your collection agency should have a special correspondence response department whose job it is to communicate with customers who dispute invoices, make partial payments, or have other out-of-the-ordinary responses.
4. Make sure your agency employs a courteous and professional staff that treats your customers with dignity and respect at all times.

Legal action?

What about legal action? Small dollar balances make going to court impractical in most cases. However, an attorney demand letter (collection letter on law firm stationery) may prove profitable in many cases.

10

SALES LETTERS

Sales letters are intended to persuade, inform, alert, or perform another sales-related function. However, they are not strictly speaking, "direct mail." Sales letters:

- Are designed to generate an inquiry, present a quotation, follow up a proposal, or perform some sales or other persuasive task.
- Are personalized and mailed to a single prospect or customer at a time.
- Are often contrived because of their repeated use. The letter is often customized to a particular prospect from a prewritten template stored on computer.

A writing formula that sells

Most sales letters follow a pattern known to professional letter-writers simply as "AIDA," for "Attention, Interest, Desire, and Action." This simple but effective formula, first discovered by advertising writers, lets you cut through jargon and messy language to create straightforward writing that works.

Why do we need a formula for persuasion? Shouldn't we be able to simply state our proposition directly and get the action we desire? The obstacle is the glut of similar messages in your prospect's in-box, fax machine, and e-mail. A recent TV commercial informed viewers that the U.S. Post Office handles 300 million pieces of mail every day. That's a lot of letters.

But how many letters actually get their messages across and motivate the reader? Surprisingly few. In direct mail marketing, for example, a two percent response rate is high. A manufacturer who mails 1,000 sales letters will expect that fewer than 20 people will respond to the pitch. If high-powered letters written by ad agency copywriters produce such a limited response, you can see why letters written by busy business executives (who are not professional writers) may not always accomplish their objectives.

Failure to get to the point, technical jargon, pompous language, or mis-reading the reader are the poor stylistic habits that cause others to ignore the letters we send. Part of the problem is that many managers and support staff don't know how to write persuasively. The solution is AIDA, a sequence of psychological reactions that happen in the mind of the reader as he or she is sold on your idea. Briefly, here's how it works:

- **Attention.** First, the letter gets the reader's attention with a hard-hitting lead paragraph that goes straight to the point or offers an element of intrigue.
- **Interest.** Then the letter hooks the reader's interest: The hook is often a clear statement of the reader's problems, needs, or wants. For example, if you are writing to a customer who received damaged goods, acknowledge the problem.
- **Desire.** The letter should create desire and demand. Your letter is an offer of something—a service, a product, goodwill, an agreement, a contract, a compromise, a consultation. Tell the reader how he or she will benefit from your offering. That creates a demand for your product.
- **Action.** Finally, the letter states a call for action. At this point, you should ask for the order, the signature, the donation, the assignment.

What follows is an example of how each of these steps can be used to create one persuasive business letter.

Attention

Getting the reader's attention is a tough job. If your letter is boring, pompous, or says nothing of interest, you'll lose the reader—fast!

One attention-getting technique used by successful writers is to open with an intriguing question or statement—a " teaser" that grabs the reader's attention and compels him or her to read on.

Here are two types of attention grabbing openers:

Is freelance a dirty word to you?

It really shouldn't be. In public relations, with its crisis-lull-crisis rhythm, good freelancers can save you money and headaches. Use them when you need them. When you don't, they don't cost you a cent.

Use me. I am a public-relations specialist with more than 20 years of experience in all phases of the profession. My services are available to you on a freelance basis.

Even if you hate freelancers, you can't help but be curious about what fol-lows. And what follows is a convincing argument to hire the writer:

Another freelance writer succeeded with a more straightforward approach:

> Dear Mr. Mann:
>
> Congratulations on your new business. May you enjoy great success and receive much pleasure from it.
>
> I offer my services as a freelance public relations writer specializing in medical and technical subjects.

Here, the writer gets attention by opening with a subject that has a built in appeal to the reader, namely, the reader's own business. Most of us like to read about ourselves. And just about everybody would react favorably to the good wishes expressed in the second sentence.

Interest

Once you get the reader's attention, you've got to provide a "hook" to create real interest in your subject and keep him or her reading. This hook is a prom-ise to solve problems, answer questions, or satisfy needs:

> To stay ahead, you need aggressive people willing to take chances. People who are confident, flexible, and dedicated. People who want to learn and who are not afraid to ask questions.

What better way to hold someone's interest than to promise to solve his problems for him?

A principal rule of persuasive writing is remembering that the reader isn't interested in you. The reader is interested in the reader. Because we want to hear about ourselves, the following letter was particularly effective in gaining and holding my interest:

> As you may know, we have been doing some work for people who have the same last name as you do. Finally, after months of work, my new book, *The Amazing Story of the Blys in America*, is ready for printing and you are in it!
>
> The Bly name is very rare and our research has shown that less than two one-thousandths of one percent of the people in America share the Bly name...

Desire

Get attention. Hook the reader's interest. Then create the desire to buy what you're selling. This is the step where many businesspeople falter. Their corporate backgrounds condition them to write business letters in "corporatese," so they fill paragraphs with pompous phrases, jargon, clichés, and windy sentences.

Don't write to impress—write to express. State the facts, the features, the benefits of your offer in plain, simple English. Give the reader reasons why he or she should buy your product, give you the job, sign the contract, or approve the budget. Create a desire for what you're offering.

With the reader's interest in hand, you can proceed to create a desire for your service or product:

> I am one of those people—one of the people you should have on your list of top freelancers. As a freelancer, I can offer you and your company many benefits. I work only when you need me. I don't require a desk in your company, nor a phone, or stationary or medial benefits, or sick or personal days. There are no "lazy" days for a freelancer: I will always hand you my very best, hoping to be hired again.

Benefits are spelled out. Anxieties are eliminated. The reader is given the reasons why he or she should hire a freelancer.

Action

If you've carried AIDA this far, you've gained attention, created interest, and turned that interest into desire. The reader wants what you're selling, or at least has been persuaded to see your point of view. Now comes the last step—asking for action.

If you're selling consulting services, ask for a contract. If you want an interview, ask for it. If you're writing a fund-raising letter, include a reply envelope and ask for a donation. In short, if you want your letter to get results, you have to ask for them.

> Read over the attached list of my clients and credits. It shows I can take any challenge and succeed.
>
> Then pick up the phone and call me today. Even if you have no project to assign immediately, let's talk about how my experience can help you get things done in the future.

An exchange of business letters is usually an action—reaction situation. To move things along, determine the action you want your letter to generate and tell the reader about it.

Formulas have their limitations, and you can't force every letter or memo into the AIDA framework. Short interoffice memos, for example, seldom require this degree of persuasiveness.

But when you're faced with more sophisticated writing tasks—a memo to motivate the sales force, a mailer to bring in orders, a letter to collect bad debts—AIDA can help. Get attention, hook the reader's interest, create a desire, ask for action, and your letters will get better results!

Sales series

For most firms, sales is a multistep process involving multiple communications with a given prospect. For this reason, many businesses develop a standard library of sales letters to address each stage in this multistep selling process. Here is a model series you can adapt to your own business and sales cycle.

The following series can be used for any product or service. Simply replace "computer systems" and any related language with your product or service. You can also substitute the benefits you offer (price savings, better service) for the benefits listed in the sample letters.

This is a fairly complete series. Use whatever letters fit into your selling cycle, in the order that makes sense for your business. Keep in mind that you do not have to use all the letters. Some may not apply to your product or fit your selling methods.

Initial inquiry generator

We all come across people and organizations who are a good fit for our products or services. A short, simple letter, like the one below, can be used to gauge their initial interest and get them to ask for more details about who you are and what you do.

Customize your own letter to generate an inquiry:

Follow the AIDA formula:

1. Your opening should grab attention with something catchy (such as a quote, a statistic, or an interesting fact).
2. Create interest by acknowledging the reader's needs.
3. Build desire by explaining how you can meet those needs.
4. Call for action by explaining what the reader should do next.

Dear Ms. Gladstone:

The tremendous recent improvements in hardware and software have made this adage truer than ever:

"Improve your computer systems, and you improve your business systems. Improve your business systems, and you improve your business results."

There's no longer any doubt: In today's business world, if you want to improve your business results, you need to have your business fully computerized and networked.

When it comes to helping you improve your computer systems, we can help.

Using the latest technology and proven software, we can increase your efficiency and productivity, while giving you faster access to important data for improved decision-making and business management.

For more information on how we can give your business a competitive edge through better computer systems, call us today. There's no cost to talk to us. There is no obligation of any kind.

Sincerely,

Sales lead: Offering free analysis of a prospect's requirements

Many prospects may be wary of meeting with a salesperson. They either are afraid of being on the receiving end of high-pressure sales tactics, or don't realize how they can immediately benefit from the product or service. You can use a letter to set up an appointment by positioning the initial meeting with the customer as an opportunity to assess their needs and recommend a solution.

Customize your own offer of a free analysis of prospect's requirements:

The key here is to make the reader believe that this is not just a ploy to get a salesperson in the door. The letter should include:

1. An opening that gains attention by requiring readers to ask themselves how they can benefit from the service or product you want to sell.
2. An answer to that question that builds interest in you.
3. The details of the analysis that create a desire to find out more.
4. Instructions telling the reader how to take advantage of this opportunity with repeat assurances that the service is absolutely free.

Dear Ms. Johnson:

Do you think that upgrading your business computer system might make sense, but not sure what you need or what to do next? Our free Business Computing Needs Analysis might be the answer.

Here's how it works:

One of our business computing specialists will visit your offices and, at no cost to you, conduct a complete audit of your business processes. We'll look at your operations, what's computerized, what isn't, and which areas could be made more efficient through better computing.

Within 48 hours of our visit, you'll receive a written report that gives the results of our Business Computing Needs Analysis. It includes specific hardware and software recommendations, along with cost estimates for purchase or lease of the recommended systems and applications.

There's no cost for this free Business Computing Needs Analysis. There is no obligation or sales pressure of any kind. Even if you don't have us put in a system for you, you'll find this analysis of your business processes and computing needs interesting—and useful. Call us today.

Sincerely,

Letter preceding a sales meeting

Many sales meetings are unproductive simply because the seller does not help the buyer prepare. In a quick fax or e-mail memo, tell your prospects how they can help you serve them better in the meeting, what you need, and by when.

Customize your own letter preceding to a sales meeting:

This letter serves to both confirm that you have a meeting and also make sure that everything you need to make the meeting productive is available:

1. Open with a confirmation of the time, date and location of the meeting.
2. List each of the things you need the other person to have prepared for this meeting.
3. A cordial close.

TO: Joseph Jones
FROM: Bob Allen, phone 123-456-7890
RE: Our Tuesday meeting

I'm looking forward to meeting you Tuesday the 5th at 9 a.m. in your office. To make our session more productive, here's a list of items it would be nice to have at hand for the meeting:

1. Sample printout, or "dummy," of the standard report.
2. Sample printout, or "dummy," of the gold report, including the trade area map we create from their customer data.
3. Brochures or other promotional materials you have on your firm and consulting services.
4. Testimonials from satisfied consulting clients.
5. Client list.

Ideally, if you give me the go-ahead to create a direct mail package for you, I'd like to take as much of this as I can back with me.

Thanks,

Catalog insert letter

Catalog marketing is an effective way to sell a broad line of related products by mail. But catalogs—professionally typeset, colorful, with lush photos and illustrations—are a rather impersonal medium. To add warmth, personality, and selling power to their catalogs, many marketers include a cover letter with their catalog mailings. You can use the letter to talk about your company, your products, your catalog, your service, your commitment to quality, your track record, benefits you offer to customers, or your guarantee. Or you can point the reader to specific features of the catalog or bargain items on various pages.

Customize your own catalog insert letter:

This letter is a friendly version of the AIDA formula. It includes:

1. An attention-grabbing opening.
2. A message that talks to the needs of the reader to gain interest.
3. Information that promises a way to help the reader meet those needs.
4. Directions explaining what the reader should do next.

Dear Friend:

The new catalog is out with a long list of brand new items you've never seen before!

Are you looking for a unique gift for the person who has everything? Are you redecorating and need that "just right" accent piece? Have you been meaning to replace that worn out (but much loved) bed quilt? Are you running out of time to browse for a gift that that's just perfect?

Now you can solve all your most difficult shopping dilemmas, without ever leaving the comfort of your favorite armchair. Browse through the pages of this new catalog and you'll see high quality products at prices that make them among the best values in the marketplace today. This is why shopping at XYZ is always a pleasure and not a chore. Our money-back guarantee assures you that if your selection does not meet your expectations, you can return it, postage-paid, with no questions asked.

Send us your order today. You can call the toll-free number 24 hours a day or fax or mail the order form enclosed.

Go ahead—sit back, put up your feet and enjoy the fun of slowly browsing through our products.

Happy shopping,

Encouraging customers to reorder

Sales letters sent to customers often generate responses many times more than responses you'll get from sales letters sent to rented lists of potential customers you don't know and who don't know you. With a mailing to existing clients, your company name on the outer envelope alone is enough to get them to open and start reading.

Sending customers letters reminding them to reorder can be very profitable—especially if you can time the letters so the customer is likely to get one when his supplies are beginning to run low.

Customize your own letter encouraging customers to reorder:

This letter is a kindly reminder that should include:

1. A reminder that the customer has ordered from you before and a statement of that order.
2. A statement that you appreciate the customer's business with words of encouragement to reorder before supplies run out.

3. A very simple order form that lists the products, leaves room for new products, and gives ordering instructions.
4. A statement of the company policy on warantees and guarantees.
5. A thank you.
6. A discount mentioned in the postscript, to encourage the customer to place the order.

Dear Sy Ackerman:

Back in February, you ordered the product(s) listed below. We appreciate your business. Now is the best time to reorder, *before* your inventory is low.

All the information needed to reorder is preprinted below. Simply verify this information, make changes in quantity if necessary, even add new products. Just mail or fax this form to us, with your updated imprint samples, at 123-456-7890 or call us toll-free at 800-123-4567 and we'll take care of the rest.

As a Business Products customer, you've recognized us for our quality products and our 100 percent Satisfaction Guarantee. This extended guarantee—along with our new, faster order turnaround time—separates us from *any* other discount professional supplier! Thank you for your continued confidence in Business Products, "Publishing's Reliable Supplier Since 1959."

Sincerely,

P.S. Now you can reorder and save 10%. All you have to do is order within 45 days from the date of this letter and mention code 9801524 to receive your discount. The price on the order form below already includes the discount. Thanks again for your business!

Sales proposal in memo format

Writing a formal proposal is a complex writing task that takes a lot of time many of us don't have. I prefer to send proposals in memo style. It's less time-consuming, more informal, and in most instances, equally or more effective.

Customize your own sales proposal:

Most sales proposals include the following five sections:

1. **Overview:** This outlines the proposed project or service. It may include your objective.
2. **Concepts and methodology:** Here you map out step-by-step what you will do to meet the objectives set down in section 1.
3. **Assignment:** Repeat back to the client what they are hiring you to do.
4. **Timing:** State when the assignment will be completed.
5. **Cost:** State your fee and other costs involved in completing the assignment.

TO: Anne Chopin
FROM: Brian Davidson, phone 123-456-7891
RE: Copywriting—direct mail package for XYZ Company

Dear Anne:

Thanks for taking the time to chat with me. Here is the memo I promised to fax today. Questions? Call me at 123-456-7891.

I. OVERVIEW

XYZ Company markets credit card enhancement programs to banks, department stores, and oil companies.

Sales have been primarily via telemarketing. XYZ Company is looking to develop profitable direct mail packages as an alternative. The objective is to bring in new members at a cost per order of $40 to $43.

II. CONCEPTS AND METHODOLOGY

Here are the steps normally involved in having me write a package for you:

- Research.
- Presentation of concepts (package outline).
- First draft of copy.
- Revisions.

III. ASSIGNMENT

As discussed, my first choice would be to work on travel arrangements. I've done a lot of work in the travel industry, and wrote a package offering a similar set of enhanced benefits to magazine subscribers.

My second choice is health trends. With changes in health care today, people are uncertain about the status of their coverage. Again, almost everyone is going to use the service at least once or twice, so it will pay back its cost.

IV. TIMING

If you can turn around copy reviews within a week or so, it's realistic for us to have final approved copy in November, in time to make a January mailing.

V. COST

Copywriting: $6,500. Includes outline, copy, and revisions. Design to printer-ready disk or cartridge: $2,500 to $10,000, depending on the design studio selected, package format, use of color, and photography or illustration required.

Keeping track of sales leads

You can use this form to track sales leads generated by your various letters. The form can be stored in a file, three-ring binder, or on a database program to organize your follow-up efforts. A well-organized follow up of leads is likely to increase the number of prospects who become customers.

Date _____ Source of inquiry_____

Response via_____

Name_____ Title _____

Company _____ Phone _____

Address_____ Room/floor _____

City _____State _____ Zip_____

Type of business:_____

Type of accounts (if an ad agency):_____

Type of projects:

For: ☐ immediate project ☐ future reference

☐ project to be started in: _____ (month/year)

Status:

☐ Sent package on (date): _____

☐ Enclosed these samples:_____

☐ Next step is to: _____

☐ Probability of assignment: _____

☐ Comments:_____

_____

Contact Record:

Date: _____Summary: _____

_____

_____

Inquiry fulfillment letters

When you respond to an inquiry by mail, fax, or e-mail, you are usually sending the recipient information that they requested. This information can include fact sheets, brochures, catalogs, and other types of sales literature. The inquiry fulfillment letter is the cover letter that goes with this package. Let's take a look at how to write an effective inquiry fulfillment piece by examining one that is ineffective.

Suppose you had responded to an advertisement from a manufacturer of forged steel valves and requested more information. How would you react to this reply?

Dear Sir:

Chemical Equipment magazine has informed us of your interest in our line of valves for the chemical process industry.

Enclosed please find the literature you requested. We will await with interest your specific inquiry.

Sincerely,

Joe Jones, Sales Manger
XYZ Valve Corporation

That letter doesn't call for action, build trust in the letter writer, or tell the reader why he should want to buy valves from XYZ. There's no salesmanship in it, just a blunt acknowledgment that an inquiry has been made. A fulfillment package should help move the sale along. However, this letter will not.

The tragedy is that most letters mailed to fulfill business inquiries are just about as horribly written. Too many marketers treat a cover letter as an afterthought thrown together after the pros from the ad agency have written the "important" elements of the communications program— the ads, brochures, and catalogues.

This is a big mistake. As creative consultant Sig Rosenblum aptly puts it, "Ads go through a long process of rough, layout, and finished art. But those are just devices to put ideas into the reader's mind. Your simple letters can carry powerful ideas just as easily as your complex ads."

But do they? Request more information on products and services you read about in ads or see on Web sites and see for yourself. The responses you receive will include weak, dreary cover letters that rely on hackneyed expressions such as "enclose please find," "pursuant to your request," and the ever-so-boring "as per your inquiry." That's not selling. When clichés substitute for copy that expresses a company's desire to help prospects solve problems, hot leads can quickly turn cold.

Part of the problem is that nonwriters, such as product mangers and engineers, often write cover letters. Management reasons that the advertising agent's time is better spent on ads and the like. Yet the letter provides the toughest writing challenge. It must sell on words alone, without the embellishment of color, photos, or artwork.

Tips for writing successful inquiry fulfillment letters

The key to successful cover letters? Be friendly, courteous, and helpful. Tell the reader how you will help him solve his problem better, faster, or cheaper than the competition. Here are seven letter-writing tips:

Thank the prospect for the lead

"Thanks for your interest," is a common opener. It may be becoming a cliché. However, it's still a necessary courtesy.

Highlight key sales points

Don't try to summarize your sales literature, but instead pick one or two of the important sales points and emphasize them in your letter. Letters are handy supplements to literature because they can include any recent developments that a color brochure, with its longer shelf life, may not reflect. Your letter can focus on a recent case history, a new application, a product improvement, or an addition to your manufacturing facility.

Tell the reader about the next step in the buying process

Make it easy for him or her by explaining exactly what to do next.

Write in a conversational tone

Your sales letter is communication from one human being to another—not from one corporate entity to the next. Warmth, humor, understanding, and an eagerness to be helpful are what make you the super-salesperson you are. Why not endow your letters with those same positive qualities?

Eliminate "whiskers"

One way to achieve an easy, natural style is to eliminate "whiskers" from your writing. Whiskers are those hackneyed expressions that drain life and personality from sales letters. Antiquated phrases from the vocabulary of the bureaucrat make a person (and his company) come across as a stuffed shirt. Here are 10 hackneyed expressions to avoid:

1. *Enclosed please find...*
   The reader can find it on his own. Just say, "I'm enclosing," or "here is."

2. *When time permits...*
   Poetic, but inaccurate. Time doesn't permit, people do.

3. *Please don't hesitate to call...*
   You really mean, "feel free to call."

4. *We are this date in receipt of...*
   Say instead, "today we received."

5. *As per your request...*
   Say instead, "as you requested."

6. *Of even date...*
   Translation: "today."

7. *Pursuant to your orders...*
   That's too formal. Just say, "as you requested" or "following your instructions."

8. *Whereas...*
   Use "where" or "although."

9. *Kindly advise...*
   As opposed to "unkindly"? This phrase is unnecessary.

10. *Hitherto, whereby, thereby, herein, therein, thereof, heretofore...*
    Avoid these archaic, stilted words.

Have a "you" orientation

Good letter-writers know that the word "you" may well be the most important word in their vocabulary. A "you" orientation means thinking about what the reader wants, needs, and desires. Having a "you" orientation does not mean tooting your own horn. It means translating the technical features of a product into benefits that help the reader do his job, serve his customers, and pleases his boss. And it means addressing the reader directly as "you." Remember, a sales letter is a personal communication, not a cold recitation of features and facts.

Be concise

Use small words and short sentences. And break the writing up into many short paragraphs. Brevity makes writing easy to read. Run-on sentences and long chunks of unbroken text bore and intimidate readers.

Make it look professional

All letters must be typed and proofread to eliminate errors in spelling, punctuation, grammar, and content.

A word on bounce-back cards

In addition to the literature and cover letter, a fulfillment package should contain a reply element. It can be a specification sheet, an order form, or a questionnaire known as the bounce-back card.

Bounce-backs are postage-paid postcards addressed to you. They ask the prospect to qualify herself by answering a few questions. Typically, a bounce-back questionnaire asks the prospect's name, address, and phone number, the name and size of her company, whether she specifies or recommends a particular type of product, current buying plans, applications, the names of others in the company involved in the buying decision, whether the prospect currently uses the advertiser's products or those of a competitor, whether the prospect wants a salesperson to call and whether the inquiry is for an immediate need, a future need, or reference information only.

Bounce-back postcards may be separate from the rest of the package, or they may be printed as tear-out inserts in brochures or catalogs. Some companies combine the bounce-back questionnaire, cover letter copy, and catalog information on a single sheet.

Most industrial marketing experts agree that the bounce-back is an integral part of the fulfillment package. "If you're not contacting the respondent personally, you should have a bounce-back card," says Robert L. Sieghardt, president of Professional Sales Support, a company that screens sales leads by telephone. Sieghardt says that as many as 55 percent of prospects will respond with a bounce-back card after a series of three follow-up mailings.

Some advertisers respond to inquiries by mailing a bounce-back card without any accompanying literature. They hope to avoid sending expensive sales brochures to students, competitors, brochure collectors, and other nonprospects. But other firms criticize the practice because it delays getting information to respondents by creating an additional and unnecessary step in the sales sequence.

"I think you're trying to kill responses by not sending a brochure," says Larry Whisehant, advertising manger of Koch Engineering, a manufacturer of chemical equipment. "The proper literature—what the respondent is asking for—is the most important piece of the package."

Robert Sieghardt agrees: "By trying to screen leads with the bounce-back, manufacturers are asking prospects to do some of their work for them."

No two marketers agree on what makes the perfect fulfillment package. But one thing is clear: The advertiser who casually tosses a brochure in the mail with a hastily dictated cover note is wasting sales opportunities.

The entire package must be designed to generate action that leads to a sale. To accomplish this, you need three things: a clear, crisp cover letter that motivates prospects, a brochure that informs them, and a bounce-back or other reply element that makes it easy for them to respond.

Inquiry fulfillment: Securing an appointment for a salesperson

When a potential customer inquires about your service or product, the next logical step is to meet with the prospect to make a sales presentation. This inquiry fulfillment letter uses all the eight tips mentioned above.

Customize your own letter to set up an appointment for a salesperson:

When someone has asked for information, you already have your foot in the door. Then it's time to sit down and visit. Your letter should:

1. Grab attention by immediately noting that the letter (and enclosed information if appropriate) are sent to respond to the reader's request.
2. Build interest by stating the reader's needs.
3. Create desire by explaining how you can solve the reader's problems.
4. Encourage action by explaining what the reader should do next.

Dear Mr. Loman:

Thanks for asking about high-performance, tailored computer systems to run your business more efficiently and profitably. Literature describing system capabilities is enclosed.

The next step is to sit down and discuss your business computing requirements in detail. We'll take a look at what you have, what you need, current business processes, where computerization can help, and what hardware and software would best meet your requirements.

Then we'll provide recommendations on the system that's right for your business. We'll give you a detailed cost estimate for purchases and a low monthly lease payment quote for the system.

To schedule an appointment with one of our business computing specialists, simply give us a call. The consultation, as well as our recommendations, are free. There's no obligation to buy.

Sincerely,

Inquiry fulfillment to accompany literature

A common mistake in inquiry fulfillment is to send an overly long and redundant letter that repeats product facts and features covered in the accompanying literature. Don't reproduce the text of your brochure in the letter. Rather, the letter should just hit the highlights, leaving the detail for the brochure or fact sheet to cover.

Customize your own letter to accompany requested literature:

Your literature speaks for itself; the accompanying cover letter should move the potential customer to actually read the literature. It should include:

1. A thank you for requesting the literature.
2. An explanation of what the literature covers.
3. A brief overview of what the service or product offers the customer.
4. An offer to discuss the service or product by phone, in person, or through an enclosed survey to meet individual needs.

Dear Mr Ramnstein:

Thanks for requesting the enclosed information on PS plumbing systems.

The enclosed literature will give you a good idea of PS' ease of use, flexibility, power, and speed. You'll also discover the many advantages of PS over conventional plumbing systems.

Your *real* question, of course, is "How can PS save ME time and money?"

Fortune 1000 companies worldwide have documented cost savings of 70 to 90 percent using PS. But the only way to determine the benefits to **your** company is to call 123-456-7890 and talk with a sales representative.

A preliminary and free phone conversation will quickly enable you to determine whether PS implementation is worth exploring further. If so, a company representative can perform a free, on-site evaluation of your current system and recommend improvements.

To find out how PS can meet your needs, simply call 123-456-7890. Or complete and return the Plumbing System Needs Assessment form enclosed. As always, there is no cost or obligation of any kind.

Sincerely,

Follow-up letters

Making contact with customers or making a first sale is just the beginning in creating a business relationship. To bring customers in and keep them loyal you'll often have to write follow-up letters.

Follow-up letter: Following up after literature has been mailed

It is unlikely that you will get to meet with every prospect or even the majority of prospects right away. For this reason, follow-up is key. According to a study by Thomas Publishing, publishers of the popular purchasing directory Thomas Directory, 80 percent of business sales are made on the fifth follow-up, but most marketers follow up only three times or less. A series of well-crafted follow-up letters can ensure you contact prospects frequently enough to gain their attention, and ultimately, their business.

Customize your own follow-up letter after literature has been mailed:

Don't sit around waiting for potential customers to respond to your sales literature. Use the mailing as a hook that gives you line to reel them in. Follow-up letters should include:

1. Mention of the literature that was previously sent.
2. A statement about the benefit to the reader of your product or service.
3. Instructions to act now.
4. An offer to send the material again if it was not received.

Dear Mr. Thomas:

Recently I sent you literature describing the computer systems, services, and solutions we have created for businesses like yours.

If you need to computerize your business, call us. We may be able to help you with an innovative computer solution costing much less than you'd think.

The sooner you modernize your business procedures and computer systems, the sooner you'll begin to enjoy the benefits of increased productivity, reduced paperwork, and faster access to critical information for better decision-making.

We're ready when you are. Phone or fax us today with your requirements.

Sincerely,

P.S. If you didn't receive the information, or need additional literature, let me know. I'll make sure to send the information to you via fast fax or e-mail.

Follow-up letter: After a phone conversation or first meeting

This letter is sent as a follow-up immediately after a first meeting in which you have mapped out your service or product. A copy of the cost estimate, printed on a separate sheet, should be enclosed with the letter.

Customize your own follow-up after an initial meeting or conversation:

This letter keeps you and your product or service on the customer's mind while they are making this business decision. Be sure to include:

1. Mention of your recent conversation.
2. Cost estimates of the product or service you had discussed, tailored to the customer's requirements.
3. Available financing.
4. Instructions how the customer can take the next step.

Dear Ms. Poplar:

It was a pleasure chatting with you today concerning your company's business computing needs.

Based on our discussion, I've enclosed preliminary cost estimates for several different systems that meet your requirements.

As you see, our flexible financing terms enable us to tailor the low monthly lease payment to meet any budget. The system can also be purchased outright.

If these figures look good to you, the next step is to discuss the specific system configuration and options in detail. After doing that, we'll give you a final cost estimate detailing all system components, pricing, and purchase and lease options for your approval.

Sincerely,

Follow-up letter: After a purchase

Salespeople are painfully familiar with "buyer's remorse," where the customer calls the day after the purchase and says, "I'm not sure about this...maybe I made a mistake...you have a return policy, don't you?" A follow-up letter after a purchase can help assure customers they made the right decision.

Customize your own letter to follow up a purchase:

To cut down on buyer's remorse calls, send an immediate post-purchase letter affirming the buyer's decision as a wise one to make. The letter should include:

1. Thanks for the purchase.
2. A review of all the positive features of the product.
3. A reminder of any guarantees, rebates, or other "extras" included with the product.
4. A psychological plug that assures the customer how smart he or she is for making this purchase.

Dear Ms. Kelley,

Thanks for your recent purchase of the Axirionn-2000 personal computer.

As you will discover, your Axirionn-2000's high-speed Pentium Processor, enhanced graphics board, and built-in ISDN modem give you the fastest and sharpest access to the Internet you have ever experienced. As you browse, you'll experience click-through navigating and Web downloading at up to twice the speed of conventional 56 Kbps machines.

Your Axirionn-2000 also comes with American Online and Netscape Communicator loaded and ready to go, with 50 free hours on American Online and one month's free direct Internet connection through Eagle Network, the Internet Services Provider (ISP) we recommend to our local customers.

New customers also get a one-year free membership in our WebWise Users Group, which includes a quarterly Internet newsletter and discounts on our Internet seminars. A schedule of our seminars is also enclosed.

The Internet is the future. You're now part of it. Others ride the Information Superhighway in the equivalent of a horse-and-buggy. You're doing it in a souped up sports car, the way it was meant to be done. Congratulations on a wise purchase decision!

Sincerely,

Follow-up letter at one-year anniversary

Selling does not end with purchase. The real profits in most relationships are in repeat orders and referrals. To get repeat business, you must ensure customer satisfaction with your products and services on an ongoing basis. A customer notice should be sent at least once a year to verify satisfaction and uncover any problems that require correction.

Customize your own one-year anniversary letter:

This is a great way to build good will and customer loyalty. Include:

1. A happy anniversary message.
2. A request for positive feedback (great for testimonial advertising).
3. An offer to answer questions or lend a hand.
4. An offer to solve any problems that have come up with your product.
5. An upbeat closing that looks ahead to a business relationship continuing into the future.

Dear Mr. Towers:

I was checking my records and noticed it's been one year since you acquired your computer system from us. Happy anniversary!

If you are thrilled and delighted with your computer system, please take a moment to let me know. We always enjoy hearing from our customers about the benefits our systems have brought to their businesses.

If you have questions, or need help mastering a particular application or function of your system, call us. We know the answers...and will be happy to share them with you. All you have to do is ask!

If there is a problem, if something isn't working the way you expected, or a particular business need is not being met, please call us. We're here to help.

Again, happy anniversary! Here's to many more!

Sincerely,

Letters for quotations

Before you begin a job or sell a product, many companies require a written quotation of cost. These quotations require a well-written cover letter that encourages the customer to sign the agreement.

Quotation cover letter

This letter accompanies a contract, formal quotation, or other document requiring signature of the customer to process the order or begin the work. A duplicate of the original quotation or cost estimate should be enclosed with this letter.

Customize your own quotation cover letter:

This letter should show the customer that you want to meet his or her needs and begin a business relationship as soon as possible. It should include:

1. A statement that tells the reader a quotation is enclosed for a specific product or job.
2. A request to verify that the specs match the customer's needs and a willingness to change the quotation if necessary.
3. An encouraging note to order now while prices are in effect.
4. An explanation of how long the terms will be offered.

Dear Ms. Compt:

As we discussed, here's a preliminary quotation for a computer system for XYZ Company.

Does this reflect everything we discussed, and what you expected? If not, let us know, and we can quickly revise the quotation to reflect your needs.

If the quotation is on target, tell us how you want to proceed. We can arrange a lease with low monthly payments tailored to your operating budget. Of course the system is also available for outright purchase.

But I urge you to hurry. Several of the major hardware and software vendors have announced planned price increases. When their prices go up, so do ours.

We can only hold the prices in this quotation for 60 days from the date on the proposal. To ensure the lowest prices, place your order now.

Sincerely,

Quotation follow-up: first reminder

If after sending the contract, you don't get a response, you need to send a reminder. Enclose a copy of the original quotation. Send this letter a week or two after you mail the original quote.

Customize your own first reminder following up a quotation:

This letter is a friendly nudge that gives the reader a reason to contact you. It should include:

1. A reminder that the attached quotation is still in effect.
2. An acknowledgment that the customer may be shopping around and looking at several different products/services.
3. An offer to requote to any new specifications.
4. An offer to answer any questions or resolve any uncertainties.

RE: Quotation and proposal for XYZ Co.

Dear Ms. Compt:

This is just a reminder that the terms and prices on the enclosed quotation are still good for several weeks.

If you've been shopping around, you may be thinking of a system that is slightly different than the one we quoted you.

In that case, give me a call. We'd be happy to requote on your new specification. We can even provide several different quotes for various configurations, to aid you in your decision-making.

Just one other thing to keep in mind: There's rarely just "one solution" to a given business computing challenge. If you're still uncertain, please call us. We can recommend hardware, software, and service alternatives that can satisfactorily meet any requirement—and budget.

Sincerely,

Quotation follow-up: second reminder

The second reminder is sent about two weeks after the first follow-up letter, again with a copy of the contract or quote enclosed.

Customize your own second reminder following up a quotation:

This letter implies that you may be able to change your quote, but it can also mean that you can suggest substitute or alternate products/services to save money. It should include:

1. A reminder that the attached quote was submitted a while ago.

2. A request that if the customer is considering another company, he or she contact you before sealing the deal.

3. A suggestion that you can help the customer save money as compared to other companies.

4. A thank you for the opportunity to offer a quote.

RE: Quotation and proposal for XYZ Co.

Dear Ms. Compt:

It's been some time since we quoted you on a computer system for your business. So I have one favor to ask.

If you're considering another system, please give me a call *before* you sign any contract or issue a purchase order to another vendor. We may be able to provide additional ideas to save you money or enhance system performance in ways these other vendors may not know about.

Thanks again for giving us the opportunity to quote on your system.

Sincerely,

Quotation follow-up: final reminder

If the prices and terms you quoted are good only for a certain period, send this letter a couple of weeks before the period is about to expire, warning the customer that after that date, the prices may be higher or the product unavailable.

Customize your own final reminder following up a quotation:

In this letter be sure to keep your tone friendly and keep the door open to future business. Include:

1. A notice that the terms in the attached quotation are in effect for only a short while longer.

2. A request to let you know if they want to go ahead.

3. A request to let you know if they would like a different product/service and therefore need a new quotation.

4. An offer to extend the quotation if the customer is still thinking.

RE: Quotation and proposal for XYZ Co.

Dear Ms. Compt:

The terms and pricing on this quotation are guaranteed for only a few remaining days.

If you have made a decision in favor of our system, please let us know right away. We'll lock in the prices and begin the paperwork that moves your transaction forward.

If you think you might want a different system than is described in our quotation, no problem. Just tell us what you have in mind. We'll give you a revised quote immediately.

If you are unsure as to whether you're going to go ahead right now, but think it's a possibility, call me. I'll extend the terms and prices on the enclosed quotation to you for another 60 days. That's ironclad, regardless of whether our suppliers raise their own prices to us during that time. (If they do, *we'll* absorb the difference).

Sincerely,

P.S.   If you have acquired a system from another vendor, we are always here to help you with software, equipment upgrades, consulting, training, service, support, supplies, or whatever else you may need—now or in the future.

Letters of agreement

Even if a prospect agrees over the telephone to use your product or service, a formal closing of the sale should be done in writing.

Letter of agreement, informal

For simple uncomplicated projects, you can confirm assignments in writing with a brief letter of agreement, such as the one below. Be sure to include a second copy for the customer and a self-addressed stamped envelope so he or she can easily return the signed form to you. For more complex projects, you should consult an attorney who can draw up a formal business agreement.

Customize your own informal letter of agreement:

This letter serves as a contract between you and your customer. Include:

1. A thank you for being given the specified work/order.
2. A request for the signed form to be returned to you.
3. A detailed description of the service/product.
4. The fee for this service/product.
5. Any exceptions that would change the fee (overtime, revisions, changes in specs, and so forth).
6. If appropriate, the terms for payment of business expenses.
7. A payment schedule.
8. A place for the recipient to sign and date.

Dear Mr. Jones:

Thank you for choosing XYZ Ad Agency to handle your Job #3333. The following agreement spells out the terms and conditions of this project. Please keep a copy for your records and return a signed copy to me in the enclosed envelope.

Job 3333 is a series of three capability brochures. I will write these brochures for you and provide such marketing and editorial consulting services as may be required to implement the project.

My base fee for the services I describe above is $10,000. That fee estimate is based on 100 hours of working time at my hourly rate of $100, and includes time for copywriting, editing, teleconferencing, meeting, consulting, travel, and research.

Copy revisions are included in my base fee. At such time as the total time devoted by me exceeds 100 hours, I shall bill you for additional working time at the rate of $100 per hour.

Out-of-pocket expenses, such as long-distance telephone calls, photocopies and computer printouts, fax charges, messengers, local and out-of-town travel incurred in connection with the project will be billed to you in an itemized fashion.

Payment of the base fee will be made as follows: One-third of the above-mentioned base fee is due upon my commencement of work, one-third due upon delivery of first draft copy, and one-third is due upon completion. Payment for expenses will be made within 10 days following receipt of invoice.

Sincerely,

ACCEPTED AND AGREED:

by:_____ date_____

Terms and conditions of fee structure

If the pricing, fee structure, terms, or conditions are complex, they can be listed in an attachment rather than being incorporated into the body of an agreement letter.

Customize your own addendum of terms and conditions:

This list of terms and conditions is dictated by the particular service. It should include all the terms including hourly fees, project fees, reimbursable expenses, and contingencies such as revisions, changes in specs, overtime, and so forth.

STATEMENT OF GENERAL TERMS & CONDITIONS

1. Fee Structure

All time, including travel hours, spent on the project by professional, technical, and clerical personnel will be billed. (Travel time is billed at half-hourly fees, portal to portal.) The following approximate ranges of hourly rates for various categories of personnel are currently in effect:

Hourly Rate	Category
$400	Principal in charge
$100 to $200	Senior consultants
$40 to $75	Marketing analysts
$30 to $50	Research technicians
$15	Computer/Typists

Hourly rates will be adjusted semi-annually to reflect changes in the cost-of-living index as published. If overtime for nonprofessional personnel is required, the premium differential figured at time and one-half of their regular hourly rate is charged at direct cost to the project. *Unless otherwise stated, any cost estimate presented in a proposal is for budgetary purposes only, and is not a fixed price.* The client will be notified when 75 percent of any budget figure is reached.

2. Reimbursable Expenses

a) Travel expenses necessary for the execution of the project, including rail, taxi, bus, air, rental vehicles, highway mileage in company or personal vehicles, which will be charged at 20 cents per mile.

The following expenses will be billed at direct cost:

b) Accommodations, all meals at cost.

c) Telephone/fax charges.

d) Postage and shipping/courier services.

e) In-house printing and reproduction.

f) Other project expenses: photocopying, laser printing, and so forth.

3. Art Production (typed layouts, type specs, mechanical assembly)

Artist's time charged at $50/hour or estimated on project fee basis.

Letters for add-on support

If your product comes with a warranty, or a support contract, you should be in touch when that contract is about to expire and again if it does expire. These moments are selling opportunities.

Selling add-on support contract

One way to profit from satisfied customers is to sell more products and services to them. Here's a letter you can use to sell a service contract to customers who have bought your products and whose warranties have expired.

Customize your own letter selling add-on support:

This letter should make the recipient feel he or she is getting something extra or special. It should include:

1. An opening offering to make the customer a top priority.
2. An announcement that a service/support contract is enclosed and is offered at a discounted price.
3. The benefits of the service.
4. Instructions to sign and mail to gain the coverage.

Dear Mr. Smyth:

We can't be everywhere, all the time, for everyone. No one can.

But now there's an easy way to ensure we're always there for you, when and where you need us to be.

The enclosed Service and Support Agreement spells out the various levels of service and support we offer businesses in our area. As one of our system users, you receive a discount of 30 percent off compared with what we charge for support to businesses who do not own or lease one of our systems.

You rely on computers to keep your business running and to access critical information. When the computers stop, so does business. Our Service and Support agreement ensures speedy repair or replacement to get you up and running with minimum downtime.

To activate your Service and Support, simply sign the agreement and mail it back to us. Service and support become immediately available the minute you sign. For faster service, call or fax us your instructions today.

Sincerely,

P.S. No need to enclose payment now. We will bill you later.

Renewing a support contract

When a customer's maintenance, service, or support contract is close to expiring, send a letter asking them to renew. Insert support contract renewal for signature. Include a reply envelope.

Customize your own letter asking for renewal of a support contract:

This letter is sent to customers who have already shown they are interested in paying for additional support or service. Its job is to convince them that the price is worth renewing. It should include:

1. An announcement that the support contract is about to expire.
2. Instructions to sign the enclosed renewal contract to ensure uninterrupted service.
3. Assurance that payment need not be sent with the contract. You will bill the reader later.
4. The benefits of the service or support program to the customer.
5. Information about the price of the contract (and any upcoming increases if applicable).
6. Instructions to renew now.

RE: Service and Support Contract #87396

Dear Ms. Crocker:

Our records indicate that your Service and Support Contract with us will expire soon. A Renewal Agreement is enclosed. To ensure uninterrupted service and support, please sign and return it right away. There's no need to enclose payment with your renewal instructions...we'll bill you later.

Our fast, responsive service and support keeps your critical business computing systems up and running. When there's a problem, we're there in a flash. Speedy repair or replacement minimize downtime and keep your business going.

As one of our system users, you get year-round service and support for a discount of 30 percent off what we charge to businesses who do not own or lease one of our systems.

Rising parts and labor costs will soon force us to raise our support and service fees to new customers. Renew now to lock in your current low contract rate for the next 12 months before our prices go up.

Sincerely,

P.S. To lock in the discount renewal rate and avoid paying full contract price, act now before your current contract expires. Renewing now also ensures that your service coverage will continue uninterrupted.

Renewing support contract: second effort

It is often profitable to mail several renewal notices instead of just one. With each, insert a support contract renewal for signature with a reply envelope.

Customize your own second request asking for renewal of a support contract:

This letter repeats the offer of the first letter and adds an additional warning. It includes:

1. An announcement that the support contract has expired.
2. An offer of a grace period during which the customer can renew the contract.
3. The benefits of renewing during this grace period.
4. A warning stating that when the grace period expires, the customer will be required to pay a higher rate than currently being charged for this service.

RE: Service and Support Contract #87396

Dear Ms. Crocker:

Our records show that your Service and Support Contract with us has expired.

For the next 30 days, we will offer a grace period during which you can renew your Service and Support Contract.

When you renew within this grace period, your service continues uninterrupted. And you renew at the Discount Renewal Rate, which is 30 percent less than what new service contract customers are currently paying.

If you renew after the grace period, we cannot hold the Discount Renewal Rate, and you may be required to pay the higher standard rate for service and support.

Sincerely,

Letters that open or close the door

Letters that say thanks after you've made a sale open the door to future business relationships. On the other hand, sometimes it's time to "zap" an inactive customer from your files. These letters will show you how.

Thank you letter for an order, including confirmation

Upon receipt of the signed contract or order, send a brief thank you note to the customer. Include a copy of the approved quotation with any changes made from the original estimate reflected in the final order.

This is a handy form letter you can file in your computer and send out easily to confirm every order you receive.

RE: Order #655321

Dear Mr. Ericson:

Thank you for your order.

This is a written confirmation of the items you have requested—described in the enclosed quotation.

If you want to make a change, please call our office *immediately* so we can accommodate your request. Otherwise, we'll proceed as outlined. Once again, thanks for your business.

Sincerely,

Zap letter

A "zap" letter is used to remove old names from your mailing list. If the person doesn't respond, his or her name is removed from your active database and put into an archival file.

Zap letters prevent customers and prospects from being annoyed by mail they do not wish to receive. They also remind customers that they have agreed to receive any material you are sending them, and are not sending mail without their permission.

Customize your own zap letter:

This is a sales letter to someone who hasn't used your services/product in a while. It should entice him or her to renew the business relationship, but also offer the opportunity to be dropped from your mailing list. It should include:

1. An announcement that because not ordering, the customer is about to be dropped from the mailing list.
2. A description of what the customer will lose if this happens.
3. A review of what your company offers.

4. A request for the customer to indicate (either by filing out an enclosed response card or calling) whether he or she would like to remain on your mailing list or be dropped. (Be sure to include the "favor" you're offering if the customer is not interested: you will reduce their load of bothersome advertising mail.)

5. A reminder (or warning) of what the customer will lose by not responding.

6. A final request to respond today.

You are about to be zapped.
Don't let it happen!

Dear Mrs Ericsson:

It's been some time since we heard from you. Unless we hear from you within the next 10 days, your name will be removed from our mailing list. You will no longer be getting exciting **free** offers from Studebaker-Worthington in your mailbox.

Studebaker-Worthington has a nationwide reputation for providing resellers with flexible, competitive leasing programs and **free** tools to help you increase sales.

But we have not heard from you in quite some time. You haven't called us about a lease. And you haven't responded to any of our recent free offers.

So, we're wondering if you're no longer interested. In that case, we don't want to clutter up your mailbox.

Here's what we're asking. Let us know, either way, whether you have any interest in our leasing programs and freebie offers, and whether you want to remain on our list. Simply use the handy reply card enclosed. Or call us toll-free 800-123-4567 today.

Warning: If you do **not** respond, you risk being "zapped" from our mailing list! To ensure that you continue to get exciting **free** offers from Studebaker-Worthington, including new sales aids and software upgrades, call or mail us now. Thank you.

Sincerely,

11

DIRECT MARKETING LETTERS

In this chapter, we discuss how to write direct marketing letters. Known as "direct mail," these letters:

- ▣ Are designed to bring checks, purchase orders, credit card information, and orders (or at least an appointment with a salesperson).
- ▣ Are usually sent in mass mailings to thousands of prospects simultaneously.
- ▣ Can be mailed to existing customers and prospects, but are most often mailed to rented lists of people likely to be interested in what your company is offering.

Model direct mail letter

Here is an example of a direct mail letter used to generate sales leads for a chemical company. The letter, mailed to environmental engineers and consultants, generated an 11 percent response. (A typical response rate for a lead-generating letter mailed to a mailing list is one to three percent.)

Mr. Joe Jones,
XYZ Company
Anytown, USA 00110

Dear Mr. Jones:

Do you have a potable water supply or waste stream that contains organic contaminants?

Have you considered activated carbon as an ideal treatment—but rejected it because of the cost?

Ecofilter may be the answer for you.

These patented, carbon-containing precoats handle high flow rates, and can be utilized at reasonable cost for many temporary applications where a one-time cleanup of contaminated water is required. Activated carbon in Ecofilter has an extremely high adsorption capacity, so Ecofilter can readily remove many types of organic compounds.

Ecofilter's unique composition makes it all possible. In an Ecofilter precoat, discrete particles of activated carbon are attached to fibers. The result is a large exposed surface area of activated carbon for superior absorption. The open, porous structure can handle large flow volumes with minimal pressure drop across the filter. In addition to adsorption, Ecofilter can remove suspended solids, too.

Is Ecofilter right for your application? We'd be delighted to evaluate a water sample to see if Ecofilter can handle your particular requirements. To find out more, give me a call or check off the appropriate box on the enclosed reply card and mail it, today.

Sincerely,

The direct mail reply card

A business reply card should be included as part of every direct mailer you send out. If you are using a self-mailer, the bottom third portion of the trifold mailing piece should be a business reply card. The fold between this business reply card and the rest of the self-mailer should be perforated to make the reply card easy to remove. A bold dotted line can be printed horizontally across the perforated fold to graphically emphasize the fact that the reply card is designed to be torn off.

A design technique that works well is to affix the mailing label directly to the reply portion of the self-mailer, then fold the self-mailer so the label shows through a die-cut hole on the address panel. This way, the reply card is already filled in with the prospect's name and address, and you get the label back when the reply card is returned to you.

The benefit of getting the label back is that, if you are mailing to multiple lists, you can tell which list generated the response. Labels from varying lists can be assigned a key code by the list broker that identifies which list a label came from. The cost of key coding is only an additional one to two dollars per thousand names, and it is well worth the price.

If you send out a direct mail letter, print the reply card on light blue, pink, canar, or some other brightly colored paper stock so that it stands out from the letter. Make the design as simple and clutter-free as possible.

Conventional wisdom says to make the reply element a business reply postcard, which means you, not the prospects, pay the postage (plus a small handling fee) for all cards returned to you. Your local post master can give you a booklet with complete instructions on how to get a business reply permit and prepare business reply cards and envelopes.

In consumer mailings, using business reply mail is clearly beneficial, because many people do not have a supply of stamps on hand (especially because the stamp rate required for postcards is not the same rate as that used for everyday mail).

In business mailings, use of business reply permits is less critical, because most businesses have postage meters, and most prospects simply run the reply card through the postage meter.

Reply cards for direct mailings generally contain these elements:

- A headline restating the key selling proposition or offer.
- A box or series of boxes where the prospect can indicate his or her desired response option.
- Space for the prospect to fill in name and address (or space to affix a mailing label, if you place the reply card so the label shows through a window on the outer envelope).
- Perhaps an optional brief questionnaire that indicates the prospect's areas of interest or that is used to prequalify leads.

The front of the card is addressed to you and contains the appropriate business reply permit number, bar codes, marks, and so on. If you elect not to use business reply mail, put your company name and return address in the center of the front panel of the card, and in the upper right corner put a box containing the words "place stamp here." Do not place stamps for return postage on reply cards. This is a waste of money, as you'd be paying for postage on every card, yet 90 percent or more will not be mailed.

Sample Reply Card

YES, I want to learn how Venus Software can upgrade my business!

☐ Please send me a brochure on your Pro business software system

☐ Have a Business Computing Consultant call to discuss my specific requirements

Name_____ Title_____

Company_____ Phone_____

Address_____

City_____ State_____ Zip_____

Business functions that I want to computerize: ☐ accounts payable ☐ accounts receivable ☐ inventory ☐ order entry ☐ general ledger ☐ others:_____

We currently use accounting software: ☐ yes ☐ no
Program used:_____

For fast service, call toll-free 800-123-4567. Or, fax this form to 123-456-7890.

Direct mail sales letters
Selling multiple items in a single mailing

In one mailing you can include any number of inserts with photos and descriptions of various items. To accompany this kind of direct mailing, you'll need a cover letter that makes the recipient want to carefully look through all of your enclosures.

Customize your own letter selling multiple items in a single mailing:

The letter above focuses not on the product (since there are many), but rather on the prices and the limited supply. This creates a sense of urgency and also makes the author or the letter look like the good guy who is trying to make a real effort to hold down prices for me personally. Your letter should include:

1. An attention-getting opener about a general characteristic of your products—usually price, supply or quality.
2. An urgent message about the price, supply or quality of the items advertised in the enclosed inserts.
3. Instructions to order now.

Dear Mr. Bly:

My accountant tells me I am going to have to raise my prices to offset our spiraling operating costs!

But I said, **"NO! NOT YET!"**

I know that customers like you, Mr. Bly, expect the **best value** for their money when they shop at ABC Company...and that's why I'm going to hold the line on higher prices just as long as I possibly can!

So, in the next few minutes, while you're looking through the enclosed group of bargain slips, please keep in mind that I may not be able to guarantee such terrific low prices in the future.

To be sure of your selections for a week's free trial, mail your order TODAY in the postage-paid envelope attached.

Sincerely,

Selling a single item by mail

Here's a letter selling slippers by mail. Because slippers are an item you can buy at a store, one of the sales arguments in the letter is to convince readers they can get a better product at a better price buying direct from the manufacturer.

Customize your own letter selling a single item:

This letter does a number of things right:

1. Short paragraphs and short sentences make this long letter extremely easy to read.
2. The copywriter does a good job of building up the readers' perceived value of, and desire for, the slippers.
   Freelance copywriter Burton Pincus says that good direct mail letters "dramatize the offer in a way that dwarfs the product's or service's cost when compared to the value of what is being purchased." This letter does just that.
3. Graphic devices—indented paragraphs, words in all caps, underlines—help make the letter appealing to the eye.
4. The last two paragraphs talk about a free, no-risk trial rather than "buy these slippers!" The copy makes it seem like the company is loaning you a pair of slippers to try on rather than making a sale.
5. The postscript gives strong incentive to order immediately. In this case, it is a five dollar discount that will expire in 10 days.

Dear Friend,

Are your feet tired at the end of a long day? Are they sore from walking and standing all day in stiff and unrelenting shoes? Are they cold and exposed as you pad around your home?

Your feet need slippers that pamper them with a soft-wool lining and genuine leather upper soles. The kind that cost you an arm and a leg at high-class boutiques and shoe stores. The kind you have probably never owned before.

But now "Comfies" can give your feet what they need to feel warm, indulged and relaxed. In stores, you'll pay $50, $65, or even more for slippers with these "extras."

But not if you buy DIRECT from Slippers For Sale!

See for yourself. Order at no risk. I'll rush you ON APPROVAL "Comfies" slippers with all the style and comfort your feet deserve... for only $25.

Thanks to Comfies, your feet no longer feel pinched, cold, or sore in your own home. Instead, they're cradled by our soft-wool lining and supported by our supple leather upper soles. You've got to feel Comfies yourself to believe the comfort.

How can we do it? All this luxury, all this comfort, AND guaranteed fit— at your price?

By dealing with you DIRECT from one central warehouse. You pay NO middleman's markup or costly store overhead. We've been saving customers money this way for more than 80 years now.

You risk **NOTHING** by trying a pair. Wear them for a full 30 days. Compare looks, comfort, and fit with ANY other slippers at ANY price. If ours aren't the most comfortable, the best value, I'll buy them back. No questions asked, regardless of wear.

Order today so I can rush your Comfie slippers by return mail. If you like, just say "charge it" to your favorite credit card.

Sincerely,

P.S. To encourage you to give us a try, I've enclosed a special coupon that gives you five dollars off your first order, <u>in addition</u> to the 30 to 40 percent we already save you off store prices. But it's only good for the next 10 days—so redeem it right away!

Selling a new edition/version of product

Another use of direct marketing letters is to get existing customers to buy a new edition or version of a product they already own. Such a letter must make a compelling case that the old product is out of date and the new product is superior. It should also remind the buyer of his or her satisfaction with the product they already own.

Customize your own letter selling a new edition/version of product:

The sample letter convinces through flattery:

1. Be up-to-date.

2. Stay on the cutting edge.

3. Have the new information before the rest of the industry.

4. Have it now at a discount.

5. The cost is insignificant compared to what you gain: "changes, revisions, and new material providing thorough and up-to-date coverage on dozens of vital topics."

6. A money-back guarantee.

7. Order now to lock in the price and put yourself ahead of the pack.

**Software technology is changing at a breakneck pace.
Now YOU can be <u>totally</u> up to date!**

Introducing the all-new, fully revised *Starset Companion: Second Edition,* the largest and most comprehensive *Starset Companion* update ever, yours for approximately **half** the cost of our other supplements.

Dear Valued Customer:

As a current subscriber to *The Starset Companion,* you need to keep current with the continual changes and improvements in available software.

To keep you on the cutting edge of technology, we've substantially revised and updated *The Starset Companion.* Our new Second Edition is enclosed for your review.

In a few weeks, we will begin offering *The Starset Companion: Second Edition* to the industry at a list price of $105.50 ($99 plus $6.50 shipping and handling).

But as a current subscriber, you may keep the enclosed Second Edition for only $27.50 ($25 plus $2.50 shipping and handling). <u>That's a savings of $78...a discount of 74 percent off the regular rate!</u>

**Why is upgrading to the Revised Second Edition of
the *Starset Companion* for only $25 is a good deal?**

First of all, it's only $25. Not a huge sum to lie on the table. Especially considering your current technology investment or what you spend on a weekly basis to operate and maintain your network.

Second, look at what you get for only $25—a fully revised and expanded *Starset Companion Second Edition*—with more than 100 pages of changes, revisions, and <u>new material</u> providing thorough and up-to-date coverage on dozens of vital topics.

Importantly, the coverage of these topics is fully updated, going beyond what we published in earlier editions and supplements.

Third, your satisfaction is guaranteed. If you are not 100-percent enthusiastic about the enclosed *Starset Companion: Second Edition,* simply return it within 30 days. When our bill arrives, tear it up, and you will owe us nothing.

To lock in your special low $25 Preferred Customer discount price, and ensure that you keep up-to-date with the changes and advances in technology, keep the new manual. Simply honor our invoice when it arrives.

Sincerely,

Lead-generating letters

Do you ever find yourself wishing you had a steadier stream of quality sales leads? Does your business depend on a continual flow of fresh inquiries to keep the cash registers ringing? Do you ever have periods when sales leads slow down, or even dry up? What would happen to your business if you didn't get the new inquiries you need every month?

Many businesses today struggle because they have difficulty with the one process that can virtually assure them all the sales they can handle: lead-generation.

It's a fact: The company that can cost-effectively generate a large volume of qualified leads, rapidly and inexpensively, whenever needed, will be over-whelmed with inquiries, appointments, business, sales, and new customers, with minimal expenditure of time and money. They will never have to fret about finicky customers, competition for new business, bad economic times, rejec-tion, or up-and-down business cycles. When you have more leads than you can handle, your revenues stay high, without the fluctuations that keep other busi-nesspeople up at night.

The main purpose of generating sales leads is to identify the best prospects for your product or service. By following up on those sales leads, your sales force, representatives, dealers, distributors, and others who sell your products can generate sales they might otherwise not have gotten on their own. In a sur-vey of some of its advertisers, Penton Publications found that 88.1 percent gen-erated direct sales of their products from sales leads. In a separate study, the Advertising Research Foundation found that one out of five prospects who make an inquiry eventually purchased the product.

A good lead-generating sales letter will generate response rates of between 1 and 5 percent—and sometimes higher—when mailed cold to a rented mailing list of prospect names. This response rate is for producing quality leads with a genuine and serious interest in your product or service, or at least in the prob-lem your product or service solves.

Most lead-generating letters are brief. Usually, they are no more than one or two typed pages, depending on the audience and the complexity of the subject matter. Letter copy should be simple, clear, conversational, and concise.

Successful lead-generating sales letters are usually simple in style, tone, content, and proposition. Lead-generating copy is designed to accomplish only one part of the selling task: getting a qualified prospect to reply. In effect, the letter should get a customer to raise his or her hand and say, "Yes, I'm inter-ested; tell me more."

Therefore, the copy must contain just enough information to gain attention, arouse curiosity, and generate interest. Additional information will be commu-nicated in conversation or other sales materials requested by the prospect. The lead-generating mailer only needs to present enough information to make the prospect interested in the product or service. More detail is not required and may even serve to decrease response. After all, if there is nothing left for the prospect to find out, they have no reason to call you.

Letter generating leads for a service business

Here is the sales letter I used to launch my freelance copywriting business in 1982. I mailed it to creative directors at 500 advertising agencies that handled industrial accounts, pulling the list from the Standard Directory of Advertising Agencies. I received 35 replies; a healthy seven percent response. I mailed this letter in a business envelope with a reply card to potential clients.

Customize your own letter generating leads for a service business:

This letter follows a classic formula for writing sales copy:

1. The headline grabs attention.
2. The first paragraph shows the reader that he has a need for freelance help.
3. The short second paragraph satisfies the need by showing the reader where to get help ("This is where I can help").
4. The rest of the letter gives reasons why the writer is the person to call when you need help.
5. The last paragraph asks for an inquiry.

HOW AN ENGINEER AND FORMER AD MANAGER CAN HELP YOU WRITE BETTER ADS AND BROCHURES.

For many people, industrial advertising is a difficult chore. It's detailed work, and it's highly technical. To write the copy, you need someone with the technical know-how of an engineer and the communications skills of a copywriter.

That's where I can help.

As a freelance industrial and high-tech copywriter and a graduate engineer, I know how to write clear, technically sound, hard-selling copy. You'll like my writing samples: ads, brochures, catalogs, direct mail, PR, and A/V. And you'll like having a writer on-call who works only when you need him.

Here are my qualifications:

I have an engineering background (B.S., chemical engineering, University of Rochester). I started out writing brochures and A/V scripts for the Westinghouse Defense Center. After I left Westinghouse, I became advertising manager for Koch Engineering, a manufacturer of process equipment.

In my freelance work, I've handled projects in a wide variety of industries including computers, software, chemicals, industrial equipment, electronics, publishing, banking, health care, and telecommunications. My articles on business communications have appeared in *Business Marketing*, *Computer Decisions*, *Amtrak Express*, *Chemical Engineering*, and *Audio-Visual Directions*. I'm also the author of *The Copywriter's Handbook* (Dodd, Mead), *A Dictionary of Computer Words* (Dell/Banbury), and nine other books.

I'd like to help you create ads, brochures, and other promotions. Call me when your creative team is overloaded, or when the project is highly technical.

I'd be delighted to send you a complete information kit on my copywriting services. The package includes a client list, fee schedule, biographical information, and samples of my work. Just complete and mail the enclosed reply card and the kit is yours at no cost or obligation to you.

Sincerely,

Bob Bly

P.S. Mail the reply card today and I'll also send you a free copy of one of my most popular articles: "10 Tips for Writing More Effective Industrial Copy."

Reply card for a lead-generating letter

Here's what my reply card for this letter looked like:

Bob:

☐ Please send more information on your copywriting services.

☐ Give me a call. I have an immediate project in mind.

☐ Not interested right now. Try us again in (month/year).

Name_____ Title _____

Company_____ Phone _____

Address _____

City _____ State _____ Zip _____

My business is: _____

Type of copy I need: ☐ Ads ☐ Direct mail ☐ Brochure ☐ A/V script ☐ PR
☐ Other:_____

Letter generating leads targeted to a specific industry

Following is a version of the above sales letter aimed specifically at potential clients in the software industry. It generated a response of five to 10 percent using various lists.

Customize your own letter generating leads for a specific industry:

When writing your letter, keep these tips in mind:

1. There's a problem in your industry that I can solve.

2. State what it is you do.

3. Refer to other companies in the same industry you have worked for.

4. If appropriate, give proof that your service works with results you've achieved with other companies.

5. Instruct the recipient about what to do next.

Dear Software Marketer:

"It's tough to find a copywriter who can produce result-getting copy for software, computers, and related high-tech products and services," a prospect told me over the phone the other day.

Do you have that same problem? If so, please complete and mail the enclosed card, and I'll send you a free kit describing a service that can help.

As a freelance copywriter specializing in direct marketing, I've planned and written successful lead-generating and mail order copy for more than a hundred software and high-tech companies including Computron, Hyperion Software, IBM, On-Line Software, DataFocus, Cartesia Software, Mortice Kern Systems, Yourdon, Syncsort, Samsung, Micro Logic, Citrix Systems, Plato Software, McGraw-Hill, Ascom/Timeplex, U.S. Robotics, Sony, Weka, Atech, Value Line, Medical Economics, among others.

Does my copy work?

- Convergent Solutions was getting a one- to two-percent response to mailings for its CS/ADS application development tool. A simple wording change to the beginning of their sales letter increased response to five percent—more than double what they were before.

- Another mailing campaign, promoting disaster recovery services, pulled a whopping 56 percent response and generated an immediate $5.7 million in sales for U.S. West. (The mailing won a Gold Echo award from the Direct Marketing Association.)

- On a space ad for Chubb Institute, a computer training company, we doubled the number of inquiries produced over all previous ads, simply by changing the presentation of the offer.

- For the Novell Companion, a book and diskette product I wrote pulled double the number of orders vs. the control.

To see some of these successful ads and mailings and others more related to your product, just complete and mail the enclosed reply card today. You'll receive a complete information kit including copywriting samples, client list, testimonials, fee schedule, and more. For fastest delivery, call 123-456-7890.

Sincerely,

Bob Bly

P.S. Respond now and I'll also send you a free tip sheet, "20 Secrets of Selling Software in Print." This reprint is packed with proven techniques for increasing the selling power of your software ads, direct mail, and brochures.

Letter generating leads for an in-house corporate training seminar

My friend Dr. Gary Blake mailed 200 of these letters at a cost of about $200 to generate leads for one of his workshops. The result was approximately $7,500 in new business.

Customize your own letter generating leads for a training seminar:

The sample letter above shows you how to include the six pieces of information that get responses:

1. A statement of a problem in an attention-getting opening.
2. An offer to solve that problem with an in-house training program.
3. A description of the program's goals and objectives.
4. A list of notable clients.
5. Instructions what to do next to schedule the seminar.
6. An offer in the postscript of a free offer for a quick reply.

Important news for every systems professional who has ever felt like telling an end-user, "Go to...."

Dear IS Manager:

It's ironic. Today's users demand to be treated as *customers* of IS. Yet many systems professionals don't have the customer service skills to make the relationship work.

Our training program, "Interpersonal Skills for IS Professionals," solves that problem...by giving IS staff the skills they need to deal effectively with end-users and top management in today's service-oriented corporate environment.

Presented by The Communication Workshop, a leader in teaching "soft skills" to technical professionals, "Interpersonal Skills for IS Professionals" quickly brings your team to a new level in listening, negotiating, teamwork, customer service, and other vital skills for communicating complex systems ideas and technical processes to managers and end users.

For more information, including an outline of our "Interpersonal Skills for IS Professionals" program, just complete and mail the enclosed reply card, or call 123-456-7890. You'll be glad you did.

Sincerely,

Gary Blake, Ph.D., Director

P.S. Reply now and we'll also send you a **free** copy of our new tip sheet, "The IS Professional's Guide to Improving Listening Skills." It will answer any questions you may have about dealing with the public, by creating educated consumers who are easier and more reasonable to deal with.

The reply card for the lead-generating letter

YES, I'm interested in learning more about your on-site seminars in:

☐ "Interpersonal Skills for IS Professionals"

☐ "Technical Writing for Systems Professionals"

Name_____ Title_____

Company_____ Phone_____

Address_____

City_____ State_____ Zip_____

☐ Call me now. *Number of people requiring training:*_____

☐ Call me in _____
                              (month/year)

For immediate information, call 123-456-7890

Or fax this card to 123-456-7899

Letter generating leads for seminar requiring paid registration

Direct marketing letters can also be used to get people to attend a seminar for which there is a registration fee. The following letter, mailed to 3,000 writer's magazine subscribers, prompted 57 people to pay $99 each to attend the seminar being advertised. Mailing cost, at $600 per thousand, was less than $2,000 total. Revenue from the mailing was more than $5,600, so the mailing did almost three times break-even, making it profitable.

The response was slightly less than two percent. Seminar mailings typically generate registration from between one-quarter to two percent of the recipients, and sometimes less.

Customize your own letter generating leads for a seminar requiring paid registration:

The letter above gives the reader everything he or she needs to know about the seminar, as well as offering to fulfill a dream. This letter includes:

1. Attention grabbing opening, telling the reader you share a common desire.
2. An opportunity to learn something you need/want to know.
3. The title of the seminar.
4. Bold subheads that direct the reader's attention to:

- What will be taught.
- Testimonials from others who have taken the seminar.
- Biographical info about the presenter.
- Date and location of the seminar.
- How to register (including the cost).
- The guarantee and cancellation policy.
- A contact number for more information.

5. A registration form attached to the end of the letter.
6. A free bonus for registering in advance.

"HOW TO BECOME A PUBLISHED AUTHOR"
A one-day Saturday seminar

A personal message by Bob Bly

Ever since I can remember, I've dreamed of becoming a published author, of seeing my byline on book jackets and magazine articles. Maybe that's a dream we share. But seven years ago, I discovered the secrets professional writers use to get their works published, while others flounder on the rejection pile.

Now I want to share those secrets with you.

Introducing "How to Become a Published Author—The Seminar"

If you live in New Jersey, New York, or the surrounding area, you can learn how to make the transition from unpublished writer to published author in my new one-day seminar.

Whether you want to publish magazine articles, essays, nonfiction, fiction, children's books, a regular column, or whatever else, this seminar reveals powerful marketing and sales techniques that professional writers use (and amateurs don't know) to break through the rejection barrier and get their writing published and into print.

What you will learn:

In Mr. Bly's talk, you will learn tips and strategies to get your manuscript published, including:

- How to write a good article proposal *without* doing a ton of research.
- The five things to look for when studying potential markets for work.
- Sample query letters you can use.
- Analysis of article proposals—what works, what doesn't.
- How much of an advance should you be paid?
- How to get your book written by deadline.

PLUS: How to earn an extra $20,000 a year part-time, or $85,000 a year full-time, writing material for commercial clients.

What people are saying about this seminar:

"Because it was all new to me, I found it all helpful, particularly the material that had to do with fiction, which is what I'm interested in."
–Donna Box, West Orange, NJ

"The marketing information was very well honed for nonfiction writers. The proposal is dynamite..."
–Marilyn Nestor, Robbinsville, NJ

"Comprehensive, positive manner of presentation. Good nuts and bolts...this is as much as can be absorbed in one bite."
–Marjorie Baines, Paterson, NJ

About your instructor

Bob Bly is the author of 17 books, including *Dream Jobs: A Guide to Tomorrow's Top Careers* (John Wiley), *Ronald's Dumb Computer* (Dell), and *How to Promote Your Own Business* (NAL). His articles have appeared in such magazines as *Cosmopolitan, New Jersey Monthly, Writers Digest, Amtrak Express, New Woman*. Monthly column in *Direct Marketing* magazine. In addition to his writings, he is also a professor of writing at New York University, a consultant to Fortune 500 corporations, as a frequent seminar leader and speaker.

Date and location

Brook Hotel, 50 Tenney Place, Brook, NJ

Saturday, November 12 from 9:30 a.m. to 4:30 p.m.

Fee: $99 advance registration by mail ($129 at the door)

Seminar fee does not include lunch. Confirmation and directions will be sent upon receipt of payment.

Register now and save $30!

To register, fill out the Registration Form (see reverse side) and mail with your check for $99 to: Bob Bly. If more than one person is planning to attend, write their name(s) and address(es) on a blank piece of paper. Attendance is limited; so please register today to ensure admission. At the-door registration is $129, so advance registration saves you $30!

Guarantee

If you diligently apply my advice and techniques and do not sell at least one book or article within one year after taking my seminar, I will refund your money in full.

Cancellation Policy

You will receive a full refund if cancellation is received at least five days before the seminar; 50 percent refund for later cancellations.

Questions?

Call Bob Bly at 123-456-7890.

Free Bonus!

Attendees who register in advance by mail receive, at no extra cost, our writer's manual #205, "How to Write a Winning Book Proposal" a seven dollar value, yours absolutely **free**!

Here's the form that was included with the letter:

REGISTRATION FORM

☐ Yes, Please reserve _____ place(s) at "How to Become a Published Author" at the advance registration discount fee of $99 per person.

My check for $_____ is enclosed (made payable to Bob Bly).

Name_____Phone_____

Address   _____

City_____ State _____ Zip_____

Detach and mail to:

Bob Bly
999 Riverview Drive
Somewhere, NJ 07000

If you've ever dreamed of becoming a published author, now you can take the next step toward making that dream come true.

Letter generating leads for a regional meeting

Another use of lead-generating letters is to invite customers, prospects, and other people to regional meetings or briefings, such as a breakfast roundtable or lunchtime seminar.

Customize your own letter generating leads for a regional meeting:

The letter above covers all the bases:

1. An opening that states a valuable advantage some people have over their competitors.

2. How this advantage is gained by attending the regional briefing.
3. What participants will gain.
4. How to register.
5. A note regarding limited seating, encouraging a prompt reply.

Dear Ms. Divan:

Financial institutions whose customers travel throughout the northeast can now gain a sustainable edge over their toughest competitors.

How? Through new electronic funds transfer (EFT) capabilities described in our upcoming Regional Briefing, "Connections: Enhancing System Performance with NYCE."

By participating in NYCE, you can reduce out-of-state ATM charges for your customers traveling in the northeast by 10 to 20 cents per transaction vs. Plus or Cirrus.

What's more, NYCE offers a wide range of value-added services—including remote banking services, ATM terminal management, card authorization, and off-line debit card processing.

Processing almost half a billion electronic transactions a year, NYCE is the third-largest regional EFT network in the nation and the *only* regional EFT on the east coast with its own dedicated data center (located in Secaucus, NJ). We currently have more than 17,000 ATM and 33,000 POS locations, making us a viable alternative to other EFT providers.

At the *free* Regional Briefing, "Connections," you'll see how NYCE can complement your existing EFT infrastructure, reducing cost and enhancing customer service. You'll also discover new and improved NYCE capabilities that let you open new profit centers for increased revenue.

To reserve your *free* space at the Regional Briefing nearest you, complete and mail the enclosed form. Or fax it to 123-456-7890. To register by telephone, call 123-456-7899.

Sincerely,

P.S. Although attendance is free and there is no commitment, obligation, or sales pressure of any kind, seating at regional briefings is limited, so please register today.

A fund-raising letter

If you work for a nonprofit organization, you may use direct marketing letters for one additional purpose: to generate contributions to your organization or cause. Because there is no direct benefit to the recipient and no benefit, aside from a possible tax deduction and perhaps receipt of a small gift, you have to appeal to the recipient's kindness. The following letter was sent along with a picture of an adorable young boy, to tug at the heartstrings of the reader.

Customize your own fundraising letter:

This letter should contain:

1. An opening that brings the reader's attention to the people who benefit from the charity (putting a face on the organization).
2. The goal of the charity.
3. What you want the reader to do to help the charity accomplish that goal.
4. The valuable deeds of the charity and its dependence on the generosity of others.
5. Instructions how to contribute.
6. An ending that returns to the people highlighted in the opening.

Dear Friend,

I think you'll be sad to learn that Chandler may not be going home for the holidays. You see, Chandler has been diagnosed with acute lymphocytic leukemia.

We try to send the children home for the holidays. But some children are just too sick. So, we try everything possible to bring a smile to their face.

You can help by sending a St. Agnes child a holiday card.

I've even enclosed a card for you to send. I wish you could see their brave little eyes light up when they get a card, knowing that someone is thinking of them.

The kids at St. Agnes hospital are very special, and they need cheering up at this time of the year. They know that other kids, who aren't sick, are at home baking cookies and giving their wish lists to Santa Claus.

Our kids can't. A man on staff plays Santa, but being in the hospital is never any fun. However, your gifts have given these children hope. If St. Agnes' Hospital wasn't here, few of these precious children would even be alive today. Your gifts make miracles happen.

Please send your card. It will do so much to brighten the season for a sick child. And with your card, will you send a special holiday donation a gift that can help make it possible for children, like Chandler, to spend all their holidays at home, and forget how close they came to dying too young?

We continue to count on you in this season of joy and compassion, to help a desperately sick child stay alive. I can think of no greater gift you might give.

God bless you,

P.S. Each child hangs a card on the little tree we've set up. I'm hoping that your card will be one of them. Thanks...from Chandler and me.

Letter inviting customers to visit your Web site

A letter or postcard can be sent to customers encouraging them to visit your Web site. The letter can be used to announce a new Web site or a new feature on an existing Web site.

Customize your own letter inviting customers to visit your Web site:

Like any piece of direct mail, this letter has to push the reader to do something to gain a personal benefit. It should include:

1. An opening that boasts the great resources available at your Web site. Be sure to give the name and Web address.
2. The details of the resources found at that site.
3. Benefits of visiting that web site.
4. Instructions how to log on (repeat the name and address).

Dear Mr. Gahan:

You may have seen our ad in DM News telling direct marketers all about the great FREE resources available to them on the Roman Web site at http://www.roman.com.

Resources like instant online counts from more than 30,000 different lists...a downloadable library of information-packed "how-to" articles on direct marketing, an online calculator for accurately determining the optimum size of test cells, and much, much more (see the enclosed ad reprint for details).

But as a Roman customer, you are automatically entitled to premium Web site access, called "Gold Level."

As a Gold Level browser on the Roman Web site, you can get many additional valuable resources that other direct marketers can't, including unlimited onscreen viewing and downloading of the complete and up-to-date data cards for all Roman lists.

For details, and to activate your exclusive Gold Level access, simply log onto the Roman Web site right now at http://www.roman.com.

But be warned...Once you see how fast, easy, and convenient it is to access list counts and data cards online at the Roman Web site, you may never go back to paper data cards again.

Sincerely,

Instructions for direct marketing letter design

Now that we've looked at some sample letters, let's examine some of the mechanics that go into designing a successful marketing letter.

I asked Ted Kikoler, one of the leading direct mail designers in North America, for some guidelines for typing and laying out direct marketing letters. Here are his personal recommendations.

- Never layout the body copy of the letter using graphic design techniques. Always word-process it.

- Use a serifed typeface. The best is either Prestige, Times New Roman, or Courier. If you are using Word for Windows and a laser printer, you can set the body copy in Times New Roman and the headlines and subheads in either Times Roman Bold or Helvetica Bold.

- Indent all paragraphs five characters.

- Use wide margins—long line lengths with narrow margins fill too much of the page, making it look like there's more to read than there actually is. A good line length is 6.5 inches.

- Add one carriage return of space between all paragraphs.

- Make the right-hand margin ragged right. Never justify it.

- Try to avoid paragraphs longer than six lines deep. If you have a longer paragraph, break it into two or more paragraphs.

- Indent entire paragraphs you want to highlight by 10 characters on each side.

- Typeset the headline of the letter for emphasis. If you are not typesetting the heading of the letter, set it off by putting it in a ruled box or a Johnson Box (a border around the heading), putting white space around it, or using a second color.

- The main body copy should be black but an accent color can be used for subheads.

- Make the signature legible.

- Shorten the first name of the reader to sound friendlier and to close the gap between reader and writer. Bill sounds better than William, Tom sounds better than Thomas.

- When using a personalized letter, try to avoid using subheads, especially all caps and centered above the paragraph. Do not typeset the heading in this type of letter. Keep the logo on the front page. Use a blue signature.

- Underscore words that should be emphasized. A good technique is to read the copy aloud and listen to the words you emphasize. These are the ones to underscore.

- Indent the entire body copy of the postscript (P.S.) by five characters so the letters "P.S." stand out. If it's all flush left, it gets lost.

- If you are mailing small quantities (a few hundred at a time), you can print the letter without a signature, then sign each one individually with a blue pen. This creates a look and feel very close to a personal letter. Signing a stack of a few hundred letters can be done without much pain during the evening while sitting in front of the TV.

Direct-mail faxing

One of the problems with mail is that there is so much of it. Consequently, it's difficult for your letter to compete for attention with all the other correspondence in the recipient's mailbox. One way to resolve this problem is to compose and transmit your letter electronically as a fax.

Tips for effective fax broadcasting

To gather many of these tips, I talked with my colleague Maury Kauffman, author of *Computer-Based Fax Processing* and fax columnist for *Computer Telephony Magazine*. Maury's articles on fax communication have appeared in numerous business and trade publications including *DM News, Target Marketing, Information Week, Folio* and *Voice Processing Asia*. He is active in the direct marketing industry and is a regular speaker at voice/fax and marketing conferences worldwide.

According to Maury's research, there are 86 million fax machines installed worldwide, and thousands of fax modems sold monthly. A recent survey by his firm showed that 90 percent of the direct marketing professionals surveyed have tested enhanced fax technology. And a Gallup poll of large and mid-size companies found that 60 percent of daily fax users are faxing more than last year.

Fax broadcasting allows you to send a personalized document to hundreds, even thousands of different locations automatically. It's an amazingly effective, yet often overlooked, marketing tool.

To increase response rates, try fax broadcasting, and:

- Personalize each and every fax, and use data from customer files to communicate.
- Add a response mechanism to your fax.
- Broadcast at night when rates are lower, for maximum impact in the morning
- Keep the fax medium in mind; photos and detailed graphics will not transmit well.
- Use white paper. Colored paper does not fax well.
- Use plain paper, not rag or weave. The texture of textured paper shows up as gray marks when faxed.
- Don't overuse the fax, or you may lose the sense of urgency.
- Know the law. Read the Telecommunications Consumer Protection Act.

"I think it is very risky to broadcast fax to cold or new leads, people with whom you have not established a relationship," writes Dan Kennedy (*Marketing Briefing*). "This can and does work. You can make sales, but you will really aggravate a lot of people, and I wonder if doing that is smart, especially in a market you wish to live in for any length of time."

At time of this book's printing, cold-faxing is illegal. Although regulations change over time, as of this writing, the Telephone Consumer Protection Act prohibits the use of telephone facsimile machines to send unsolicited advertisements (Section III, Part D.2, Paragraph 54: Facsimile Machines). Marketers should use faxes to communicate only with companies with whom they have a prior relationship, and not to broadcast fax to cold prospects who don't know you. However, a "prior relationship" doesn't necessarily mean the people receiving your fax are customers; they may just have made an inquiry at one time, requesting a catalog or brochure.

"Keep an internal 'Do Not Fax' list," advises Maury. "Anyone who dislikes fax messages, or who has communicated that they do not wish to receive faxes should be taken off your fax broadcast database." He also advocates adding the following message to the bottom of fax broadcasts: "If you wish to be removed from our fax distribution list, call us."

I've found that the majority of complaints about fax broadcasts come from SOHO businesses (small office/home office). Large corporations rarely object to fax broadcasts. The reason is simple: The SOHO typically has only one fax machine. When you send unsolicited advertising, you're tying up that machine and using up their paper, which they pay for out of their own pocket. The corporate prospect, on the other hand, has access to many fax machines, and often has an assistant to send faxes. Fax broadcasting doesn't tie up his only fax or waste his time.

Here are some hints on saving money with fax broadcasting:

- Broadcast at night when the rates are lower.
- Limit graphics, as they transmit much slower than text. Use text and line art without halftones.
- Keep your fax to one page. Incorporate the recipient's information on the page to eliminate the need for a separate cover sheet.

When compiling fax lists to use for broadcasting, keep these tips in mind:

- Request fax numbers on all business reply cards and other response devices.
- Make sure fax numbers are up-to-date by verifying them periodically.
- Double-postcards should do double duty. Use them to clean your list and update fax numbers.
- Consider offering an incentive to those who mail or call with updated fax information.

- ⌨ Your sales force should always update fax numbers with addresses and phone.
- ⌨ Customer service should verify fax numbers when customers call in.
- ⌨ Ask your mailing list house whether they can, for a fee, append fax numbers to records in your customer and prospect database that don't already contain them.
- ⌨ Consider broadcasting to an association list—typically most people in your target group belong.
- ⌨ If you need fax numbers immediately, use telemarketing to locate and verify.
- ⌨ Once your list is compiled, make sure updates are made on an ongoing basis.

Direct mail via the Internet

Everyone has too much to read, and that's especially true for people who have e-mail. Author Dan Poynter says that 30 million people use e-mail each day, and it will keep growing year after year. With all of that clutter, how do you make your e-mail stand out from the crowd? The following guidelines can help.

Finding e-mail lists that work

Unless you live in a cave, you know that Internet marketing is growing in popularity exponentially. In a recent online survey, more than 50 percent of direct marketers polled by Edith Roman Associates said they now use the Internet as a marketing tool.

More and more e-mail lists (or "e-lists") are emerging on the market today. But how do you tell which ones are the quality e-lists? These five questions can help you determine which lists can produce profitable results for your product or service.

1. What is the Web site's method for opting-in the people on their list? There are dozen of databases with fancy names and big descriptions, but after digging through the promotional information, they turn out to be nothing much. Prospects who have not requested anything do not remember how or when they got on the list, and probably will not respond. These lists might have a chance with all those free offers that have been circulating the Web, but serious direct marketers are looking for genuine Internet buyers.

For promotional e-mail, response lists are generally superior to compiled list. In e-mail, there are numerous lists on the market compiled from Internic, which is the organization with which all Web advertisers must register their domain names. Other compiled lists consist of Internet addresses of people who visit use groups.

Response lists, by comparison, consist of Internet-enabled prospects who have either responded to an e-mail offer or registered at a particular Web site. By doing so, they have actively indicated interest in a particular subject area. Another plus is that, in addition to just the Internet address, the list contains additional information as name, address, phone number, and sometimes even buying preferences and demographics.

Results from Internet marketing programs indicate that the best response is obtained using opt-in lists. The true definition of "opt-in" is that people on an e-list have registered at the site or through some other electronic or paper form, and checked the option requesting additional e-mail information from other companies.

Different list owners use different definitions of "opt in," resulting in lists of varying quality. When you visit Web sites and fill in guest pages, note that some Web sites have pre-checked the "Yes, I want to receive e-mail from other companies" option. So when you complete and submit the guest form, you opt-in automatically.

Other Web sites require the registrant to proactively check "yes" to the opt-in option. The latter is indicative of a more responsive, qualified e-list.

"Make sure the opt-in language explains clearly that other companies will be e-mailing to the Internet user," advises Michelle Feit, vice president, Internet marketing, Edith Roman Associates. "If Web surfers visiting the site are not presented with the choice to opt-in, they may respond negatively to receiving e-mail from direct marketers, including you."

How can you find out what opt-in means to the e-list you are considering testing? Ask for their opt-in language. Or go to their Web site and register. If an e-list owner won't give you their opt-in language or the URL address of their Web site, questions the integrity of their list.

A number of lists use a form of "reverse opt-in." They broadcast e-mails to Internet addresses with an advertising message that includes the promise of future promotional e-mails. They state that if the recipient doesn't want to receive future e-mails, he or she must click on "unsubscribe."

Therefore, these so-called opt-in lists aren't really opt-in at all, since the prospect who takes no action is considered qualified, which isn't true. (This is the electronic equivalent of mailing qualification cards for a controlled circulation publication, and considering anyone who does *not* send in the qualification card with a note saying "I *don't* want to subscribe" as a qualified subscriber.)

2. What type of relationship does the site have with the people on its list? The most responsive lists have ongoing relationships between site and registrant. "Whether they are receiving a monthly magazine, weekly newsletter, or are purchasing products from the company, look for lists of people who have an ongoing relationship with the site and are not just surfers," advises Feit.

"You want to know how often the people are returning to the site, how often the site is contacting them, and the last contact date."

3. How is the e-list maintained? Well-maintained lists add new names, match e-list names to e-mail preference files, update address corrections, and remove bounce backs and opt-outs. Thanks to the speed of the Internet, there is a lot of activity on e-lists. A inaccurate file can decrease response and increase flaming, bounce backs, and costs. Look for e-lists that are updated monthly or more frequently and guarantee 100 percent delivery.

When you rent a quality response e-list, don't be surprised when the list owner refuses to transmit the names to you, and insists on transmitting your e-mail themselves, for a fee.. This is standard practice among owners of quality lists. It's the electronic equivalent of a conventional list owner who won't send his list directly to mailers, but ships only to bonded letter shops.

For the e-lists on the market today, about one-quarter the list owners insist on doing the transmission, while the other half will release their e-mail lists to mailers. Research shows that most of the firms who release their e-mail addresses have compiled lists.

Why do owners of quality response lists insist on controlling their lists so closely? One reason is to ensure the integrity of the list by eliminating tampering. More importantly, it prevents the people on the list, whose trust the owner values, from receiving unwanted offers. And it ensures that Internet users get only offers of interest...including yours.

4. What selections are available on the e-list? Selections are essential for target marketing. E-lists have two types of selections: Web site data and individual data.

Site data is generated from log reports, and a "quality" e-list will have them available. Examples of site data include original registration dates, last time visited, and number of times visited.

Individual data is gathered directly from the registrant or by enhancement. Examples of individual data are consumer vs. business trafic, age, gender, job title, industry, and special interests. Selections allow you to target only those Internet prospects most likely to respond to your offer.

5. Does the e-list owner offer any value-added services? Some e-lists offer value-added services that can increase the effectiveness of your marketing. You can turn your message into a personalized offer by putting the person's name in the body of your copy. Immediate "click through" reports show how many people took the next action by clicking through to your Web site.

Other value-added services available include split tests for multiple messages, list owner endorsements, address corrections, e-mail address appending, data enhancements, and e-mails with graphics, to name a few. Many of these services can increase response and reduce cost per order.

Sample promotional e-mail

The low cost of e-mail lets you target promotions toward different market segments. In this e-mail, the targets were all XYZ managers with e-mail addresses. The lead of the e-mail uses this fact as the rationale why the reader should pay attention to the message received.

Customize your own e-mail promotional letter:

E-mail that promotes your business should include the same elements of direct mail writing found in snail mail. They should:

1. Immediately attract the reader's attention by pointing out a problem or situation the reader can relate to.
2. Offer a solution to that problem.
3. Create a desire to know more about your product or service.
4. Offer proof that you are the best.
5. Tell the reader what to do next.

```
TO: XYZ Management
FROM: John Johnson
RE: Proprietary data management solutions
Dear XYZ Executive:
ATTENTION XYZ PERSONNEL: IF YOU CAN RECEIVE AND READ THIS E-MAIL
MESSAGE, THE INTEGRITY OF YOUR CRITICAL DATA MAY BE AT RISK....
With the proliferation of distributed computing throughout the XYZ
organization, more and more critical XYZ data resides on
client/server networks for which no coordinated, centralized data
management strategy exists.
As a result, an increasing number of XYZ systems are at considerable
risk for data loss, data corruption, downtime, and other problems
that can result from lack of effective data management systems.
Our company, Techo Systems, provides effective, flexible data
management, storage, back up, and recovery solutions for over 250
Global 2000 companies worldwide.
Within the last 12 months, Techo Systems has experienced explosive
growth, increasing revenues by 70 percent and doubling customer
service staff. We've recently installed systems for Sprint, GTE,
Siemens, and other major telecommunications companies. BUT XYZ
CONTINUES TO REMAIN OUR BEST CUSTOMER.
Techo offers its XYZ customers effective, centralized data
management solutions customized to meet their specific data backup
and recovery requirements. Today there are more than 100 Techo
systems within XYZ protecting over 30 terabytes of XYZ proprietary
information.
```

SPECIAL OFFERS FOR XYZ ONLY!

For a limited time, Techo Systems is making these valuable FREE offers to XYZ customers and potential customers only. Please check as many as you would like to receive:

/ / FREE Techo Advisor software enables you to analyze your data management needs and compare storage options costs

/ / FREE TechStore98 Demo Disk and Information Kit

/ / FREE no-obligation Storage Management Analysis

/ / FREE Reference List of Installed Techo systems for XYZ

Name_____

Company_____

Address_____

City_____

State_____

Zip_____

Phone_____

Fax_____

E-mail_____

You can mail or fax a printout of this reply form to:

Techo Systems, Inc.

Anytown, USA

Fax 123-456-7899

For any questions, call 123-456-7890, or e-mail mdinfo@Tech.com.

Sincerely,

P.S. These special FREE offers are available until September 15. Once they expire, they may never be available again.

ABOUT THE AUTHOR

Robert W. Bly is the director of the Center for Technical Communication, a consulting firm that helps businesspeople improve their communications and interpersonal skills. CTC presents seminars to associations and corporate clients nationwide on topics such as direct marketing, business and technical writing.

Bob Bly is the author of more than 40 books including *The Elements of Business Writing* (Macmillan), *The Copywriter's Handbook* (Henry Holt), and *Selling Your Services* (Henry Holt). Other titles include *Creative Careers* (John Wiley), *Business to Business Direct Marketing* (NTC), and *Keeping Clients Satisfied* (Prentice Hall).

Bob's articles have appeared in such publications as *Computer Decisions, Writer's Digest, Business Marketing, Direct, Amtrak Express, Cosmopolitan, Science Books & Films, Chemical Engineering,* and *New Jersey Monthly.*

Organizations that have hired Bob as a trainer and speaker include the Cincinnati Direct Marketing Association, Thoroughbred Software, Walker Richer & Quinn, ARCO Chemical, Creative Group, Cardiac Pacemakers Inc., U.S. Army, Dow Chemical, Mail Order Association of Nurseries, Foxboro, Computron, IBM, McGraw-Hill, The Pricing Institute, and the International Laboratory Distributors Association.

In addition, Bob has written sales letters, direct mail packages, and other marketing documents for such clients as Agora Publishing, Phillips Publishing, KCI Communications, Lucent Technologies, McGraw-Hill, Lane Laboratories, BOC Gases, Alloy Technology, AT&T, Intrasoft, Isogon, and Rodale. He has won several awards for letter-writing, including a Gold Echo Award from the Direct Marketing Association, an IMMY from the Information Industry Association, and two Southstar Awards. He is the editor of the magazine *Bits & Pieces for Salespeople,* published monthly by Economics Press.

Questions and comments on *The Encyclopedia of Modern Business Letters, Memos, Faxes, and E-Mails* may be sent to:

Bob Bly
Center for Technical Communication
22 E. Quackenbush Avenue
Dumont, NJ 07628
phone 201-385-1220, fax 201-385-1138
E-mail: rwbly@bly.com Web site: www.bly.com

INDEX